Royally Chosen Christmas

Royal Bastards MC 7
Elle Boon

By Elle Boon elleboon@yahoo.com

© Copyright 2020 Elle Boon

All cover art and logos © Copyright Lou Grey

Royally Chosen Christmas

Royal Bastards MC 7

Copyright © 2020 Elle Boon

First E-book Publication: 2020

Cover design by Lou Grey

Cover Model: Lewis C of BigCartel.com

Photographer: Kevin Floyd of Floyd Co.

Edited by Tracy Roelle

PUBLISHER:

Elle Boon

Royal Bastards Code

PROTECT: The club and your brothers come before anything else and must be protected at all costs. **CLUB** is **FAMILY**.

RESPECT: Earn it & Give it. Respect club law. Respect the patch. Respect your brothers. Disrespect a member and there will be hell to pay.

HONOR: Being patched in is an honor, not a right. Your colors are sacred, not to be left alone, and **NEVER** let them touch the ground.

OLE LADIES: Never disrespect a member's or brother's Ol'Lady. **PERIOD.**

CHURCH is **MANDATORY.**

LOYALTY: Takes precedence overall, including well-being.

HONESTY: Never **LIE, CHEAT,** or **STEAL** from another member or the club.

TERRITORY: You are to respect your brother's property and follow their Chapter's club rules.

TRUST: Years to earn it...seconds to lose it.

NEVER RIDE OFF: Brothers do not abandon their family.

Royal Bastards MC Series

BASTARDS MC SERIES SECOND RUN
E.C. Land: *Cyclone of Chaos*
Chelle C. Craze & Eli Abbot: *Ghoul*
Scarlett Black: *Ice*
Elizabeth Knox: *Rely On Me*
J.L. Leslie: *Worth the Risk*
Deja Voss: *Lean In*
Khloe Wren: *Blaze of Honor*
Misty Walker: *Birdie's Biker*
J. Lynn Lombard: *Capone's Chaos*
Ker Dukey: *Rage*
Crimson Syn: *Scarred By Pain*
M. Merin: *Declan*
Elle Boon: *Royally F**ked changing to Royally Saved*
Rae B. Lake: *Death and Paradise*
K Webster: *Copper*
Glenna Maynard: *Tempting the Biker*
K.L. Ramsey: *Whiskey Tango*
Kristine Allen: *Angel*
Nikki Landis: *Devil's Ride*
KE Osborn: *Luring Light*
CM Genovese: *Pipe Dreams*
Nicole James: *Club Princess*
Shannon Youngblood: *Leather & Chrome*
Erin Trejo: *Unbreak Me*
Winter Travers: *Six Gun*
Izzy Sweet & Sean Moriarty: *Broken Ties*
Jax Hart: *Desert Rose*
Royal Bastards MC Facebook Group- https://www.facebook.com/groups/royalbastardsmc/
Links can be found in our Website: www.royalbastardsmc.com

Table of Contents

Dedication

First and foremost, I'd like to thank all you amazing readers for loving my Royal Sons and the Royal Bastards enough to want more. I hope you like Hollywood and Talena as much as I loved writing their stories.

To my amazing team of Beta's, y'all rock sooo effing hard, Debbie Ramos, Maureen Ames and Karen DiGaetano; thank you ladies for helping with this story. Thank you all, for all you do to make my books so amazing. Thank you to my editor Tracy Roelle for always putting in those long hours for "that client" LOL. And a huge thanks to you readers who are simply the best ever. FLOVE y'all soo hard. And last but definitely not least a huge shoutout to Lou Gray for this amazing cover. The absolutely stunning guy gracing the front is Lewis C. The photographer is Kevin Floyd of Floyd Co. Be sure and check them out on Instagram. Happy reading, y'all.

XOXO,
Elle Boon

Character List

**TO AVOID SPOILERS THIS LIST ONLY INCLUDES
THE CHARACTERS MENTIONED
IN THE PREVIOUS BOOKS**

ROYAL MC Members:
King Royal – President – Son of King Royal SR, brother to Duke VP (Royally Tempted book 3)
Duke Royal – Vice President – Son of King Royal SR, brother to King (Royally Treasured book 4)
Traeger – Sgt at Arms (Royally Taken book 2)
Keys – Enforcer (Royally Broken book 5)
Hollywood aka Scott Haven – Enforcer (Royally Chosen Christmas book 7)
Digger – Road Captain – Owns Royal Towing
Cosmo – Enforcer and money man (Royally F**ked changed to Royally Saved book 6)
Timber – Tattoo Artist (Royally Twisted book 1)
Alexa – King's ole' lady
Ivy – Timber's ole' lady, former best friend of Luke Royal twin to Duke Royal who committed suicide.
Kailani – Traeger's ole' lady – Mob boss's daughter the Royals took out
Lennox – Duke's ole' lady – Doc's daughter – Doctor and old timer
Palmer – Keys' ole' lady
DaiTai – Cosmo's ole' lady

Former Originals: None have books or have been mentioned except King SR...yet "wink"
King Royal Sr – President – Deceased
Ryno Marx – VP - Deceased
Argo Peters – Sgt at Arms – Deceased

Crazy Jax – Treasurer – Deceased
Torpedo (Tinny) – Deceased

Royally Chosen Christmas Playlist

Lonely - Justine Bieber

It Will Come Back - Hozier

Goodbyes - Post Malone

Finally//beautiful stranger - Halsey

Memories - Maroon 5

You Broke Me First - Tate McRae

Falling - Harry Styles

Without Me - Halsey & Juice World

I Fall Apart - Post Malone

Tell Me You Love Me - Demi Lovato

Starting Over - Christ Stapleton

Someone You loved - Lewis Capaldi

I hope - Gabby Barrett & Charlie Puth

Hold On - Cord Overstreet

Love Lies - Khalid & Normani

Bad Intentions - Niykee Heaton

Sex On Fire - Kings Of Leon

Apologize - Timbaland & OneRepublic

Bring Me To Life - Evanescence

You Don't Own Me - SayGrace Ft G-Eazy

If You Want Love - NF

Hero - Enrique Iglesias

Let's Hurt Tonight - OneRepublic

If the World Was Ending - JP Saxe & Julia Michaels

Die From A Broken Heart - Maddie & Tae

Prologue

He scanned the area to the east of the village. The fucking newest royal couple visiting the camp couldn't have come at a worse time. You got a US Official there as part of some damn mission and two countries in the middle of a war because, well, the one side didn't like anyone who didn't believe in their cause. Nope, not a good time at all. The call had come in three days ago that something was going to go down, something big that would make the Americans look like the bad guys, again. Newsflash fuckers, America already looked bad in the eyes of the world. However, that didn't stop them from sending him and his team out to the middle of bumfuck nowhere, where the temperatures reached triple digits during the day. Nobody gave a single fuck about any of that. What they cared about was ensuring the royals, who had arrived yesterday, lived long enough to get the fuck out of the village, without a national incident being blamed on America. The US official had his own team watching his six, which was ironic since he and his team weren't privy to who and or where they were. Hollywood was pretty sure he'd seen something earlier on the other side of the village but wouldn't swear on his life.

Movement caught his eye. He adjusted his scope, sighted in what he hoped like fuck he wasn't seeing. "Don't be what I think you are," he murmured. For the last forty-six hours and eleven minutes he'd been lying in the same spot without moving. The sandy hill offered very little coverage except a few sparse bits of foliage he and his team had burrowed under; their clothing matched the land almost perfectly. Hollywood was used to being patient during a mission, had known he'd have to hold his position for an extended period of time. The rest of his team were spread out a little farther back in case he needed them. If that happened it, all Hell would break loose, something their government was hoping to avoid at all costs. It was why they were sent in to do the dirty work nice and quiet like. Get in, take out a target, or rescue the mark without incident and come home. If you don't make it back, that sucks for you but don't go thinking they're going to admit what happened to the world.

Time slowed as he tracked the young girl's progress toward the village, her bare feet kicking up dust behind her. He shut down everything else around him, focusing on her. Long black hair gleaming in the sun overhead. Her dress was white, too white, billowing out behind her. Through the scope, he noticed the protrusion on her chest. Where she should be flat since she couldn't be more than ten, a fucking kid like his little sister. Only this girl walked with determination and clearly had something under her dress that wasn't natural, boxy in appearance.

"Hollywood, you got eyes on the girl?" The question was barely a whisper in his ear.

He took a deep breath, knowing he only had two minutes to line the shot up before all Hell would break lose. They'd chosen him to take the shot because not many could hit a target over a mile away with accuracy. He could, every time. "Yeah, I got her. She's packing."

"Thirty seconds and then our window close for the in and out without incident." Lieutenant Diamond was calm like always. Hollywood would hate to see the man pissed.

Hollywood didn't respond, his team trusted he'd make the shot in time. Instead, he watched the young girl as she walked forward, noticing the way her hands bunched at her sides into little fists. He zoomed in on her face, seeing a tear roll down her cheek. *"I'm sorry, little girl."* He didn't say the words out loud. With one small adjustment to the scope, he took a breath and squeezed the trigger. Many would've began moving away. He wasn't made that way. With the scope still in position, he watched as her body jerked and then fell, almost gracefully to the ground. Some thought he stayed to admire his work, but the truth was, he felt he owed it to those lives he'd taken. It was his way of showing them respect , sort of like saying goodbye. Fucked up maybe, but it was his last moment with their souls.

"You done doing your last rights and shit, Hollywood? Maybe we should've called you Priest instead of Hollywood. Come on, we need to move before they start looking for your ass. You may be further out than they'd think a shooter should be, but they'll start casting a net. Let's move it," Lieutenant Diamond barked.

With his clothing soaked in sweat and grime, and other shit he'd had to lay in from over forty-six hours of being in the same spot without moving, he broke his rifle down quickly and silently. Once he had his precious in the sand-colored case, he eased backward, ensuring he didn't make much more than a slight shift in the earth. He'd just earned the right to head back to the states, he hoped.

Chapter One

Two weeks later...

"What do you mean you're pregnant?" Hollywood asked Angel. He could feel his world spinning out of control, and he'd only been in California for a handful of days after being debriefed in North Carolina at Fort Bragg. His Lieutenant had given him a heads-up last night to get his shit together and be back in forty-eight hours for another mission, he had no time for this shit.

"Scott, don't make me repeat myself," Angela pleaded, her dark eyes swam with unshed tears.

Fuck, he was always careful, and they hadn't fucked in over seven, maybe eight months. She didn't look like she was ready to have a baby or close to it. He did a mental calculation as to when the last time he'd been in California and when they'd slept together. She'd be closer to eight months. When he'd tossed the condom, he knew for a fact it hadn't broke or leaked.

"Say what?" He stared down at her dark head and her too thin frame. Aside from her medically enhanced chest, she didn't look any different. He was sure she'd have a belly if she was as far along as she was supposed to be if she was

17

carrying his child. She was confusing the fuck out of him, and he wasn't a stupid man.

"I need your help. You said you'd always be there if I needed you, and—I need you now more than ever." Angela moved forward, brushing her body against his.

He lifted his arms, gripping her biceps in his palms. "Dammit, Angel, don't. We'll get to your announcement in a minute. Are you on one of those stupid ass diet fads again?" When he'd first met her, she'd been a couple years older than him without an ounce of shyness. She'd been a fucking bombshell who knew how to use her body to get what she wanted. His friends called her a dark-haired Marilyn Monroe. He never saw the comparison except that she had an hourglass figure like the other woman, and she was petite at a little over five foot three with curves in all the right places. His teenaged body had reacted in the most obvious way anytime she'd entered the same room he'd been in. It had been lust at first sight. She'd taught him more that summer than he'd known in all his seventeen years. Of course, he could teach her a few things now. If her father, his stepfather had known all the places he'd fucked her, he'd probably have had a fit. The thought almost made him smile.

"No, I'm not on some stupid diet, unless you call pregnancy a diet." Her dark eyes flashed up at him. "I'm pregnant and sick every hour on the hour." She put one hand on her stomach, the other one over her mouth. She was clearly battling the urge to throw up.

Where he and their sister Talena were blond and blue eyed, like their mother, she was like her father, dark haired and dark eyed. She'd told him her mother was Hispanic and spoke very little English, which at the time he hadn't thought much of, but later he realized Gary had taken advantage of the woman, like he did all women. Gary had married Scott's mother when he'd been a boy, but the prick hadn't introduced Angela to them until the summer he'd graduated high school. He often thought his stepfather had hid his past from all of them for some nefarious reason, but once she burst into their lives, it hadn't matter why. For one thing, she was only there for the summer that first year. For another, he found fucking the man's daughter he'd come to despise, made him hate Gary a little less, and then he'd left for the military. Now, years later, he and she only saw one another when he flew in occasionally. If they fucked, it was no biggie. They were more friends than anything else. He definitely didn't look at her like a stepsister, most assuredly not a future mother to his child. Fuck.

"How long have you been sick?" Her wan face, and thin appearance was concerning.

Angela shrugged out of his hold, turning her back to him. "You're going to hate me," she whined.

"For the love of all. Why would I hate you? You and I both know we were never a thing, Angela. I'd never hate you for anything you did. Just spit it out and get it over with. You know I care for you," he said gently. Hell, she was his stepsister. What the hell was she thinking? It wasn't like he'd ever given her the impression they were more. He could literally count on one hand the number of times they'd hooked up in the last two years and still have a finger or two.

Angela lifted her tear-streaked face, lower lip trembling. He'd known her for over five years and knew every little trick she played. They were almost brother and sister, yet there was no blood relation between them. Angela's mother had been his stepdad Gary's second wife. He'd divorced her mom when Angela was five, and although they'd only been married for six years, Angela said Gary had been a good father, until he moved in with them when she was ten. After that, his visits had become few and far between, although he'd made up for it with money. He never said what he thought good old Gary's reasoning for up and divorcing Angela's mother was, the timing was too close to his own father's death and him marrying his mother. Oh, he didn't think his mom and Gary had anything going on prior to his dad's death, but he did think the prick had seen an opportunity and took it, leaving his other family to move up in the world. Even though the man appeared to love Angela, he'd left her and her mom for another family.

The first time he'd seen Angel standing next to Gary, her dark eyes had been dancing with knowledge that he'd found hard to ignore. Luckily for him, he'd been in the pool, so his sudden boner was hidden by the water. His stepdad had been a condescending fucker who'd expected him to toe the line, but Scott had never played by his rules. That summer, he'd just graduated from high school and had scholarships to some of the best universities in the country. He had a folder piled with letters of acceptances from colleges waiting for him to choose one. He hadn't accepted any of them, deciding to enlist in the Army. Which was the complete opposite of what was expected of him. At the time he hadn't been a hundred percent sure what he was going to do, until he'd looked at Gary in his suit and tie standing on the side of the pool with his arm around Angela, glaring down at him. He'd known right then and there was no way he wanted to be like that fucker and go into business. That had been his dad's life and maybe if he'd still been alive, he'd have a different outlook, but Gary wasn't a man he wanted to be like.

He could still remember the fear that had assaulted him before he broke the news to his mother and wondered if that same emotion was eaten at Angela. She'd walked into his apartment with her shoulders hunched, not how he was used to her carrying herself. Yet, just as he'd waited until the end of summer when he'd finished packing his bag to go, he had pulled his big boy pants on, Angela was going to need to do the same damn thing. Because if there was one thing he'd learned, shit didn't disappear because you put it off. And there was no doubt in his mind that the baby she carried was not his, not even a slim chance in hell.

Of course, that summer all those years ago was different, because he'd looked up from the lap he'd been doing, spellbound by the gorgeous girl standing next to Gary, and he'd known he would have her. If he'd been standing next to them, they'd have seen the way his dick had leapt to life in his swimming trunks. His saving grace had been the fact he'd been in the water so the two of them couldn't see the hard-on he was sported as he'd looked up, getting a view of her panty-less state. He'd listened to his stepdad inform him his daughter was there for two weeks. All he'd heard Gary say was it was going to be his job to make sure she felt welcomed. Gary had no clue just how welcoming Scott had made her. Angela though, she'd taught him things he hadn't known. He'd laughed when she'd told him her nickname had been Angel, especially since at the time he'd been balls deep in her. There had been nothing five years ago, nor now, that was angelic about Angela. Not at nineteen, nor twenty-five. Up until then, he'd gotten a few decent blowjobs from girls his age, but she'd shown him that porn stars weren't the only ones who could do the things he'd seen on DVDs. He'd done his best to take care of her throughout the years, and not just sexually. Shit they hadn't really fucked much in the last few years since he'd been in the military, yet she always called him when she was in a bind. Like now, but never this extreme.

"Angela, what do you want me to do? I'm only here for a couple more days and then I'm gone again." he asked, needing her to understand he wouldn't be here.

"It doesn't matter. Please, I need you to take care of us." She put one hand on his arm, the other on her small bump, running the tips of her fingers up to his face.

Scott grabbed her hand, stopping her. "Listen, I'm sorry, Angela, but I don't know what you expect me to do. Whoever the father is, you need to contact him. If he's not an upstanding guy or whatever, then you know you can do it on your own." He released her hand after giving what he hoped was a reassuring squeeze. He was the last man who would be a good father figure. He'd moved up the ranks in the Army to Delta Force. Shit, most of his assignments were so highly classified, he didn't know where they were going until they got there and wasn't sure if they'd make it out. The only thing he made sure of before each mission was that he called his mom and Talena.

"You don't understand. He'll kill me," she cried.

He shook his head, seeing the girl he'd known for years doing what she did best. "Look, I know you think this is the end of the world, but you're twenty-five, not sixteen, Angela. My mom will help you, but I'm not claiming a child that isn't mine. Hell, Talena loves you, and she's your half-sister, same as mine. They'll both help you, but I won't claim paternity for someone else's baby."

Anger flared in her dark eyes. "You're so stupid. Talena's no more my sister than she's yours. God, how could you be so smart, yet so fucking dumb? Your mom couldn't have kids after you. They adopted Talena."

Shock held him rooted to the spot for long seconds after she spat the words at him. His father had been killed in a car accident when he'd been eight, leaving him and his mother shattered. Gary had been his father's business partner, a man his mother had trusted and relied on. When she fell in love with him, and then married the man just two years later, the entire community had been overjoyed for her. As for him, being a ten-year-old boy, he'd only wanted a father figure and he'd know Gary for a long time, he'd been like an uncle. However, Gary was the farthest thing from what he'd deem a father, or maybe he hadn't wanted to be a stepfather. Gary had hidden his dislike of Scott from everyone, until after the wedding, and then he made sure Scott knew how things were going to work. He'd been a child and hopeful he and Gary could...he didn't really have a clue what he'd thought, but he'd been young and missed his dad something fierce. What he hadn't known was he'd been the one who ultimately held all the power within Haven Corp, which in turn made his stepdad hate him even more. However, it did make the other man have to be nice to him, or at least, he had to pretend when they were in public. He'd always wondered if the other man wished him dead, but again, his father had protected him through his will, leaving the company to him, and if in the event of Scott's death, the company went to trustees, not the widow. Smart man, his father. Haven Corp was built by his grandfather, then made into more by his dad. Scott decided he wasn't making it more, though. Gary could continue working for him and the company while he went out and did good for his country.

Angel though, she was throwing a curveball into his life.

How the hell could he not have known they'd adopted Talena, his beloved sister? Gary, his stepdad loved Talena like she was his own, yet he'd treated him as if he was a second-class citizen at best. It made absolutely no sense whatsoever. Surely, his mother would've told him? They were close, always had been. Hell, they all three looked alike, from the light blond hair to their blue eyes. Sure, he and his mother's eyes were lighter, but they'd been told their entire lives how much they resembled their mom.

"You don't believe me?" Angela asked, wiping the tears from her cheeks, tears she could turn on or off just as quickly.

"We look alike," he blurted. Fuck, that sounded stupid even to his own ears. Many people resembled others without being related.

Her mirthless laugh had him clenching his jaw. "Listen, I'm sorry about—your situation. Hell, it feels awful calling a baby a situation. You should be overjoyed. I'll support you as a friend and a brother. You know as good as anyone I'm not a good catch." No more fuck buddies for them, that was a given.

She sliced her hand through the air, a scream escaping her. "You'll support me? You don't have a clue what's going to happen to me. Oh god. I've got to get out of here."

Scott stepped in front of her when she moved toward the door. Her wild outburst different than any he'd witnessed. "What are you going to do? You need to calm the fuck down."

"It's none of your business. I needed you to help me, but you clearly won't. I'll *handle* it." She shoved at his chest.

"What do you mean, you'll handle it?" Shit, was she going to get rid of her baby? He raked a hand over his head. His hair was in need of a good cut, but when they went out on missions, they needed to blend in. Fuck, he didn't have time for this bullshit. When he came home, he wanted to see his family, rest a bit, then go back in with a clear head after fucking a woman or three.

"Listen, Hollywood, you worry about yourself like you always do, and I'll worry about myself, like I've always done. As for our little sis, remember what I said. She's no more blood than I am, and daddy dearest will have his sights set on her next," she sneered.

While he was trying to come to terms with what she was saying, she managed to push past him, using his confusion to her advantage. In those few moments, Angela was down the hall and entering the elevator.

"Angela, hold up, let me help you." He rushed into the hall, his bare feet slapping against the concrete floor.

She met his eyes seconds before the doors closed, resolution in her own, confusion in his. Scott thought about running down the stairs and demanding she tell him what she was going to do, but he really had no say. She wasn't his anything except stepsister he slept with when he was on leave occasionally. Sure, he loved her, but he wasn't in love with her, and she didn't love him like that either. "Fuck," he muttered, walking back into his apartment, slamming the door behind him. There's one thing that was drilled into him to remember to do when he was in combat. No matter what the situation, no matter whose life was at stake, or how high the risks, always stay in control, never panic. Right now, he was doing his best to remember that.

"It's never as good as it seems, and it's never as bad as it seems, but keep your head and there's always a way out," he murmured, wishing he'd said that to Angela.

The day after tomorrow he was due to go back to North Carolina before his next assignment sent him out for God knew how long. Shit, for all he knew, he'd be gone when Angela had her baby. Shit, he needed to call her and then call his mom. Although he wasn't going to claim the child, he needed to make sure she was okay. Angela's bombshell about Talena's paternity had sent him reeling. There was one thing he was certain of, and that was if you wanted to know the truth, you go to the source.

He padded to the kitchen island, swiping up his cell and hit speed dial for his mom, Tara Haven-Dupont. Although she'd married Gary Dupont, she'd never dropped his dad's name. Strangely enough, she'd also given his sister Talena the hyphenated name as well. The ringing on the other end seemed to go on and on. Scott was sure it had probably only rung a few times, but he was about to hang up, so he didn't go into her voicemail. He jerked the phone back to his ear at the sound of his mom's sweet voice coming across the line.

"Hey, Scotty, what's the matter?" she asked, concern lacing her words.

She'd always worried about him and his sister growing up, that concern included Angela when she'd been in their home. "Hi, mom. Are you at home?" For some reason he didn't want to ask her such an important thing over the phone.

"Yes, I'm watching Talena and a couple of her friends swim. Why, is everything okay? Do you need me to come over there?" Panic had her tone getting sharper.

"No, nothing like that. I was going to come over and see you before I fly out," he told her.

"I really wish you would consider getting out at the end of your term."

He was used to her request; she'd been saying the same thing since he'd reenlisted a year ago. He still had three years to go, unless he was injured, which he hoped like hell didn't happen. "We'll see, mom. If it's okay with you, I'm gonna come on over." He wouldn't tell her it was called End of Active Service, or EAS, many called it term or enlistment.

Tara was his mom, and she didn't care what they called it. She wanted him to quit and come home, end of story.

"That sounds serious. Are you sure everything is okay? Oh, no, are you sick or hurt? Did you get shot again?"

He groaned, knowing full well she'd go on and on worrying if he didn't shut her down. "Mom, you saw me a week ago. Did I look like I'd been shot?"

"No, but you're a soldier, you can hide that stuff."

"I'll be over there in about an hour or less, mom. Don't fret," he said, using one of her favorite terms. God, he loved to hear her joy; both her and Talena were the reasons he knew the things he did when he loaded up and flew to some godforsaken hellhole were worthwhile. They were the innocent, and he was the...shit, he wouldn't say brave. There had to be ones willing to do what was needed to eliminate threats. That was the altruistic version. The reality was, he was damn good at killing. A vision of Angela at the end of the hall, a look of resolution on her face made him grimace.

He didn't correct his mom when she called him and his team soldiers. Operatives is what they were called. His fellow Army brothers could be called soldiers. His team and others like them didn't go by such. The government used them because they were deadly and they were good at getting in, getting shit done, and getting out without the world knowing about them. He hated that his mom wasn't as aware of what he did, but they say ignorance is bliss. He wished he could've been left in the dark about Angela's situation, only knowing now he had to let his mom in on the secret.

Luckily for him, his sister Talena must've yelled for their mom, eliminating his need to reassure her that all was fine.

"I need to get a group of hungry teen girls something to eat or they turn into hangry teen girls. Trust me, you don't want to see that. I'll see you in a little bit. You be careful and watch your speed," she said.

"Will do," he agreed.

He heard his sister laughing, calling out their pizza choices. In a moment of indecision, he almost changed his mind about going over there. His mother hung up before he could. "Putting shit off was for pussies," he growled out loud staring at the silent phone.

He snatched his keys off the counter, slid his phone into his back pocket, and checked to make sure he had his wallet before shoving his feet into a pair of shoes by the door. Damn, he had to admit how much he loved a nice pair of loafers, something he didn't get to enjoy much when he was at Fort Bragg or on a mission. The blister on his big toe hadn't even fully healed yet, but he was set to head back to wherever he was needed.

The drive to his mother's house; he never referred to the home as Gary's, didn't take nearly long enough. Pulling into the exclusive neighborhood memories assailed him. It had been the home they'd had when his dad was alive. Even though the memories were fading, he remembered the big man who he was named after.

Navigating through the light traffic hadn't taken more than forty-five minutes. He wished it had taken longer, thinking he could've used a little more time to figure out what he was going to say, how he'd ask his mother why she'd lied to him all these years. Huge gates blocked the entrance to the exclusive neighborhood, with each home having several acres of land, it was prime real estate only the truly wealthy could afford. He punched in his private code, waited on the gates to open, then made his way to the entrance to their driveaway, where he had to do the same thing again. Some might think the safety protocols were a bit much, but when you were worth over five hundred million dollars, you didn't take safety for granted. Haven Corp was worth at least that the last he'd checked and only grew.

He eased his Ferrari into the garage after waiting for it to open, the quarter of a million-dollar ride fitting right into the surroundings. His fellow Delta guys had no clue about his true wealth, which suited him. He pushed the door up, easing out of the low-slung ride, glancing at the vehicles parked in the eight-car garage. Gary's Bentley was missing, as usual. The other man was never around.

Pocketing his keys, he entered through the mudroom, then turned left instead of going into the house, heading toward the back where the pool was located. The home and land were all part of his trust, left to him in his father's will. It was something he and Gary had butted heads over and one of the reasons he'd joined the Army, then accepted placement in Delta Force. He would never sign anything over to the fucker, ever. His will stated everything went to Talena if he was to be killed, but there was a caveat that she couldn't sign it off to anyone else except her children upon her death. He'd followed his own father's footsteps and made sure Gary was privy to this. Even if she wasn't his biological sister, he still loved her the same. His jaw ached from grinding it, making him angry at the bastard all over again. The only reason he tolerated the shithead was his mom and Talena loved him. Otherwise, he'd have...what the hell would he have done?

The man ran the company when Scott didn't want to, ever. He'd been his dad's best friend, and now, he was married to his mom. "Shit," he said hating the bastard with a passion that didn't sit well with him.

He followed the sounds of young girls' laughter. The pool area was more like a damn waterpark on steroids. There was an outside kitchen, a pool house, two hot tubs, multiple slides built into the rock walls, making it appear as if they were part of the scenery. The pool itself was a huge L shape that disappeared into a cave-like grotto. He'd helped in redesigning it when he'd been a teen, showing the architect pictures he'd liked. What they ended up with looked like it was set in the jungle, with rocks and foliage that some high-end contractors had come in and created. His mother had laughed and said it was an oasis. Most days if he wanted to find her or his sister, all he had to do was search outside since it was where she spent most of her time, lounging by the pool with Talena. All the kids who came over loved to climb up the rocks and jump into the pool like they were in the forest, kind of like Tarzan. The entire thing had taken a couple years to completely grow to what it was today, but it was nothing less than magical.

Scott stood back, unseen for a moment and watched as Talena lifted her arms above her head at the top of the fake mountain. Her form was much more graceful than the other girls, and then she let out a yell, making him grin as she dove gracefully into the deep waters. Scott hated to upset their mother and ruin her time with Talena with his questions, but fuck, he loathed the fact she'd lied to him. No matter what, Talena was his family.

Laughter filled the air, girls cheering one another on, completely oblivious to the demons plaguing him or the shit he was about to wreak on his mother. Talena climbed out of the pool, her long blonde hair was almost white, the sun making it look like a halo. His chest ached at the thought of losing her as a sister.

"There's my baby boy." His mother moved in front of him, blocking his view of Talena.

"Hi, mom. You look gorgeous as always." It wasn't a lie. At forty-three, she could easily pass for a woman ten years younger. She too was in a bathing suit, her two-piece showing off the fact she was still in excellent shape.

She slapped his arm, then pulled him down to kiss his cheeks. "Come over into the shade and have a seat."

Following her over to the area where huge fans were set up, blowing mist all around, he toed off his shoes so they wouldn't get wet. Damn, he was definitely going to need to get his head back into warfare before going into whatever shithole they sent him.

One of their staff placed a glass in front of him, filling it with his favorite drink. A Shirley Temple with extra grenadine. "Thank you, Louisa."

"You're welcome, young man. I must say, you're looking well." Louisa nodded, walking away with her tray.

Scott laughed, sipping his drink before looking at his mom who was watching him with knowing eyes. She'd always been able to tell when he had something on his mind.

"Alright, tell me what's got you coming over here looking so pensive." She held up her hand. "While I'm very happy to see you, you and I both know you were just here, and you said you'd call when you landed. I assumed that meant we wouldn't see you until, well until the next time." Her voice hitched.

He reached out, putting his hand over hers. "Don't, mom."

With a deep inhale, he opened his mouth preparing to ask her the question that was eating at him. The familiar trill of her phone ringing had him snapping his mouth shut.

She held her finger up, her smile sunny like always. "Just a second, honey. Hello? Yes, this is her stepmother."

He sat up straighter, watching his mother as she listened to whatever the person on the other end had to say. Her tan complexion paled; the hand holding the phone began to shake so much he worried she was going to drop the little device.

"What's wrong?" he asked when she didn't speak.

His mother opened her mouth and closed it a couple times while still holding the phone to her ear. Scott gently took the phone from her. "Hello, this is Angela's brother. What's going on?" He didn't mention they weren't biologically related.

"This is Officer Bradshaw. We tried calling Angela Dupont's father as he was listed first on her contacts but were unable to reach him. This number was the second on her list. She's being airlifted to the hospital for emergency surgery." There was a pause while he could hear the sound of a helicopter in the background.

Scott listened as the officer explained about the accident. "She's pregnant," he told the officer, unsure if Angela would've been able to tell them herself. His mother's sharp intake of air almost distracted him from what the other man was saying.

"I'll let the hospital know, but you need to understand— the accident wasn't. It appears to have been intentional."

The words dropped like an anvil on his head. Moving away from his mother, he asked more questions, getting frustrated at the lack of response. Finally, he hung up after he had all the officer could give him.

"Where's Gary?" It was Saturday, the bastard should've been home.

"I don't know. He left a couple of hours ago for a meeting. Oh god, I need to go to the hospital." His mother's grief-stricken face took him back to a time when he was a boy, a time he had buried from when his father had been killed in a car accident.

"No, you need to stay here with Talena and try to get ahold of Gary. Tell him to meet me at the hospital." He cradled his mother's face between his palms, trying to infuse her with his strength. "She's going to be fine." He rattled off the hospital the officer had told him they were airlifting

Angela to, waving at Talena as he made his way back the way he'd come. Normally he'd have made sure to spend time with his little sister before leaving, and he could see the hurt on her youthful face as he left without doing so this time. After he made sure Angela was okay, he'd come back.

How he wished his words and prayers would've been the truth hours later as he sat in a plastic chair looking down at his loafers, his cellphone gripped in his hand while he waited for someone to come and speak to him. He'd prayed and hoped, which he should've known better than to do.

"Mr. Haven?"

He hurried to his feet, moving swiftly toward the doctor, already knowing what he was going to say by the set to the man's shoulders. Scott had been in situations where death occurred. The man in the clean scrubs had clearly taken the time to make himself presentable before coming out to break the news to him. Fuck.

"I'm Scott Haven, Angela's brother." Obviously, there wasn't anyone else in the surgery waiting area but him.

"I'm Dr. Obrien. I was part of the trauma team that tried to save your sister. I'm sorry, but she and the baby didn't make it. Your sister didn't have her seatbelt on when she went over the cliff. Even if she had, at the high rate of speed she was traveling, I don't think anyone would've survived. The fact she was driving a convertible and went over the rocky edge—it was a miracle she was alive when she made it here. I'm truly sorry for your loss."

Scott could see the man meant what he said. He listened to him say he was sorry again and then go on to explain how hard he'd tried to save her. Which didn't mean shit to him because she was still gone, but he knew the man needed to say the words, so he let him. Angela loved to drive fast, especially with the top down. What she didn't do was drive or ride without buckling up. "Are you sure she didn't have her seatbelt on?" he asked for verification.

Dr. Obrien rubbed the back of his neck before answering. "In a crash like this, if she'd have been wearing a seatbelt, there would've been bruising along her torso from the belt, even if she'd have been ejected. Your sister's body"—he took a deep breath—"May I be frank with you?" He'd been making motions across his chest as he was speaking and then dropped his hands.

Scott nodded, taking a moment to steady his thoughts, waiting for whatever shit was going to fall out of the man's mouth.

"Ms. Dupont had more broken bones than any trauma patient I've ever encountered. To be honest, she had very few bones that weren't fractured when they brought her in. She also sustained significant damage to both lungs, ruptured her spleen, and her intestines were compromised due to her pelvis being fractured. I can only say her saving grace was the head trauma that knocked her unconscious. What I mean, is that she was completely unresponsive. The injuries, Mr. Haven, would've been excruciating for anyone, but a woman—I wouldn't want anyone, especially a young woman to suffer like that. The head injury would've occurred immediately upon impact. My diagnosis would be that she wasn't cognizant when she went over, nor when she sustained the rest of the damage. I hope that gives you and her family some measure of relief."

"Thank you, doctor. How...how about the baby?" Shit, did they deliver her child?

"There was no chance for the baby to survive. My guess, from the size of the fetus, she was probably around twelve weeks. Even with the best medical intervention, that's too early for a baby to be born."

The doctor went on to explain the size of a twelve-week baby, comparing them to a plumb and some more technical shit he let go in one ear and out the other. His heart was breaking for Angela and her child and the life they wouldn't get to have.

The distance to where they had Angela's body felt like he was walking through waist-high mud. He'd known either he or her dad would have to identify her. The fact it was him, had guilt slicing through him worse than the knife he'd taken in the thigh a year ago in Cambodia. If only he'd done or said something differently, made her stay and talk to him. Anything instead of letting her get on the elevator and leave.

"You can look through the window if you'd prefer?" the doctor offered.

They stopped outside the door, but if there was one thing he wasn't, that was a pussy. He gave respect in the field when he took a life; Angela deserved better. She deserves someone to identify her properly, someone to do the right thing. He was her someone. With his strength wrapped around him, he motioned for the doctor to lead the way. In all his years, through deserts and jungles, shitholes he'd thought he'd seen the worst he could've seen when he'd had to pull the trigger and watch a child's life leave their body. Yet nothing could've prepared him for the feeling of loss assaulting him when he looked down, seeing the once beautiful woman who'd come into his life like a whirlwind lifeless.

"Dammit, Angela, you look so damn broken," he choked out. He thought of the sassy vixen she'd always been, the one who'd looked up at him, begging him to help her only hours before.

"Oh, Angel," he whispered, smoothing his hand over her forehead, shocked at how badly his entire arm shook and was afraid he'd damage—fuck, how goddamn stupid to think he could hurt her more. "What happened to you?" Tears burning his eyes.

A sheet covered her from shoulder to feet. From what he could see they'd tried to make her look...better. He would pay the best make-up artist to come in and see that he or she worked magic so that Angela would look beautiful one last time. A choked sob shook him at the thought of never seeing her vivacious personality again. He may not have been in love with her, but he loved her. One day he had imagined seeing her settle down with a husband and kids and getting to be a doting uncle. Some might think that was fucked up since he and she had hooked up, but he and Angela had understood each other. They were friends, or so he thought.

Three months. She was three months pregnant. He had no clue who she'd been seeing or if it was a casual hookup. Her words before she'd left his apartment about the other man killing her sprang forward.

After saying all the right things to the doctor, or at least he hoped he had, he walked out of the hospital. His phone gripped in his right hand remained silent, no word from Gary or his mom. Taking a deep breath, Scott made his way to his car, the sleek silver Ferrari sat where he'd left it. Most people would've been afraid to leave a vehicle that cost over two hundred grand in a crowded lot like he'd done. His only thought had been to get to Angela. Their last conversation played through his mind, making him wish he could go back and change things. No, he wouldn't have agreed to claim the baby, but fuck all if he'd have allowed her to leave like she had. "Damn you, Angel," he whispered, wiping his eyes with the heels of his hands; the feel of his phone digging into his forehead was a welcome bite of pain.

Settling into the driver's seat, he drove back to his mom's house, trying to figure out a way to break the news to her and his sister. Shit, how the fuck did he go from having a stepsister and a half-sister, to what he was facing to this? He just learned he and T weren't truly related either.

This time outside the large gates he hesitated. His Lieutenant Colonel needed to know what was going on since he didn't think he'd be flying out on schedule. Instead of punching in the code on the pad to get in, he hit the number programmed into his phone.

"Yo, Hollywood, what's going on?"

"Sir, I have a problem."

His team called him Hollywood, saying since he grew up in California and because he looked like he stepped off the set of a movie, it was appropriate. He'd always laughed when they'd said it. When he'd began getting tattoos, a few of his teammates had pretended to be outraged, joking that his Ken image was being ruined. He felt like the furthest thing from the sunny image in that moment.

Realizing his superior had spoken but he hadn't been listening had him wincing.

"I'm sorry, Sir, can you repeat that?"

"I asked what your problem was, Haven."

Shit, when the man goes from calling him Hollywood, to Haven, he knows he's in trouble. Without pause, he explained about the accident, leaving out the gruesome details and his relationship with her.

"My condolences, Haven. I'll get your paperwork handled on this end. I'm really sorry to hear about your sister. The team was set to leave in seventy-two hours but as things go, there's been a development, so it's actually been moved back. You've got a week, but if you need more, give me a call. However, if the mission gets the go ahead after the week is up, I'll need you on the next flight. Understood?"

"Understood, Sir," he agreed.

After disconnecting the call, he punched his code in and drove through the gates, parked back in the spot he'd occupied before as a heavy weight settled over him. At the sight of Gary's Bentley, anger boiled in his veins. Motherfucker hadn't picked up his phone or returned his half a dozen messages, but he was home?

He pushed his door open, waiting for the batwing door to lift up before he climbed out of the car. Every step he took made him even more pissed that Gary hadn't showed up at the hospital or called.

The first place he checked was his dad's old office, the space Gary had taken over and acted like he was king of the castle. Shockingly, he wasn't there. He didn't expect to find him outside with the girls, so he went upstairs, his hands balled into fists. The second story master suite's door was closed, which normally he'd have been polite and knocked. Polite had left the motherfucking building when he had to identify Angela's lifeless form. He slammed the door open, the crash as the heavy wood hit the wall fueled his anger.

"Scott, what's the meaning of this?" Gary asked, his tone outraged.

He looked the older man up and down, noticing he had developed a belly in the last year or so. "Why the fuck haven't you returned my call or picked up your fucking cellphone when I called?"

Gary jerked the robe that was lying on the end of the bed up, before answering. "I was driving, boy. It's illegal to call or text in California. What did you need?"

The smooth way the other man spoke set his anger to a degree past boiling. He took a deep breath, knowing if he eliminated the space between them, he'd beat the shit out of the fucker, and then he'd probably go to jail. With short succinct words, he told him about Angela, watching Gary's every reaction.

"Thank you for handling that, Scott. I'll take care of the other details." Gary turned away from him, his back straight.

Scott noticed the other man's back was scored with fingernail marks just before the robe covered them. His mother didn't have long, cat-like nails that would make grooves in a man's back.

"What about my mother and sister?" he asked, wanting to hear the sadness a parent should feel knowing their child was gone. Hell, speaking about his own father still had the power to choke him up, images of Angela lying nearly brought him to his knees.

"If you'd like to break it to your mother you may but let her tell your sister. A woman is much better suited for those kinds of things. Don't you think?" Gary moved to his closet, his voice getting fainter the farther he walked away.

Scott had heard enough. There wasn't an ounce of sadness, or remorse, no inflection whatsoever in his stepfather's tone. In fact, if he'd been asked how the other man sounded, he'd have said indifferent.

A quick glance around the room, made him clench his teeth together. As he stared around the space, all he saw was stark furniture and expense. He knew his mother had her own suite downstairs, the master she'd shared with his father, but he'd thought something of her would show in Gary's space.

He turned away, heading down to the pool area. Telling his mother was going to break her heart all over again.

Chapter Two

Talena held her brother's hand during the funeral, wiping at her burning eyes from all the crying she'd done in the past couple of days. Scott handed her another tissue, taking the crumbled one from her. She tried to say thank you, but her throat hurt from swallowing so many times in her bid to not cry. It wasn't that Angela had been one of her favorite people. In fact, her sister was truly horrid to her growing up, always saying the most awful things; things that made Talena feel absolutely terrible about herself. No, what made her cry was the memory of what Angela had said to her the day before she'd died, words that made her grip her brother, or rather, Scott's hand harder. She needed to find a way to tell him what Angela said. Scott would protect her and make sure what happened to their sister—what happened to Angela didn't happen to her. For the last two nights she'd locked her bedroom door, which she'd never done before.

She felt the weight of disapproval being directed toward her, knowing her dad didn't like Scott. He definitely didn't like that she was staying close to her brother and not him. Oh God, she didn't think she could pretend to not know the truth. The anguish she'd held in since Angela's bombshell escaped in a hiccupping cry. All the little things that had been happening over the last year, she could no longer brush off as her dad not wanting to let her grow up, like he'd claimed.

Dads didn't do what hers did to their daughters. She knew the truth now and Angela, she may have been mean and spiteful, but in the end, she'd tried to protect Talena.

"Ah, pipsqueak, don't. You're breaking my heart, and I only got one to give," Scott whispered, pulling her in closer to his side.

"I...I'm sorry. It's just so aw...awful," she cried.

Their mom moved closer in her chair, wrapping her arm around her back with a murmur. Her own eyes were filled tears and red from crying. Tara Haven wasn't even Angela's mother, but she was torn up, unlike her father who like a statue.

Feeling both her mom and brother surround her, she felt safe and loved. They sat that way for the rest of the service, while her dad was on the other side of her mother, dark shades hiding his eyes. Not once did she see him look sad. She never had, in all her years, no matter the circumstance. Before, she'd thought that meant he was strong and brave. The blinders were off now that Angela had ripped all of her stupid childish innocence away with her revelations. She was glad to know the truth, but at the same time she wished...well she couldn't say she wished she didn't know. Knowledge was good to have if you could do something with it. For her, knowing meant she now had to be on guard.

When the minister closed the Bible, everyone stood up pulling her from her inner turmoil. Again, her dad didn't move to take her mom's hand. It all was so odd all the little things she was noticing for the first time. She wasn't sure if she should be thankful Angela had opened her eyes or not.

"Thank you all for coming out today. I know how hard it must be to lose someone so young. Angela Dupont was very meticulous it seems, even before her untimely passing. She wanted a letter read in the event of her death." He lifted a blush pink envelope with a gold seal. "Strange a woman in her mid-twenties would have the forethought to write a letter such as this, but as you all must know, Ms. Dupont wasn't your average girl." He looked around the gathering.

Talena heard her dad's sharp intake of air.

"For my family's sake, I'd like to ask that you present us with the letter to read in the privacy of our home, if you don't mind." He moved around the gorgeous casket with the beautiful flowers that had been draped over it, paying no attention to where his daughter lay, his sole focus was clearly on getting to the minister and the letter he held.

It should've been a request, but her father never requested anything, he demanded.

The minister sighed and shook his head. "I'm sorry, but this was laid out and paid for prior to her death several weeks back. It was delivered to my office yesterday," he said.

"Yes, well, that is all well and good, but this entire funeral has been paid for by me and my checking account. If you'd like me to see to your payment going through, I suggest you allow *me* to decide when and where my family hears our daughter's last words," her father bit out.

The minister pushed on his ear, bringing her focus to the fact he had what appeared to be a hearing aid or some kind of device in it. The entire funeral was a huge spectacle, one that was in line with their wealthy status. She was actually shocked her father had stepped out of character to approach the man instead of allowing him to read the letter. Whatever was in the envelope was clearly something he didn't want everyone present to hear.

"Gary, I don't see any reason we can't allow the man to read Angela's letter. What could be in there that's so awful?" Scott asked.

"This is none of your concern, boy."

Talena was jarred from her own musings to find her brother had gone around the opposite direction and stood a couple feet from the minister. At her dad's words, she could see her brother's jaw harden in anger before he stood taller. Gah, she needed to stop thinking of them as such. Gary wasn't her dad, and Scott wasn't her brother. Tara wasn't her mom. She was nobody to anyone.

"Gary, you call me boy one more time, and I'll show just how much of a boy I'm not. Feel me?" Scott towered over both men anger in every line of his body.

Her father grabbed the letter, pushing it inside a pocket of his suit jacket. He looked at the crowd, his eyes harder than she'd ever seen them.

"We're in the middle of my stepdaughter's funeral. I would appreciate it if you two would please stop beating your chest and allow her to be put in the ground in peace."

Her mother didn't need to raise her voice or resort to name calling to get everyone to fall in line. With one little softly spoken sentence, she put two grown men in their places. Not that her brother needed it, but her dad, he was on the verge of an explosion, everyone could see it and feel it.

The minister let out a breath. "I will abide by the family's wishes. If you all would like to come up and pay your last respects."

Hours later, she was sure she'd cried all the tears she had in her body. Everyone had already left, gone home to their families, leaving her alone with her mom and dad. Only they weren't really her parents, not by blood.

"What's the matter, my Dove?" her dad asked, startling her from her thoughts.

She'd always thought his nickname was beautiful. Now, it scared her. She'd come outside to escape from all the sympathy from all the well-wishers.

"Today was awful." Truth since it had been, knowing she'd never see Angela again, never get to have the close relationship like other girls with their big sisters. She'd craved to have a sister who would teach her how to wear makeup and how to do all the things a girl did, like when she had her first boyfriend.

Her dad settled on the swing next to her, the loud creak made her flinch.

"Sometimes people leave us because it's their time to go. I've lost a couple people in my life, but with their passing, my life was enriched." He sounded like he was discussing the weather, not the loss of a loved one.

She was puzzled by his words. How could anyone be richer by the loss of another's life? Of a child?

He reached across the distance, running his fingers down her cheek. She jerked away, her hand covering her face. "Why do you not like me touching you?"

His touch didn't feel right. In the last year, she thought it odd how he'd begun touching her more often, in ways that didn't fit in with the norm. He said she needed more sunblock on, even though she'd just put some on, or he found a new lotion that was good for teens. In hindsight, she was aware his excuses were absurd. She wasn't that naïve or stupid. Angela had told her to watch for signs that he was grooming her. She'd been clueless, so of course she went to the internet where she googled the meaning. Good god, that had been a worm hole that frightened the bejeezus out of her.

"I don't like anyone touching me," she said, getting up from the swing, moving away from him and his touch.

The creak of the swing warned her that he too stood. She tensed with the need to run at the sound of his shoes crunching over the grass.

"That doesn't seem right or fair. I'm your father, and I need my baby girl now more than ever. I just lost my oldest child."

Something about the way he spoke and how he stared at her, his eyes didn't look sad like when his favorite team had lost a game, and really, she only thought he was upset then because he lost a bet. Her father hated to lose anything. The way he was coming toward her was more like what she'd witnessed when watching a predator in a documentary when it stalked their prey, scaring her worse than when she watched a scary movie at her friend Maureen's house.

"Hey, you two. What's going on?"

Talena turned at the sound of Scott's voice coming from behind her, unable to keep the cry of relief from escaping her throat. She didn't care what it looked like as she ran the short distance to him, flinging herself into his arms with a sob. "Scott, I don't want you to leave me."

"Talena, stop acting like a baby and come here." Her father's angry growl was like a whip cracking through the air.

She looked up into her brother's icy blue eyes, begging him without saying a word. He'd always been her protector. How did she ask him to save her from a man who was supposed to be her dad, when she wasn't sure if she actually needed saving? Angela didn't come right out and say it, but she'd said enough to scare her, and now she was gone. Her world was turned upside down and didn't look like it was going to level out.

"Mom told me to come get you. She said you needed to come in and get cleaned up before dinner. Why don't you run on in while I have a talk with Gary?" He sat her on the ground behind him, his voice gentle, his touch even more so.

"Okay, but you're not leaving without saying goodbye, are you?" she asked, uncaring if she sounded whiney. He was her big brother who she missed terribly when he was away. When he left this time she wasn't sure what would happen.

"Wouldn't dream of it, pipsqueak. Tell mom I'll be in shortly." He ran his hand over her head.

"Okay, thank you." She didn't look at her dad before running toward the house. In the last year she'd gone from loving her dad like a daughter would, to being wary, and now she was fearing him. With the loss of Angela, her life was spiraling, making her feel a lot older than she was.

"When are we going to get to read Angela's letter?" he asked Gary, knowing full well the fucker wasn't going to allow anyone else see what she'd said. What the bastard didn't know, was he'd already read a copy of the letter since she'd sent him one as well.

"Your mother and I already did. Angela was a very sick young lady, as was proven by the fact she committed suicide. I'm trying to keep that fact from your little sister. Now, what is it that you really want, Scott?" Gary said, puffing out his chest.

He would've laughed at the other man's effort at intimidation if he wasn't so fucking livid. All these years he'd thought, hell, he was sure his mother did too, that Angela was Gary's biological child. That was until he'd read the letter that had been delivered to him in the event of her death.

"There's several things I want, but let's start with the main one." He stepped into Gary's personal space, bumping Gary's chest with his own. "I want to make a few things very fucking clear, so you best listen really closely. If you so much as put one motherfucking finger on Talena, I will slice every inch of skin from you, slowly. I'll make sure you're awake as I do it, and I will then take great pleasure in removing bits of you, starting with the tip of your cock. From there, I'll work my way down until you're no more than a eunuch. I will of course cauterize you after I snip and slice so that you won't bleed out. I have ways of ensuring you will live until I am done with you. Shall I go on? Trust me. I know how to torture and make damn sure you live long enough you'll wish you'd never been born." The last was growled right next to Gary's ear.

"What's the meaning of this?" Gary asked, taking a step backward.

Oh, he'd give the old son-of-a-bitch credit in the acting department. His outrage and shock appeared genuine, but so had the years of pretending to be something he wasn't. A loving father. When in reality, he was a pedophile who took advantage of his position. Sure, Angela could've made the shit up, but the pictures she'd sent were proof that Gary had been with her, in the biblical sense when she'd been a child in his home, and even more recently. The child she'd carried hadn't been some random guy, but Gary's.

As he stared at the man his mother had married, his father's business partner and former best friend, he wanted to kill him with his bare hands. This was a man he'd known his entire life, a man he'd have sworn was honest and upstanding. A man he'd have trusted with his family.

"Scott, you need to explain what the hell is wrong with you. I understand you and Angela were close, but she was my child." Gary's eyes watered.

If he didn't know any better, Scott would've relented, maybe even apologized. However, his eyes were wide open. Little things began to fall into place now that Angela's letter had filled in the blanks. He hated that her death had to be a catalyst, but he would make damn sure Talena didn't fall prey to the same fate her sister had. She wouldn't be a victim.

"What's wrong is I also got a letter from Angela. Yes, Angela and I were close. Clearly, you and she were as well," he said, watching Gary to see how he reacted to his words. The slight narrowing of his stepfather's eyes was quickly masked when he looked away.

"Of course, we were close," Gary sputtered, moving backward, his hands going to the lapels of his jacket and jerking it down.

He was done tiptoeing around the truth and allowing monsters to destroy innocents. "A father, even one who wasn't biologically related, doesn't fuck their daughter. You took advantage of your position. Hell, let's call it like it is, shall we? You molested Angela when she was a child under you and your wife's roof. That was the reason your first wife divorced you. You raped your child for years and then when she was older, you continued it and called it an affair."

At first, Scott thought the other man was going to try to lie his way out of what he was saying, but then he should've known better. Gary was a snake who had no morals, no shame.

"You have no proof other than the ramblings of a sick girl who took her own life, rather than face the fact she was an unwed mother-to-be. Now, if you're done making wild accusations, I'm going inside to be with my wife and daughter. If you want to be welcome in my home, I suggest you not make these accusations again, especially in front of your mother and Talena." Dark eyes flashed a warning, as if he could back his words with some sort of retaliation.

Again, Scott stepped forward, halting Gary's smooth exit. It took restraint to keep him from hitting the man who'd been a part of his life since he'd been a young boy. While he stared down into his stepfather's face he let Gary see his resolve. "Let's get a few things straight, Gary. One, that's my house, not yours. It belonged to my father and is part of *my* estate. Which I will come to inherit when I turn twenty-five. That's in two years, Gare." He used the hated nickname the other man had raged about a colleague using once before. If there was one thing he'd learned, it was how to fight in any battle. Words could wound just as deeply. "Second, you and I both know that Angela was telling the truth about your fucked-up relationship. Mind you, since there was no shared blood, society wouldn't have looked down on either of you, now, except for the fact you're cheating on your wife. And for your information, it wasn't just a letter she sent to me. Did you know she'd been taking pictures of you and her and had been, for years? Hell, maybe there are videos as well. Thankfully, she didn't send me those, but she did include some incriminating pictures, spanning years. Fucking years. And, yeah, you and she were clearly fucking in them, of that there is no doubt." His anger was boiling out of control at the thought of Gary doing the same to Talena.

"You and I both know these things can be created, falsified with even a rudimentary computer program," he denied.

Scott had already thought of that. He'd sent the images to one of his friends who specializes in cybercrime. The man had verified the authenticity of the images after he'd scrubbed them of any viruses. There was no copy paste insert done to them. "No, I made sure they were the real deal before coming here. Oh, don't look so shocked, Gare. I didn't make it into Delta Force with my looks."

"Who else has seen these so-called incriminating images?" Gary pulled a handkerchief out of his pocket, wiping his brow and shook his head.

"My team leader as well as a trusted cybercrime specialist. So, you can stand there and deny till you're blue in the face, but you and I know the truth. She was a child, your child who trusted you. The first time Angela said she was barely a teen when you molested her, blaming her mother. Did I mention how detailed she was in her ten-page letter? She didn't leave much out that I could tell, obviously she'd been planning—she'd not done what she did in haste. From what I gathered, you made her believe she was special."

"You can't believe the ramblings of a...a girl who wasn't of the right mind. Look what she did," Gary yelled. "She killed herself and that of her unborn child."

"That she did, and I'll always regret not doing more to help her. You know what I think? I think that baby she carried was yours. She loved you like a woman, not a daughter. That's why you moved her out here, not because she didn't get along with her mother like you'd said but so you could have her closer to you. She was nineteen then and still thought you and she were...fuck, I don't even fucking know. Angela's letter said you and she were in love. Which is bullshit, and you and I both know it. Sick fucks like you groom kids to think that way, but she was nothing more than a victim. You belong behind bars where Bubba would make you his bitch," he spat, bumping his chest against Gary's.

"You can't prove anything. Besides, what would your precious military think if they found out you were fucking your own sister?" An unholy light glinted in the dark face his mother had ran to when her husband had been killed in a car accident, a face that Scott had thought was kind and caring. Now that man was threatening to try and tarnish his name. He wanted to laugh at the audacity, but he knew Gary wasn't joking. However, he also didn't want to give the bastard any more chances to hurt his family. His mom and sister were the two most important people in his life. He couldn't leave them unprotected and with his career, he was gone for long periods of time.

"My team is aware I had sexual relations with Angela, my non-blood related sister. What they didn't know was my stepfather was fucking her, had been molesting her since she was thirteen. Is that what you were asking?"

Sweat was rolling down Gary's face unchecked now. "What do you want from me?"

That was a loaded question. "I want you behind bars. I want Angela alive, and I want this to be a nightmare I wake up from. Can you deliver any of those for me?"

"Hey, you two, supper is getting cold," his mother called out. From the sound of her voice, she was coming toward them and would see they had been arguing in seconds.

"You better make a quick decision, because there's no way on God's green Earth I'll allow you to continue to live in my home with my mother and sister. You can't ruin my career, Gary. You may run my father's company, my company, for now. But you won't come Monday morning." He'd already had the board of trustees begin the process of removing Gary from his position. Yes, they'd needed him sixteen years ago when his father was killed, and he'd been a little eight-year-old boy. The company had been growing by leaps and bounds in the medical field. However, they were so ingrained in the world of medicine with more heads, that Gary was basically sitting in an office twiddling his thumbs. As for criminal charges? Scott wasn't sure what he'd do or could do given that Angela was no longer alive to press charges, nor did his mother deserve that kind of attention brought to their family. Fuck, he would need to talk to her first.

"Tell your mother I had a business call I had to deal with," he snarled.

"Don't do anything stupid, Gary. I got eyes everywhere," he said, the lie rolling off his tongue.

He cursed himself for not thinking that far in advance. However, his only impulse after opening Angela's letter and seeing the evidence for himself, had been to verify Angela's images were real and not faked. After that, he'd rushed to his mom's house with the need to make sure Talena was safe. Lieutenant Diamond had given him strict orders not to kill a civilian. Gary was lucky he was a well-trained operative, or he'd be a dead man. Watching the bastard stride away, like the weasel he was, had him clenching his hands into fist to keep from reaching for his gun tucked safely behind his back. The slight miscalculation could cost him, but he was able to breathe easier knowing his mom and sister were both safe with him. He had the better part of two weeks, if not longer, before he had to ship out. In that time, he'd ensure both their lives were as safe as he could make them, and Gary would be out of Haven Corp and their lives, if he had any say in the matter.

"Scott, where's Gary going?" his mother asked.

He took a deep, steadying breath before turning to face his mom, and prayed she didn't notice the anger still raging within him. "He said something urgent came up that he had to take care of. Come on, let's go inside. I'm starving. Look at me, my stomach's eating my backbone," he joked, patting his abs for affect.

His mom laughed, sliding her arm around his waist. "You're built just like your father was. You know that man could eat an entire cow and never have an ounce of fat on him either."

He didn't miss the wistful tone in her words. If he'd been Gary, he wasn't sure he'd have been so chill if his wife spoke of her deceased husband so fondly. Of course, Scott Senior was a man not many would've been able to live up to. He'd been six foot three like Scott was. If he'd still been alive, his mom said they'd have called him Scotty, or SJ for Scott Junior. Yeah, he wasn't sure he'd have been good with that nickname. Scott suited him, or Hollywood as his Delta Force Team called him. "He didn't have any fat on him because you had him running after you all the time. I remember the way we'd all go to the ocean, and you and he would run up and down the beach for hours while I played in the sand. Why didn't you ever take Talena to the beach?"

His mom sighed as they walked but didn't answer him right away. He didn't press her, his focus on the night sounds around them. The sound of Gary's car leaving a few minutes ago had eased a little of his fears but he wouldn't relax until he'd made a few calls. While they walked and talked, he sent out a text to one of his friends who was also on leave in the area. If he was free, Scott was sure he'd have no problem checking in on Gary for him.

"The beach was a special place to your father and me. It didn't seem right to go there with...with Gary. I've made a lot of mistakes in the past ten years or so, but Talena hasn't wanted for anything, even if I didn't take her to the ocean to frolic like I did with you. Trust me, she and I have our own special things we do."

"What kind of mistakes, mom? From what I've seen, you're damn near perfect. Heck, that's probably why I'm still single. They say find a woman half as good as your mom. That's something I just don't think is possible. Truly, what the hell makes you think you did something wrong?" They stopped on the veranda outside the entrance to the dining room, light spilling onto the patio highlighting her blue eyes. They weren't the same light blue as his and his dad's, but they were still a pretty blue. He could understand why people thought she was Talena's biological mother, with her blonde hair and blue eyes, similar but not.

"I married Gary too soon after your dad...after his death. He was there when I was needing someone to figure out what to do with the company, and he was your dad's best friend. It's wasn't the love like I had for your father, rather friendship and stability. He was fine with that he said, even when I told him I didn't think I'd ever love a man like your father. You needed a man to be there for things, and Gary had always been a part of our lives, so I thought I was doing the right thing." She took a deep breath, stared into the house before continuing. "I wanted a big family. Your dad and I, we were going to fill this house with children. He always joked that we'd have four or five to start. After you, we decided to wait a few years, and then we had just started trying again. The day of the accident I'd just found out I was pregnant," she choked out.

He was frozen in place. Talena wasn't old enough to be that child and Angela was older than him plus she wasn't his mother's child. His confusion must've been clear for her to see because he didn't need to ask before she was speaking again.

"His death was so hard and watching you cry for your daddy was like losing him all over again, night after night. It was like my body couldn't sustain the pregnancy. I miscarried at sixteen weeks. I decided then and there I wasn't having another man's child, when I couldn't even keep the one inside me safe. A few months after your father's death, Gary found me curled in a ball in my master bedroom. You had been at school, luckily. Gary said your father wouldn't want me to continue on like I was. He said I needed to stop grieving and start living. When he suggested a marriage of convenience, I went along with him. After a couple of years, I decided I wanted a child, but I wouldn't have one, not the conventional way. Talena—she's mine as much as any."

The fierce way she spoke and the love she had for Talena was undeniable. He was still reeling from the news, even though he'd already known thanks to Angela, but he kept his face impassive, his training coming in handy. He also felt Gary had an ulterior motive for getting his mother to marry him but kept that to himself. "Is she aware?"

His mother shook her head, still looking in through the closed patio doors. He saw Talena walk by with a platter in her arms. Their cook would've given it to her only because his sister had probably begged to help. "Are you going to tell her?" he asked.

"I had planned to, someday. Angela said it wouldn't matter because, well, you know, she was also adopted. Or did you know that?" His mother finally looked up at him, sadness clouded her vision.

"I do. I didn't until recently." No need to tell her how recently or what else he knew. Fuck, the saying about tangled webs ran through his mind.

"I need to tell you something else." She kept one hand on the door handle, meeting his gaze squarely. "Gary and me. We aren't. He and I are not husband and wife in the sense like a normal married couple. When he suggested we get married, he knew I wasn't ready and that I might never be. It's been sixteen years since I lost your father, but I still dream of him. I still wake up wanting him, only him. I know Gary has lovers, and I am fine with that. I always have been. I told him long ago if he ever met a woman he fell in love with, I'd divorce him so he could be happy. I needed you to know I would never trap him into a loveless marriage. I do love him, and he loves us, all of us, just not in that way."

"Mom, why are you telling me all of this right now?" Her confession was so out of left field he wasn't sure what to make of it.

"I saw the two of you arguing. I know the day Angela died you were upset because we couldn't get ahold of him, and well, I needed you to know I was aware he was with one of his women. I didn't want to say anything at the time but seeing you ready to pummel him made me feel as though I was making things worse. He wasn't off doing anything I wouldn't be okay with. Do you understand what I'm saying?" She didn't look away when she stopped speaking, nor did she hunch her shoulders like she was embarrassed.

"What about you and your needs? You speak about him having lovers, but what about you. Mom, you're young and beautiful and only forty-three. You have a lot of life to live. Hell, I know half my team, who are too stupid to realize I'd already marked their foreheads with my scope, thinks you're hot. The other half are smart enough to keep their thoughts to themselves, but I saw they agreed with the others the one time you showed up to greet me when I returned. What about you?" He hated the thought of her being alone or in a loveless marriage for the rest of her life.

"Are you asking if I have a lover, Scott? Because the answer is no, I have no male companion, and I don't want one. Sixteen years may seem like a long time to many, but to me, it was only yesterday I was with your father planning our future. Now, come on, let's go inside and eat. I wanted to make sure you knew everything. There are no secrets now." She patted his arm then walked in with her confident stride.

No way was he going to break her heart and tell her the bastard she was married to, even in name only, was a damn child rapist who more than likely was also the father of the baby Angela had been carrying. He wondered what other woman the prick was sleeping with since he'd obviously been with someone on the day Angela had died.

"It's about time you two came in. Charlene was getting ready to toss everything out and order me pizza." Talena grinned, her braces made the word pizza sound a little lispy.

"Hey, I'm all for pizza. You like anchovies on yours?" Scott hated seafood of any kind, same as Talena and his mother. The dual 'yucks' came from both the females in the room. Normal, they all needed normal, even if it was make believe for a little while.

After dinner he agreed to stay the night, thinking he'd get some work of his own in before going to bed. At twenty-three, he hadn't planned to take over the company anytime soon, maybe never. Shit, he didn't want to be stuck in an office wearing a suit and tie. Although it was something his father and grandfather before him had seemed to love, being stuck in an office for eight to ten hours or more didn't appeal to him. Throw him in the middle of a firefight or a rough terrain with a backpack and his wits, and he'd be golden. They may call him Hollywood, and God yes, he loved his comforts, but he'd rather be outside doing something physical. He could still appreciate the finer things, like his quarter of a million-dollar Ferrari and even the nice clothes when he was home, but to think about getting up at the asscrack-of-dawn every day, driving to and from the same place, sitting behind a desk, doing the same shit, day in and day out, he wasn't that man and never would be.

"How could he have been best friends with my dad all through college and after, then marry my mom when my dad died, yet somehow have another life so well hidden nobody knew anything about it?" he asked the empty room, still puzzled over the fact his father who was a smart man had never known the duplicity of his friend.

He could remember his father telling stories about times he and Gary had done things, or maybe it had been Gary who'd been the storyteller. However, his dad had believed in him enough to make him VP of the family business. They'd both had the drive needed to run a company like Haven Corp, making Gary the natural choice to take over after Scott Senior had been killed. Now every memory made him wonder if Gary hadn't been manipulating things, ensuring he was a staple feature in their home long before his father's death. Coming over four to five nights out of the week, eating dinner with them while they talked business around the table made sure he was a fixture. He'd been Uncle Gary, the nice guy who played ball with him and his dad.

It was after he married his mom that all changed. He changed, becoming aloof and disinterested, almost cruel to Scott.

The one thing Gary took pride in was the multi-billion-dollar corporation Silas Haven, his grandfather had started, Gary acting almost as if he was a Haven or wishing he was. His own father had loved and continued to build the huge conglomerate it had become, but it had grown even more after Gary had taken over due to the advancement that had been set in motion prior to his dad's death. Scott and the board of trustees kept quiet and let him control things because he'd never faltered when it came to Haven Corp. He had to wonder how much the man had pocketed from the company to keep his other women happy and silent.

How the fuck had he not realized his mom and Gary hadn't been a real couple? "Because you didn't want to think of your mom and him that way," he muttered out loud. There hadn't been any casual kisses or lingering looks like he'd seen other parents make. Shit, it was all there if he'd only been more aware.

A quick scroll through a folder on his phone gave him a list of the board of trustees. He'd requested the names from his lawyer earlier, before he'd sat down to eat with his family, knowing he had to move quickly. He scanned the names, double checking there wasn't anyone new who hadn't been there previously. Sure, even ones who had been there could be bought, but if they'd been around long enough, then they should be loyal to the company, not Gary, he hoped. He pulled out his cellphone, using the secure VPN, and entered the passcode into his laptop to tether the internet through the backdoor to the company. His lawyers' email came through, showing they'd already began the process of removing Gary from the business. "I'll ensure you get a nice severance package of course," Hollywood gritted out. Even though it was the last thing he wanted to do, his lawyers' had told him it was for the best. Since the fucker wasn't an owner, nor was he a shareholder, a huge mistake on ole Gary's part, he didn't have a leg to stand on.

The video feed came up on the computer of the main offices. He clicked through the different screens, unsure of what he was looking for, until the image popped up.

"Whatcha doing there, Gary?" he muttered, pulling up the camera feed in the main office. He hadn't thought he'd be grateful to his security team when they'd insisted on the installation of the extra equipment a few years back. Shit, he hadn't wanted to have another thing to monitor but they'd assured him it was necessary. They'd be getting a damn raise.

The sneaky bastard slipping into the office with a duffel bag clearly had a backup plan. Scott wondered how Gary had cut the power to the building without the generators kicking in, a breach in the system he'd make damn sure didn't occur again. His supplemental security feeds didn't run off the same grid, so he was able to watch Gary walk in with an empty looking bag and leave with what appeared to be a full one. He had planned for this it appeared, or he was stuffing the bag with something he shouldn't be.

Scott didn't waste any more time wondering what the fuck Gary was or wasn't doing before hitting the button to call the security guard at the gate. Although the power was off, the guard shack had power. When he didn't answer right away, internal warning bells off inside Scott.

"Haven Corp," the man finally barked.

"This is Scott Haven. Lock the gates and don't let anyone out, not even Gary Dupont."

"I'm sorry, but Mr. Dupont is the boss here. Who did you say you were?" he asked.

Scott cursed for allowing shit to go without ensuring he was the face of Haven, but it was something he didn't see changing. "I'm the owner of Haven Corp, boy. If you allow anyone, and I mean anyone in or out, you're fired."

"Hello, Mr. Dupont. There's a man who says he's the owner on the phone."

Scott grit his teeth as he listened to Gary's cultured voice telling the guard to hang up and ignore the phone.

"Ah, the power's out, Brian. More than likely it's some punk pulling a prank," Gary said smoothly.

Whatever else was said, he didn't hear as the line went dead. Jumping to his feet, he slammed his fist onto the desk. "Fuck," he growled out when the wood cracked.

He sat back down, shutting down access to the company. Gary would still have whatever money he had in accounts that were his, but he was out of Haven Corp's Accounts. Scott would make sure he was out of the company as well. The corporation would run itself, or rather the department managers would oversee their shit until the board appointed a new head. With three years left on his term with the military, he couldn't take over the company, nor did he want to. The last fucking thing Haven Corp needed was him at the helm. He could kill a terrorist in a single shot from over a mile away without a problem, which not many could do. That had been one of the reasons he'd been recruited to the elite group. Each team had specialists; he was their sharpshooter, having beat the record of the last man by hitting the target over a mile away, over and over again. As counterterrorist operatives, Delta Force members are trained in the art of hostage rescue in closed spaces. When they rescue captives, the hostage-takers are rarely left alive. If they had to go in and get a hostage, then they used a simple two-tap method of dealing with terrorists—two shots go into each kidnapper. Scott was who they used when they needed to take out a target from a longer distance and wanted or had only one shot to do it. The best shooters could hit a target at one mile away, he was better, hitting his target at 2000 yards consistently.

Haven Corp was a medical technology company, and his family made huge commitments to volunteerism and sustainability. Nowhere in the company handbook did his abilities for shooting a terrorist in the head at 2000 yards fit into the profile of what a good leader looked like. He wondered when the last time ole Gary had suited up to volunteer. His finger itched to lock onto the man through his scope with the little x centered on his forehead. A quick little death would be a mercy for all of them. Too good for the bastard but he'd do it without blinking an eye if he could.

A quick check at the time had him grimacing. Tomorrow he'd call an emergency board meeting and let them figure shit out. That's what he paid them for. He strode over to his closet, grimacing at the thought of putting on a suit and tie the next day just to fire Gary. Before he did that, he needed to tell his mom.

His cell vibrated on the desk. He went back over, looking down at the screen. "Son-of-a-bitch."

He'd known Gary had balls, but to take the company jet, proved he was next level balsy or stupid. He hadn't thought the man would actually up and leave the state, which was stupid on his part. Scott didn't bother calling the pilot since he had already run into the guard not listening to his direct orders. If there was one thing he didn't do, that was repeat the same mistake twice. "At least I don't need to worry about the bastard returning home tonight," he muttered.

Scott would ensure the fucker didn't think he had a right to come back to anything owned by him or his family, ever, and once the plane landed, Gary wouldn't have access to it either.

He left his bedroom, intent on telling his mother. A weight settled over his shoulders at what he had to break to her. Even though he felt she would be better off without the asshole, she still had to have some feelings for him. He nearly collided with Talena as soon as he turned the corner in the hallway outside his room.

"Shit, pipsqueak, you startled me." He knelt down, brushing her white-blonde hair back from her forehead. "What's wrong?"

Talena had her legs pressed up to her chest with her arms wrapped around them, big blue eyes staring up at him with fear etched on her face. "I didn't want to sleep in my room."

He noticed the blanket and pillow behind her. "You what, thought you'd sleep out here in the hallway?" Rage nearly choked him at the reason she was camping out in the hall by his room. Gary was lucky he was on his way to somewhere far away from him.

She nodded.

"I was on my way to see mom. Why don't you come with me?" He wouldn't be breaking the news to his mother with Talena right there but leaving her looking like a lost little lamb wasn't an option. An image of the girl in the white gown popped into his mind. He squeezed his eyes shut, banishing the memory.

They walked side-by-side down the wide hallway toward the suite, his mind churning. He'd scooped her blanket and pillow up, tucking the pastel fabric under one arm with the other draped over her shoulder. No way was he going to allow her to sleep on the damn floor. Their mother answered the door after one brisk knock, looking as if she hadn't even sat down yet, let alone taken off her makeup.

"Hey, you two. What're you doing up?"

Talena shrugged but didn't say a word. He didn't blame her knowing she was probably too scared.

"I found this one outside my room. I think she was looking at the stars," he said.

"Ah, and what sort of celestial sightings did you see?" She held her door open wider, motioning them in.

Scott urged Talena in first, going in after her. "I need to speak with you without little ears," he whispered. His mother nodded.

Shortly after they entered, Talena was curled up on her mother's bed, sleeping. Scott moved toward the door, motioning for his mother to follow him. Out in the hall, he explained about Gary, holding nothing back. As tears formed in his mom's eyes, he wanted to kill the man with his bare hands right then and there for having to be the one to break the devastating news to her. "I'm sorry," he said. Never had he felt so damn useless than he did staring down at the woman who gave him life.

She dabbed at her eyes with a tissue she pulled out of one of her pockets. "This isn't your fault." Taking a deep breath, she shoved the crumpled tissue back into her robe. "I always thought there was something odd about the way he was with Angela. But then, he and I didn't...you know. I just brushed it off as his way of being fatherly. He was very affectionate with me and Talena, but not overly so. I mean. God, I was so stupid."

"No, you're not. Dad trusted him. We all did. Things are going to be fine. They'll be a mess for a time, but shit will even out. I can't tell you what to do, but—" he didn't finish saying what he wanted to say. She needed to divorce him and keep him far away from his sister. He would do what he could to make sure the bastard wouldn't step foot anywhere near either of the women he loved.

"I'll contact your dad's lawyer, or rather my lawyer, and start the process of removing him from our lives. I don't want him anywhere around me or Talena. God, she can't know any of this." She looked backward, her fist over her mouth.

"Angela warned her to stay away from him. I think she was trying to protect Talena from the same thing happening to her. Their relationship was fucked up, even though she thought...well, I can't say what she thought other than what was in the letter she sent me. If you want it or need it for the divorce, I'll let you have it. It's not pretty though," he warned her.

"Thank you, Scott. I'll let my lawyers know in case we need it. I'm sure if Gary knows you have it, he won't contest the dissolution. He's smart, probably too smart. You said he left with a duffle bag, right? I'm sure he had a contingency plan. If I had my guess, he's probably been syphoning money from us for the last sixteen years, just in case." Her shoulders went back, the strong will he recognized filling her with purpose.

"You're probably right," he agreed.

Later that night, lying in bed, running scenarios through in his head, had him in knots. He had no clue what the future held, but no matter what, he'd be there for his mom and sister, always.

Chapter Three

Ten years later...

"Dammit, Talena, you can't be driving like you're on a racetrack. You're going to give me a damn heart attack," he growled.

Talena patted her brother's chest, her own heart racing for a completely different reason. He was so freaking gorgeous. Of course, he wasn't her biological brother, but he'd grown up being her protector. She wished he'd take that hat off and see her as a woman grown. A woman he wanted. The saying *if wishes were rainbows, we'd all have gold* came to mind. Yeah, she'd be so damn rich if that were true. Not that she wasn't technically rich, although she'd give it all away if she could have a life with Scott.

"Are you even listening to me?" Hollywood snapped, shaking her by the arms a little roughly.

She shivered at his touch. "Yes, Sir, I'm totally listening to you," she answered. Even his rough handling turned her on. She wouldn't tell him she fantasized about all the naughty things she'd like him to do to her. He'd probably turn tail and run for the nearest institution and have her committed.

His eyes narrowed at her breathless words. "You're going to get put over my knee, little girl."

Talena imagined what it would feel like to have his big palm on her bare ass. Good lord, how she would love it if he actually did follow through with his threat, the same darn threats he'd been making since she'd been seventeen and he'd caught her sneaking out with friends. "Promises, promises, big guy."

He gave her another little shake before releasing her. "I'm not kidding. You can't be driving a car like that so fucking recklessly."

She watched him pace away, enjoying the view from behind as much as the view from the front. In a pair of worn denim that fit his ass like a glove, she couldn't tear her eyes away from the way his angry strides had every muscle flexing. His thighs were also a thing of beauty. When he'd left the military, she and her mother had been ecstatic. Secretly she'd hoped he'd move in with them, back into the huge house that had seemed so empty since Angela and...the man she'd thought had been her father had died. No matter that it had been ten years since that time. The memory of their deaths and their betrayals had her stomach cramping like she'd eaten bad sushi. She and her mother hadn't told

Scott, or rather Hollywood as he was called, about her eating disorder. Her mother didn't notice at the time how dangerously ill she'd become, and neither had she, both grieving and trying to come to terms with the upheaval of their lives until it was almost too late. She hadn't told her mother she'd known about her adoption until she'd been in the ER, hooked up to life-support. Even now she had to work to maintain a healthy balance.

"What am I going to do with you, Talena. You keep pushing and pushing me. I'm your big brother, yet you push all my buttons," he growled.

"I've been pushing your buttons since before I was old enough to know that's what I was doing." She took a deep, cleansing inhale, letting it out before she said something she'd regret. "I get what you're saying, and I'll try to see if I can keep from pushing the speedometer to the limit again." Total freaking lie, but she said it with a straight face, and he wanted to believe her. Good ole Scott, he didn't want to face the fact she wasn't the little pipsqueak he remembered her being.

Hollywood turned to look over his shoulder, giving her a half grin. "I guess that's the best I'm going to get out of you, huh?"

It was best not to lie to the man since he was like a human lie detector. He didn't speak of his time in the Army or how he'd been recruited into the Delta Force much, but she knew from what she'd researched that you had to be super awesome in order to become one of their elite operators. That was one thing he'd mentioned. They weren't called soldiers but operators.

"T, why aren't you happy?"

His question and nearness startled her, making her realize she'd zoned out again, dammit.

"I'm happy," she lied.

"Bullshit. You know better than anyone about not telling me the truth. If there's something you don't want to tell me, then you just say it's none of my business. I may not like it, but I'll take that over an out-and-out lie." He ran the back of two fingers down her cheek.

She wanted to scream at him that she would be happy if he saw her as something other than a little girl or a sister. She wanted to tell him that other men didn't make her happy, that her life felt empty and meaningless. She didn't say anything because even in her head, she sounded desperate and spoiled. She had everything a girl could ask for. Money, a nice home, nice things, a mother who loved and doted on her, a big brother who looked out for her and protected her. What she didn't have was friends, real friends who liked her for her, or someone to hold her and tell her they loved her, were in love with her. All around her, she saw that kind of love, but her own foolish heart seemed to want only one man—a man who didn't see her as anything but a kid sister in pigtails and braces.

"Nah, you're not happy, you're existing."

She stepped away from his touch, confused at his frown. "I need to get going."

"Where are you going?" He tilted his head to the side, staring at her with an expression she recognized.

"I'm meeting up with some friends." Not a lie. She was going to skip out on them, but now she'd changed her mind.

"If you're going to be drinking, you best leave your car and get a ride home or call me. I'll make sure you get home safely."

Talena lifted her hand to her forehead, giving a jaunty salute. "Yes, Sir, I'll be a good little girl and do just that. Jeez, how do you think I survived all these years without your overbearing self?"

He pulled her hand down, wrapping his arms around her body. "One day, you're going to get yourself into more trouble than you bargained for."

She was struggling to breath as he held her within his hard arms, feeling his rock-hard body pressed against her own. "I can handle trouble, Scott."

"I don't think you can, baby girl." He pressed her head to his chest.

She felt his heart beating beneath her. The fast thump mimicked her own, then she felt him kiss her head and step back.

"Remember what I said about drinking and driving. I will blister your ass and take away every vehicle you have access to, trust and believe me on that," he growled.

The softness from moments ago had to have been an illusion, for the man staring down at her with the icy blue eyes, wearing black denim and a fitted black T-shirt stretched over muscles with more tattoos than unmarked skin, looked nothing like the soft-spoken man she'd heard.

"I got you and said I wouldn't. I'm twenty-three, not thirteen." She balled her hands into fists to keep from flipping him the bird. "Do you know how many nights mom and I worried over you and what you were doing whenever we saw anything on the news about terrorists and such? You were in a branch of the military that didn't seem to report to the government like—normal. All we had to go on was the few and far between phone calls and visits. I was sixteen when you retired, or whatever you call it, but you still kept your distance from me until a few years ago. Oh sure, you came around and did the good son and brother bit, but things weren't like they were before." She didn't say before our lives went to shit. "I clearly didn't get myself offed, or in some situation I couldn't get out of without my super soldier brother intervening back then," she reminded him, hating the hurt she felt at the rejection his absence made her feel. Talena turned away, her long legs ate up the short distance to where she'd parked her car outside of Cosmo's and Tai's newly built house at the Royal MC Compound. The home was stunning and showed the man didn't lack in the wealth department either.

She needed to get away before she broke down in tears. The only reason she'd come out to the compound was to drop off a few things she no longer needed for Tai, the latest woman to fall for one of the Royal MC brothers. Alright, in her own mind, she'd admit the truth; she used the excuse to bring the things out to Tai in hopes of seeing Hollywood. Most of the stuff was new that she had no plans to ever use. She'd bought the shit and never wore or needed because she was, as her big brother had so eloquently stated, a spoiled rich girl.

God, how truly pathetic I must be.

Rounding the hood of her custom built MC20 Maserati, she ignored his growl for her to stop. The sports car really was a work of art that she should be more careful with. Her allowance, paid via Haven Corp, funded her lavish lifestyle. The latest model of her car wasn't due to hit the market for another year, with the figure well over a hundred and seventy-five grand.

Once she was settled inside the smooth, dark leather interior, she popped her sunglasses on before chancing a look back at Hollywood. Tears burned her eyes, but she was made of sterner stuff. Talena had cried so much in her life. She honestly didn't think she had any more tears left to cry even if she wanted to, which she most certainly didn't. Hollywood's own icy blue eyes were hidden behind sunglasses, making her glad he couldn't see her through her designer shades. She wondered what he was looking at as he stared straight toward her. With the tint on her windows, she didn't think he could see her all that well, but he was like superman in her mind, seeing through things with his laser vision. The thought almost made her laugh as she fired the engine up.

God, she loved the way the Nettuno Engine purred. She knew for a fact it could go from zero to sixty in two-point nine seconds flat. That would be something she didn't share with Hollywood though, not if she wanted to continue driving her precious car. He'd lose his shit if he knew she'd been participating in illegal drag racing in LA for the last two years. Nope, she wouldn't be sharing her extracurricular activities with him. It wasn't like she was putting the title to her car on the line like some of the other drivers. She didn't race her precious car, not that she didn't think it would win, but in the races, she preferred to race with something much more subtle.

She shifted into reverse with ease, making sure she rolled down the driveway and out onto the highway as if she was a geriatric grandmother out for a Sunday stroll. Once she was far enough away, she let the car do what it was made for. Fly, giving her the sense that she loved, feeling free.

"I wish I was more like Tai. She's a fighter," she whispered. Anger at herself for being such a little bitch made her turn the radio up, drowning out the voices in her head while the scenery flew by.

The other woman had nothing when she'd met Cosmo, except the clothes she'd had on her back. Talena had heard Tai's story, had seen the scars on the other woman, yet she stood tall and proud. Her courage made Talena wish she was braver. She'd known in those moments, if she'd been in Tai, or any of the other women's shoes, she'd have buckled and died. They were worth a thousand women like her. While Cosmo was rich as all get out and would gladly buy Tai anything her heart desired, Talena was happy to give what she could to others, to women who deserved more than life had given them. She'd gone through her things, boxing up so much stuff she would actually need to make a couple more trips in order to unload it all. She hoped between Tai and the other ladies, her trash, would be their treasures. Next time, she'd make sure Hollywood wouldn't be there before she ventured out. One day, she'd fuck up and then he'd see her feelings written all over her face. Poor Scott would have to do what he did best and let her down easy. Of course, then he'd back away, maybe stop coming to their family home. If there was one thing sure to break Tara, his biological mom's heart, it was losing the son she loved more than anything and anyone else in the world. She'd loved Talena enough to adopt her and give her a loving home, but Scott, he was her flesh and blood. She'd never forget that truth.

Shaking off thoughts of what might happen, she glanced at her phone, smiling at the message from Tai. The woman and Cosmo were both overly grateful for the things she'd given away. Some of the things she'd given were super sexy lingerie, still sporting the tags. The heated looks Cosmo had given the other woman had been exactly what she'd envisioned Hollywood would look at her like if he'd ever seen her wearing the apparel. Of course, he never gave her the opportunity to be in anything close to the lace items, not since she'd been seventeen, and at that time, she'd been barely a twig having just started puberty. When she did start to fill out, she'd tried to be more like the women she'd seen him with, but he didn't appear to notice her as a female at all.

"I could be a virgin and need him to take away the ghastly V-card or I'd die, and he'd probably deny me." She wasn't a virgin though, not that she'd ever been promiscuous like some of her friends were. However, after her little visit to the ER and subsequent stay in the hospital when she'd nearly starved to death, she'd struggled to regain control of her life. It had taken a long time, years, to become healthy, both physically and mentally. Once she did, she'd also had to adjust to forming friendships with people who didn't know about her family. All her friends from school had known about Angela committing suicide and being pregnant, then her father dying under suspicious circumstances. Talk in her school had been vicious, with the cool kids saying terrible things that had made her skin crawl. Food became a weapon she could control when nothing else was within her ability. Her mother had been busy keeping up a façade of perfection. Not that she was a bad mom, just the opposite. She was perfect in every way; except, she wasn't her mom. It took a few months of not eating and vigorous exercise for her body to begin showing the damage.

"Poor little rich girl," she growled, driving around a curve a little faster than most would've, but she knew how her car performed and how to handle the machine. Even now, she could see the IVs in her arms, could hear the beeping of machines working to keep her alive. But the most jarring was her mother's soft sobs, the feel of her warm hands wrapped around her own.

"Please, Talena, don't leave me. I can't lose you. You might not be the child of my flesh, but you're the child of my heart. Please, baby, fight to stay with me," Tara cried.

Talena inhaled, hating the memory of how frail she'd been, how hard it was to speak. She hadn't known it at the time, but her throat was raw from the intubation she'd gone through. Fuck, the humiliation she'd suffered after she'd gone home and realized everyone in the inner circle knew she'd almost died from her stupidity.

Her mind thought back to when her body began to change, going from stick thin, to full and curvy. She'd almost fallen back into old habits out of fear, waking up at three in the morning and working out for hours while the house was quiet, then pretending to have already eaten before going on a jog. Her mother had noticed right away, her mama bear instinct kicking in. Tara, god love her, began waking up earlier and earlier until she'd found the right time and put a stop to the downward slide Talena had begun. Tara Haven was a steamroller who didn't take no for an answer. Instead of berating Talena, she showed her how to embrace her figure, and she'd forever be grateful to her mom for her tenacity, knowing many who were as sick as she'd been hadn't survived.

Although she'd wanted to be more like her mother, slim and petite, she'd learned to do as her mother had said. It took work, but she appreciated what she had. Her mother, although not a curvaceous woman, more physically fit, still drew men, young and old. Talena often wondered where she'd got her looks and build. People had always commented she looked like a Haven with her blonde hair and blue eyes, but after Angela's revelation, it was like a dagger to her heart every time someone said those words. She wanted to blurt the truth when people would look at her and refer to her as a Haven replica. Their common remark would then be something about her and Hollywood taking after their father, rest his soul. Each time someone would say that she was sure she'd grind another layer of her back molars off. She wasn't tall by most people's standards at five-feet-seven, with most of her height seemed to be in her legs, yet next to their mother, she did look like a giant. Tara also loathed exercise, other than yoga, but her mother's figure never gained an ounce of fat. Talena had to work out in order to stay slim. She often wondered if her biological parents were more like her. And then, guilt would hit her for thinking about the faceless people who gave her up when her mother was the most wonderful human being in the world.

"I will admit I do like my boobs now." She laughed, taking a peek at her cleavage quickly before focusing back on the road. At seventeen when they'd began to grow and grow, she hadn't been.

The first time Hollywood had come home on leave and seen her in a two-piece swimsuit, she thought he was going to go ballistic. Her top hadn't been anything skimpy, but with thirty-two double Ds, pretty much any suit she wore was. He might not have been as upset if his buddy hadn't been staring as if he'd never seen a woman before. That summer was when boys and grown men started to notice her. In her juvenile mind, their attention meant affection. It didn't take long for her to figure out that wasn't the case, with her V-card being given to a guy she barely remembered. Lord, if Hollywood—she pumped the brakes on her wayward thoughts. It didn't matter what he knew or didn't know. Heck, he was the last man who should cast stones, especially since she had firsthand knowledge of his dirty doings. Her treehouse was never the same after he'd fornicated in it with some bimbo. She'd been twelve and had a fight with Gary, the man she'd thought was her dad, planning to hide in her favorite place, only to come to a jarring stop on the wraparound deck of the huge treehouse. Her brother and some skank, probably Angela she now knew, were fucking right there in her space. Oh sure, it had been his to begin with, but it had become her treehouse. So yeah, she really didn't give two shits what he had to say about who, what, when, and where she'd give her body.

"As a matter of fact, I think it's time I ended my revirginized state."

She thought of Tai, Cosmo's ole lady and the shit she'd been through. If there was anyone who deserved love, it was her. She saw the way the tough looking man looked at the tiny woman. Cosmo was rich as fuck and loved Tai fiercely. Anyone who looked at him could see that burning in his dark eyes. Talena really had nothing except a college degree that she was doing nothing with, using her family's wealth like it was Monopoly money. She enjoyed giving stuff to others, but really, what she gave was stuff she bought with cash she hadn't earned. King's woman was a badass she wished she could be like. Traeger's ole lady was as well. No wonder Hollywood didn't look at her as anything but a child.

She needed to stop being such a little crybaby bitch. Between what Tai had survived, and the other ladies the men Hollywood was friends with, he had every right to think she was nothing but window dressing. Surely her little heart could handle unrequited feelings for the man who only saw her as a burden. She just needed to go out and look for someone who wasn't...him. What she needed to do was grow the fuck up and get a life that didn't revolve around lusting and loving a man who could never feel the same for her.

"That's one fine piece of equipment, and I'm not talking about your pseudo sister."

Hollywood didn't bother to look over at T-Rex. He'd heard the other man walking up a couple minutes ago and had known he'd been standing back, waiting. "That's good to hear. I think King would miss you if you were dead."

"I suppose that's true. I also suppose it's true you could do it as well, what with you being an ex-super soldier and shit."

He snorted, wondering how much T-Rex had heard. "Did you need something, or you just out for a walk through the woods?" Everyone was aware he and Talena weren't related by blood, but they also knew he'd gut anyone who fucked with her.

Dressed all in black, T-Rex looked more like he'd fit in at a death metal concert than in the woods on a nature hike.

"I'm more the big bad wolf than little red riding hood. You got someone tailing that sister of yours? I didn't like the look on her face as she drove away."

He tore his eyes away from the road where her vehicle had been. "What the fuck you talking about?"

"Brother, she had the look of a desperate woman. You were too busy trying not to notice that she's not the little girl you needed to protect or some shit. That girl who just drove out of here, is a woman who's on the verge of a freak out or maybe break out. Trust me, I know shit like that." T-Rex turned on his size fourteen shitkickers and walked back toward the clubhouse.

"Yo, T, what the hell brought you down here?" Hollywood hollered.

"You might want to check out downtown LA and the street takeovers going on. I hear there's some hot chicks who show up, some even racing."

"What the fuck, man? If you know something you need to fucking tell me instead of this bullshit." He started after the hulk of a man, unafraid of getting his ass handed to him.

"Hey what's all the yelling out here?" Cosmo walked around his house wearing a pair of slacks and a button-down shirt.

"Dammit, T, I'm not playing." He halted when he lost sight of the other man. "You'd think a giant couldn't move that fast through the woods.

Cosmo nodded. "You'd think. What did he do?"

He opened his mouth then closed it, not wanting to repeat a rumor he wasn't sure had anything to do with his sister. Shit, she had him tied up in knots and had since he'd caught her laying out by the pool in three tiny triangles. Fuck, his dick jerked beneath the fly of his jeans at the memory.

"Kid sisters would be hard on big brothers, especially ones who looked like yours. I don't know how you don't have a personal security guard following her every second of the day," Cosmo said with a shake of his head.

Hollywood had thought of doing just that but stopped short of acting on it. He did have a tracker on her cell, her car, and even on a couple pieces of jewelry he knew she never took off. Call him paranoid, but when you were worth as much money as Haven Corp, he figured it was better to be safe than sorry.

"She'd throw a fit and then rebel. I learned to pick my battles. From what Blockhead said, it looks like I need to head to town tonight and check out some street racing." He shouldn't call his friend names, especially when T-Rex hadn't done anything except warn him about something that may or may not have to do with Talena. Logic and jealousy had nothing in common when it came to him and his feelings.

"That Blockhead will bust his knuckles on your hard head if you give him any shit," Cosmo warned.

His fellow MC brothers didn't know about his background, other than the fact he was a rich playboy who owned a corporation. They thought he was the male version of Talena, and he liked it that way. "I'll send him a case of his favorite liquor as an apology."

"I'd add something for Koko too. You know that dragon is his favorite thing on this planet." Cosmo slapped him on the back before turning back the way he'd come. "By the way, tell your sister thanks for giving Tai all that shit. Most of it was brand new or close enough. I hadn't even thought to get some of what she'd brought."

Hollywood tipped his head to the side. "What did she give her?" He assumed it was clothes and shit since she had a closet the size of a normal person's bedroom.

"Shit, brother, she brought her some purses with the LV logo and matching wallets, some female stuff my woman was too shy to ask for but was so damn excited to try on right then and there. I thought she was going to break something getting out of the clothes she wore. Damn, brother, I swear to you as my witness, every motherfucking day, I find myself wishing I could kill some fuckers all over again. Each time I see her eyes light up when she gets something given to her, because she'd never received a gift before, I want to rush out and give her the world. Of course, at the same time I'm fighting a battle within myself not to hunt down anyone who had ever hurt her. I'm going to make it my mission to find out all the things she wants and see to it she gets it. Your girl, she did that for mine today. I won't forget it."

Cosmo gave a nod before walking back inside the huge house he'd built on the compound grounds.

Hearing Cosmo call Talena his girl made him wish for things he shouldn't. Fuck, his dick didn't understand she wasn't his or that she couldn't be. The stupid thing got hard anytime she was within touching distance, which was why he had a strict no touch rule. Until today, he'd done pretty damn good at keeping his hands to himself. He wondered if she noticed his dick trying to burst out of his jeans or not. He could just imagine how he'd explain that to her sweet naïve little ass. *"Sorry, pipsqueak, that's just my phone. Don't worry about it, sweetheart."*

"Why do you look like you just ate shit?"

He jerked his head up, frowning back at Cosmo. "I thought you went inside?"

"I came back to give you this." He held out a tennis bracelet.

"Where did you find this?" he asked, taking the platinum piece of jewelry he'd given to Talena when she'd turned twenty-one. It had a tracking device he'd had put inside the clasp.

"Tai said it was on the floor by one of the boxes. It must have fallen off when Talena dropped off all that stuff. See the clasp." Cosmo pointed at the end.

"Thanks, brother. I'll make sure it gets fixed and give it back to Talena." He shoved it into his front pocket, wondering if she noticed it was gone. For the last two years, he'd never seen her without it on.

"Women need us to show we care in more ways than just buying them pretty things, you know?" Cosmo's voice dropped to a low murmur. "I can buy Tai just about anything she could ever want. Hell, I could take her to any shop on Rodeo Drive and recreate that scene from Pretty Woman for her, but do you know she's happier when I hold her in my arms and listen to her talk. Not just pretend to listen, but truly hear her words. I don't just do it to get my dick in her either. I do it because seeing her eyes light up with happiness, feeling her heartbeat against my chest makes me feel alive." Cosmo put his hand over his heart. "Brother, seeing your woman happy is almost as good if not just as good as coming inside their warm, welcoming body. I'd do damn near anything for Tai's happiness."

"I get what you're saying. I've always put my mom's and sister's happiness before my own." That was the truth. Halfway across the world, he'd made sure they were happy and safe, even when they had no clue. He always had eyes on them.

"Let me ask you a question, man. But before I do, I need to be straight up with you. Before I go into any situation, I research the fuck out of every player. I know more than you've shared with the others. Now before you bull up and think to say or do something stupid, let me say I've known for years. When I came here to kill King Senior, me and my team dug deep. My guys were barely teens when I rescued them. A few of them decided military was their path to take, so they have a little experience in your field. The Army had no records of you and your team when you left Fort Bragg each time you went away. Then bam you came back, several times a man or two missing. Now, most branches of the military have protocols for their soldiers, making them keep their hair buzzed, no tattoos and shit, but there's this one that doesn't. This super secretive, some might even say non-existent branch, that operates just on the fringes. Delta Force Operatives are men who are selected and trained, sent into places that the government can't go in officially, and if they don't make it out, well, the government doesn't really recognize them. Am I hot?" Cosmo asked, leaning against the house with his arms crossed as if he hadn't just dropped a bomb that could destroy Hollywood's life.

"Where did you get your information?" he asked instead of answering.

"There's a lot you can find out if you know where to look. I don't need you to tell me if I'm right or wrong. You and I both know the truth. The reason I'm telling you this is because I also know that the girl who just drove out of here, looking like someone just kicked her while she was down, is no more your blood than I am. She was looking at you like my Tai looks at me. If you're too blind to see that, then you best be prepared for her to turn those sights on someone else, because I know that expression. That was a young girl who was lost. If T-Rex said she was taking part in street racing, you can bet your ass she's trying to find something or outrun it. That's a desperate girl. You know what happens to desperate people, Scott Haven."

"How the hell did you get so damn smart, brother?" Hollywood wasn't going to admit shit to Cosmo, didn't need to. He wondered who else knew about him. Keys and his computer hacking skills combined with the fact he was an ex-SEAL could have some idea. Shit, he was going to have to come clean to his MC brothers sooner rather than later.

"I had to be in order to survive the shit I did. You best get your ass in gear if you're going to find out where they'll be racing tonight. You might give Keys a holler. I'm sure that brother can get that shit for you in like five minutes."

He could pull up the tracker on her car or cell, but he'd have to get to his computer. Keys was a phone call away.

Chapter Four

Keys was able to get the info for him in minutes. Los Angeles was a big area. His little Talena had driven faster than he'd thought she would or should. For that, she'd be answering to him and his palm when he caught up to her.

"Damn, bro, she must've been burying that needle to get from here to there that quickly. She's lucky she didn't get pulled over," Keys muttered, the sound of the keyboard clacking away in the background continued.

"Believe me, I plan to make sure she's aware of my displeasure. Is her phone moving or stationary?" He'd given Keys the code for the tracking devices on Talena's car and the other ones he was sure were on her person.

More keys being tapped filled the air before Keys answered. "Yeah, looks like their all in the same area, although I can't say for sure she's not moving at all. If she is, then it's in the same ten to fifteen feet range. I can get satellite footage pinged if you want?"

Hollywood pulled the phone away from his ear, staring at the screen like he'd misheard his friend. "You mean you can pull up cameras from the surrounding area?"

"Sure, if that's what you want to think." Keys went silent. "I don't think you'll like what you find, Hollywood. Maybe you should take a couple brothers with you. On second thought, I'm coming with you. I'll make a couple calls and meet you out front." Keys disconnected the call without another word.

He didn't get a chance to respond or question him further. If there was one thing Hollywood hated more than watching a woman cry, it was not knowing what the fuck was going on. Keys hanging up before explaining had him wondering what the fuck his friend had seen that made him react the way he had.

"Fucker, you best tell me what the hell you saw," he growled as he punched Keys' number into his cell. He started walking quickly toward the clubhouse where he'd left his bike, intent on making his way with or without anyone coming with him. The phone rang several times before Keys voicemail kicked in.

His long strides ate up the distance in no time while he internally fumed. He wasn't a man who put off things because he was scared of facing danger alone. With Keys help he had a location that was near enough to his loft in LA. On his way down he'd make some calls and see if he could get a few men in place without involving his brothers. He had a feeling shit was going to go down that would land him on the wrong side of the law. Not that the MC had a problem with that, but with Tai's shit in Florida being recent and her status not quite legal, the last thing he wanted to do was draw attention to the club.

"See, told you he was going to try to be all bullheaded and shit. Brother thinks he's some kind of untouchable superman," Keys said nodding toward Hollywood.

"I see that. He's even got the angry walk and muttering down to perfection. Think he's got hidden scars we haven't seen? Bet I can out scar him," A big man said in a deep raspy voice.

Hollywood stopped walking, glaring at the two men standing near his bike. "What the fuck you do you think you're doing, Keys?"

"Going for a ride with my buddies. PS. You and Roq here are my buddies." Keys winked but didn't move.

He gave a hard shake of his head. "Listen, brother, I just need you to tell me what you found and then let me handle it from here. The club already has enough heat on it from everything that happened down in Florida."

"Yeah well, tough shit. Being a brother ain't about rolling with the good. It's having a brother's back whenever it's needed. I know you've had our backs lots of times, so shut the fuck up and let's ride. I'll fill you in on the trip down unless you want to waste more time jawing over shit and give your girl more time to get herself in even more trouble?" Keys took a step away from Hollywood's bike at the same time as Roq did.

While Keys was tall and muscular, built like a swimmer, Roq was even taller and more muscular. Fuck, if he was being honest, he looked as though he'd fit right in with a WWE wrestler. If Hollywood had to guess, he'd say the man stood at over six foot seven and had to weigh close to two hundred seventy pounds of pure muscle. Hell, his biceps appeared to be as big as most people's heads.

"Let's go." Hollywood wasn't going to waste time or energy arguing. In a fight between him and the two men, he was pretty sure he'd lose. Keys was a straight up tough motherfucker, but he knew he could handle him one-on-one. However, it was the other man that was an unknown, or rather Hollywood did know men like him. Roq was a straight killer. His eyes were the dead giveaway. Dark as night, staring straight at him with no emotion while his lips kicked up in a smile, telling Hollywood to go ahead and try him. Nah, he wanted someone to push his buttons, but it wouldn't be Hollywood.

He moved forward, not hesitating, showing no fear to either man. Keys and Roq were on his side, but make no mistake, if they fucked with Talena, he'd make them wish they were never born.

"Mic up on the ride and I'll fill you in on what I know. Roq's on our side, Hollywood. He's part of Cosmo's security," Keys said as he stepped around, heading to his own Harley.

"Good to know. Anything else I need to be aware of?" Hollywood asked, his voice level like he was asking about the weather.

"He's good, Keys. You were right, clearly he wasn't just a soldier." Roq spun on his shitkickers and straddled his own ride.

The words fuck off hovered on his lips, but as the other man said, he wasn't just a soldier. Hell, he never had been, they were operatives. "Let's ride."

Three deep rumbles started almost simultaneously, soothing his frayed nerves. Whatever his...Talena had gotten herself involved in; he'd be getting her fine ass out of. Afterwards, they'd be having a talk. His hand might be coming into contact with that gorgeous ass of hers she likes to show off so damn much. Even thinking about her ass made his dick hard. Most people might think it was wrong of him to think of her in such a way. Fuck, he had at one time. Until she was twelve, he'd thought she was his half-sister. That time had been such a fucking nightmare with his stepsister Angela's suicide followed by Gary's betrayal and death. Their memory was tainted by so much bullshit he had a hard time dredging up anything good, except Talena and his mom. It hadn't been until he'd come home on leave one summer expecting to find his sweet little sister like always, only to be stunned by the voluptuous young woman she'd become. She'd been only seventeen, but her body had been all woman with curves that had been barely contained in a string bikini. It had taken all he had not to kill his buddy he'd brought home with him, when the asshole wouldn't stop staring at her tits. His saving grace had been the fact he'd had on a short sleeve button down shirt that was untucked that hid his massive erection. Poor Jonathan wasn't so lucky, which was why he and old Johnny don't talk anymore. Or it could be because he'd knocked a couple of the other man's teeth out, but whatever, fucker should've known better than to keep staring at his sister.

When they hit the road, he turned the mic on his helmet, assuming Keys would have made sure Roq and he were on the same frequency. He was good at waiting, which was one of the reasons he made a good sniper for his team, but during the minutes he waited for Keys to come on, Hollywood found himself growing impatient. Shit, if his team could see him now, gripping his handlebars so fucking hard if they'd been made of weaker material, he would've bent them in half, and then he'd have been laughed right out of Delta Force.

"Hollywood, Roq, you two hear me?" Keys asked.

"I hear you so cut the shit and spit it out," Hollywood growled, uncaring if the other man was able to listen in or not.

"Go on, Keys, I'm good."

"Hollywood, have you ever heard of the LA street races that go on at night usually?" Keys tone was even.

"Vaguely."

"Well, from the intel I pulled up, they're getting a lot more active and a lot more dangerous. You know kids nowadays seem to have more money and balls than before. Of course, it's not just kids who race or show up at these things. It's a lot more organized and shit. I'm just going to say it. Brother, there's a fuckton of money and dirty shit going on in the LA racing scene. Money, drugs, and women get passed around like candy while the racing is going on. Your sister is a regular on the scene down there."

Keys' words dropped like ten thousand rocks on a lake. His Talena wouldn't be whoring herself out at some underground racing. He wouldn't believe that unless he saw it with his own eyes or heard it from her.

"Slow the fuck down or you'll get yourself killed, Scott," Keys yelled.

He eased up on the throttle when what he really wanted was to punch the bastard in the mouth for speaking. "What else did you find out?"

Keys explained more about the different groups that made up the racing scene and who Talena appeared in the different CCV images with the most. How Keys had found so much so quickly astounded him, but again, the man was a computer genius. Hollywood knew the time would come they'd have a come to Jesus moment, but that wasn't now.

"Does she have a guy she's with regularly as well?" The question was sour to get out. Already the nameless, faceless man was six feet under in his mind.

"The images didn't show her up close and personal with any one man if that's what you're asking. If you're asking if she's been intimate with anyone, I can't answer that, brother."

"Axl and Ridley are already there. They said it's a nice set up. There's a group in charge that appears to have connections. I'd say that's the reason they've been able to fly under the radar of the LAPD. He said they're no longer racing in the streets either. Did you get that on your CCV shit, Keys?"

The man's deep southern drawl became more apparent through the microphone and the more he spoke. "Do they have eyes on Talena?"

"Negative. They're looking for her without making it obvious." Roq's calmness was the opposite of Hollywood's.

"I sent them an image of her from earlier today when she arrived at Cosmo's place. They'll let us know when they see her. Besides, her car will be easy to spot," Keys reassured him.

The thirty miles that separated him and Talena's locations felt like hundreds instead of the miniscule distance it was. He wouldn't let traffic hinder him, already planning to bob and weave if needed. By the time they reached the city, night had fallen and still neither Axl nor Ridley had spotted Talena. He couldn't pull up his own tracking device to see if he could locate her either. As frustration built, he was a powder keg ready to explode when they came to a stop a couple blocks from their destination.

"Hold up, Hollywood. Let me see what I see on her whereabouts." Keys' words echoed his own thoughts.

The other man slung his backpack around, pulled out his computer, which he never went without, and had it booted up in minutes. Under normal circumstances Hollywood would've made a quip about the other man and his toy. Not this time. He sat with his feet planted on the pavement, looking around them. Unease snaked down his spine. "Roq, you good, brother?"

"Got a little chill, I think I need my jacket. You bring yours with you?"

Fuck it all. He knew this wasn't going to be an easy in and out ride. "Yep, got mine too." He moved cautiously, hoping he hadn't ridden straight into an ambush.

"I got us a match. We can now play WOW with a group." Keys pumped his fist in the air and made a whoop sound.

If shit wasn't so screwed up, Hollywood would've laughed at the other man's antics. The deep rumble of bikes broke through his musings. He shifted, grabbing his gun from the custom holder by the headlight. In one swift move, he had the Glock out and down by his thigh, hidden from view when the two men pulled up next to Roq.

"It's cool, brothers. It's Axl and Ridley." Roq kicked the stand on his bike down before getting to his feet.

Keys nodded but didn't move, his fingers continued to fly across his screen. Hollywood kept looking around the darkness, that tingle still making him feel uneasy. "You still needing that jacket, Roq?"

"It's probably because you got a spotter up on the roof looking down at you with a high-powered scope about a hundred yards to your right. Don't worry, I don't think he's that good of a shot, and if he was, Cannon's got him in three, two, got em," Ridley said.

"Eliminated the threat. Fucker was doodling you boys' pics and even drew hearts around your heads and made splatter images outside them. PS. You're welcome."

"Cannon, get over yourself and get down here. Did you clean up your mess?" Roq asked.

The man named Cannon sighed loudly. "This is not my first rodeo, daddy. The poor guy had an accident. He was playing with his knife and fell on it. Damn thing went right through his eye too. Clumsy fool, he shouldn't have been playing around. I did take his drawing though, you know, so there's no questions about who the fools he was making hearts over were."

"Bingo. I found her. Damn, brother, she's as slippery as a greased-up pig at a county fair," Keys muttered.

Hollywood wasn't going to ask what the hell Keys was talking about. All he cared about was finding Talena and getting her the hell out of the shit she appeared to have gotten herself in. "Let's move then," he said.

"Let me see if I can pull up some video of the area where she's at. We're some tough fuckers, Hollywood, but there's six of us. We could be riding into the middle of as many as a hundred or as little as one. Let's make sure we're prepared." Keys stared back at him. The computer held steady over the tank of his bike.

The last damn thing he wanted was to wait, yet he agreed it was the wise thing to do. "You're right." He raked his hand through his hair while Keys tapped away on his computer.

"While we rode around, we saw a lot of cars coming in. This isn't a throw some money in your tank and race on the backroad kind of shit." Ridley paused, looking up and down the road. "I didn't see the car Keys had said your sister drove. A vehicle like that would've stood out. Even with all the rides that did come in, I'd have noticed something flashy like that."

They'd stopped underneath a bridge where several homeless groups were gathered around dumpsters with fires blazing in them. Christmas was right around the corner, and it was unseasonably cold in California, especially when night fell. Not a single one seemed to pay any of the men on bikes no mind. Hollywood thought it strange, but maybe they were used to the comings and goings of different vehicles, or maybe the people running the races paid them to keep quiet. "How about the homeless? Did you check them out?"

Ridley went still as did Cannon.

"An oversight we'll correct." Ridley nodded at Roq once.

Hollywood looked over at the homeless men, then back at the men who'd come to help him, stunned to find they were nowhere in sight. "Shit that's spooky as fuck." He knew men who could move like ghosts, but the two men who were literally right next to him made not a sound, nor did they even stir the air. If he hadn't known they'd been there, he'd have wondered if he'd been mistaken.

"They'll know if they're homeless or not shortly. Keys, you find what you need? I don't like sitting out here like this for so long."

"Dammit there's no CCV feeds anywhere inside there." Keys waved his hand toward the area they knew Talena to be.

Hollywood shrugged. "I guess we go in and see what's what. If you don't want to go, I understand, brother. You got a kid and an ole lady to go home to. I promise, no hard feelings. As a matter of fact, I think it's best you head on back and let King know...shit, just be prepared for anything. I don't want you or any of you to get into any shit because of me and mine."

Before Keys could argue, a pearl white SUV pulled up. The tinted window on the passenger side came down soundlessly. "I can't believe you were going to have fun and not invite me. By the way, Digger's behind me with a cage to load your bikes, since I'm pretty sure none of you fuckers want to leave them on the side of the road. Get your shit and hop in. My rig will get us in and out of anything except maybe a landmine. Although, to be fair, I think even that we'd make it out with a few scrapes," Cosmo muttered, his left arm was draped over the steering wheel while he stared around them.

He shook his head, a grin tipping his lips up. Damn, it felt good knowing his friends, his brothers, had his back. Like clockwork, Digger and a prospect rolled up, jumping out of the big truck with the enclosed trailer attached. They helped the two men load each of their bikes while Ridley and Cannon did their shit. Hollywood didn't worry too much about either man since they clearly didn't need him to.

Talena rolled her eyes when Louis pulled up next to her Mazda CX9 in his Lykan Hyper Sport. He was her real competition in not only speed but everything else. His girlfriend was a real bitch who hated Talena because she thought Louis wanted to replace Rosalie with her. She could've saved the other woman a shitload of stress and told her there was no way in hell she'd hook up with the asshole but realized nothing she said would've mattered to Rosalie.

"Hola, Talena. You're looking muy caliente tonight," Louis said, eyeing her up and down.

Rosalie slapped his arm before getting out of the passenger seat, muttering something too low for Talena to hear.

"You need to be nicer to your woman, Louis." Talena didn't smile or encourage him in any way, never had. Nothing she did seemed to sway him from hitting on her either. The man was like a dog with a bone, or maybe a kid who wanted a toy he couldn't have was closer to the truth.

"She'll be back. Want to go for a ride and see how a true machine runs?" He lifted his brows, his words a clear double meaning.

"I'm good, thanks." She looked at her watch, hating the fact there was still another twenty minutes before it was *go time*. If she had to sit next to him, his overinflated ego, and his too chatty self, she was liable to do or say something she'd regret.

Talena used two fingers to lift the window buttons on the door, waiting for them to come up completely before she pulled the keys out of the ignition. She never brought her purse with her to one of the races, knowing how easily shit got stolen. Pushing the driver's door open, she got out, making sure she had her keys. Although most of the men and women hanging around could easily pop a lock and hotwire a car in less than two minutes, she'd never heard of it happening before a race when a car was on the line. Now afterward, all bets were off.

"Hey, chica, what's going on? You want a drink?"

Talena smiled and waved away the offer from a group she'd partied with on occasion. Music blared all around. The tempo varied depending on which group you neared. She was hoping to find one of the popup booths that had been there the last weekend that sold scarves. She'd bought one but had lost it.

She looked down at her watch and froze. Her bracelet, the one Scott had given her a couple years ago was gone. "Oh no," she cried, spinning around and nearly colliding with a man. "Excuse me." She hurried back the way she came, looking at the ground as she did. The entire time, she tried to remember the last time she'd seen it. "Tai's house. Oh, god, please let it be at her house."

Her phone had the clubhouse number and Hollywood's number, but she also had Tai's number now thanks to her trip today. She hit the number she'd programmed earlier, walking back to her car parked on the line while the phone rang.

"Hey, Talena. I was going to send you a thing to say thanks for all the amazing things you gave me. Um, do you want it all back?" Tai asked.

"Oh lord no, never. I...I lost my bracelet, and I was wondering—"

"Yes, I found it. Didn't your brother tell you? Cosmo took it right out to your brother. I promise, I would never keep something so precious, Talena."

She felt tears well in her eyes knowing something so sacred was safe. "Oh, honey, I know you'd never keep anything that wasn't given to you. Thank you so much for easing my fears. I thought I'd lost it, and it was gone forever." She took a shuddering breath, letting it out in a big exhale.

"Good. I'm sure Cosmo gave it to your brother. If there's ever anything you need from me, don't hesitate to ask."

She promised Tai she would, then hung up, feeling marginally better. Of course, she now needed to get ahold of Hollywood and ask him for her bracelet back. She'd do that after she raced and kicked Louis's ass. The need to release some of the adrenaline pumping through her veins was like the need to breathe.

Ten feet from her car, she almost turned back around and said fuck it when she saw the man in question and his bitch staring at her. It wasn't like she couldn't afford to leave the Mazda on the line and forfeit her entry fee. However, being a coward wasn't in her blood. Not that she actually knew whose blood ran through her veins, but she had come to terms with the fact she was making her own destiny regardless of who or what she came from. And Talena Haven wasn't a damn quitter just because Louis, his girlfriend, and his boys were bulled up around their cars like a bunch of strutting peacocks. They did it every damn time as if she'd get scared enough to quit or stall at the line. "Not today, fuckers," she whispered.

"What was that, Taloora?" Rosalie asked, purposefully saying her name wrong.

"Why, Rosa, I'm sorry, I didn't see you down there," Talena mocked, knowing the other woman tried her damndest to appear taller with her four-inch heels and still fell shorter than Talena's own five seven. Hell, if Rosalie was five-foot-tall in her bare feet, she'd be surprised.

The other woman stomped back over to Louis, yelling in Spanish curse words Talena couldn't make out.

She probably shouldn't have stooped to Rosalie's level, but it felt fucking good to piss the woman off. It was also a bonus that when Rosalie went to where Louis stood, she'd hopped into his arms, and the two began to make out, which took attention off of Talena's return. All of the pricks took a lot of enjoyment out of watching their boss make out with his woman, it appeared.

Talena slid into her car almost unnoticed. A couple of other drivers gave her a nod as she walked up, respecting her as a driver not just a hot chick they wanted to fuck. Everyone was aware of Louis and his gang and their antics. Louis usually won the races, if Talena wasn't there, but he was a sore loser and a jackoff of a winner. She and he had been neck-and-neck, the last couple months, almost every other week she won. Before that, she'd won quite a few races, lost several as well. She still wasn't sure why he'd shown up and decided to become part of the scene, other than Rosalie and her girls. The woman owned a clothing business that catered to the lifestyle of the racing crowd. Her girls wore the garb, making sure the men appreciated it and wanted their own women wearing it. What she really thought they wanted was to fuck the women parading around, which she was sure they probably did or could, but she wasn't judging, much.

In truth, Louis gave her the creeps the way he was always watching her. However, she'd brushed her feelings aside until he'd crossed the line a week ago, scaring her more than any man ever had. Talena closed her eyes and took a deep breath, trying not to think about what had almost happened. She still wasn't sure if she'd dreamed it, or if it had happened. No matter, she wasn't drinking before or after races anymore unless she brought her own liquor or if it was from an unopened bottle. Definitely not drinking any shots or whatever the fuck she'd had last time.

The sound of engines firing up startled her from memories best forgotten, or in her case, memories not remembered.

She didn't do like a lot of the drivers did and rev her engine. Many liked to show off with how loud their motors could get. In her opinion, all that did was risk overheating your engine, and she wasn't foolish enough to do something like that.

Out of the corner of her eye, she could see Louis sitting in his car next to her, his arm on the open window. If he wasn't such a creepy asshole, he'd have been a guy she'd have said was hot as fuck. He wasn't very tall, maybe just shy of six foot, but he had black wavy hair he pulled back in a low ponytail. His dark complexion was flawless and his dark eyes had many women taking second looks. It was the eyes that made you think of sin, and they were also evil as fuck in her mind. His lips were full. She'd immediately noticed them when he'd talked. Combine all that with his extremely muscular physique, and he'd have been a high nine, until he opened his mouth, or you looked into his eyes. There was no denying the depravity inside him once you did either.

The first week she'd raced him, she'd won by a small margin. He'd been all smiles and congratulations. Talena had thought he was a great guy, a great loser, until a half hour after the race. She'd stumbled upon him and a few others who were with him. The things they'd said about her and what they'd planned to do to her made her blood run cold. They'd laughed when Louis had compared her to the last bitch he'd taught a lesson to when you fucked with him. The way he reminisced about making the nameless woman suck his cock after he'd beaten her, was said with such pleasure she'd felt sick. It had taken everything in her to walk away quietly, praying they didn't hear her. The next day, she'd convinced herself they were guys just making shit up, but then she'd heard more whispers throughout the races, and then Rosalie and her girls came. She was such a little bitch, and her friends were just as bad. Yet there was no denying Rosalie got off on hurting others, especially women who she felt were her competition. On more than one occasion, she'd seen the gaggle of women gang up on someone they felt were competition or anyone they took a dislike to. Talena fell into one of their categories even though she wanted absolutely nothing to do with any of the men Rosalie and her bitch friends fawned over.

"Mind on the race," she said, making sure she didn't look toward Louis directly. From her periphery, she'd noticed Rosalie getting into the vehicle with him. Only five minutes more to go before it was time to race. She had to wonder if the other woman was going to ride with him or what but knowing every extra pound of weight could fuck with how well a car did, said he wouldn't allow it.

A girl in a pair of booty shorts and a bra like top moved up to the front minutes later, waving a flag. She forgot about Louis and his bullshit. After this race, she was going to move on. This area wasn't the only place there was to find a spot to race. Sure, it was organized, and the cops didn't seem to patrol as heavily, but the bullshit that was everything else wasn't worth it. Mind made up, she felt as if a weight was lifted from her shoulders.

Her car rumbled under her, familiar, exhilarating. She let the motions that were like second nature take over as the flag fell to the ground, shifting smoothly from one gear to the next. Her Mazda bumped ahead of Louis's Lykan. She glanced over at him, seeing the hate he didn't bother to mask as he stared back at her. Fuck, she had no doubt he wouldn't be allowing her to walk away without making her pay.

They both slid around the corner, his car overtaking her own. He used his NOS early, which sent a shiver of fear down her spine. Why he'd do so already was crazy, unless he had a plan. Whatever it was, she wasn't playing. Up ahead, the course was to turn left. She saw four cars coming up on her fast, the other drivers making headway. Talena made a calculated decision, downshifting, letting the others pass her as Louis turned left, she turned right, heading away from the race. Hollywood had told her when something didn't feel right, if you felt a tingle racing down your spine telling you something wasn't right, then listen. "I'm listening," she muttered, heading away from the races and the two thousand five hundred she'd ponied up.

"God, I'm such a spoiled little bitch." She slapped her hand on the steering wheel as she thought of all who'd have killed for the money she'd put up to race, yet there she was, leaving it without a second thought.

Chapter Five

Talena blinked hard several times, unwilling to cry. There was no crying in racing, dammit. The garage where she kept her car was a good fifteen minutes from the downtown racing scene, enough time for her to clear her head and figure out what the fuck she was going to do next. Clubbing didn't appeal but going home and moping didn't either. She wished she was better friends with the ladies back at the compound, then she'd have a reason to go back and hang out there. "Nope, I just do like I always do and hit up one of the hot spots. There's always people there who want to party with me." Having a black Amex solidified that.

She wished she had her purse on her, but that was another rule she'd made when she'd began racing. Never taking more than she could hold in her back pocket. Fucking thieves were rampant among the crowds, and they didn't look anything like you'd think. She'd been robbed and hadn't even known it until hours later, the pickpocket sliding into her bag, taking her wallet and ghosting without her being aware. The next time, she'd thought she was being more cautious, wearing a cross body, but nope, they were able to get in and out of it as well. She still wasn't sure how, so now she didn't carry anything except her ID and a little cash wrapped around it. For her entry fee she always paid it via a cash app.

The exit for the garage was coming up when she noticed a vehicle was behind her. She decided to skip the exit since the offramp wasn't well lit and neither was the neighborhood. Checking her fuel gauge, a grimace twisted her mouth. Fucking-A. It was just her luck she'd probably run out of gas, and the asshole trailing her was probably some Michael Myers like stalker. Of course, knowing her luck, he probably wasn't the slow-walker type killer.

"Let's see if you can keep up," she said as she pushed the clutch in and shifted gears. Although the freeway had cars in every lane, she maneuvered in and around them, bobbing and weaving. The big vehicle behind her tried to keep up, but as she'd suspected, whoever it was hadn't counted on her car being so fast. The next exit was coming up swiftly, with four lanes that she'd need to cross to get to it. Talena said a prayer, eased off the gas slightly, and what followed was probably the most insane driving she'd ever done. The sound of horns blaring filled the night air, and more than likely drivers calling her every name in the book, but she made the exit by the skin of her teeth. The huge white

SUV flew past her. Its tinted windows didn't allow her to see who was in it, but she assured herself if they were bad guys, they wouldn't be driving white since the bad ones in movies drove black.

"Oh sure, good analogy." She gave a shaky laugh, her hands not quite as steady as she'd have liked when she made her way back onto the freeway going the other direction. Maybe going out after switching vehicles wasn't such a good idea.

Hollywood gripped the arms of the passenger seat, unable to believe the way Talena handled the race car. He wasn't going to call the little fucking thing she was in anything other than what it was. "Remind me again why I can't beat her ass as soon as we find her?" he asked through gritted teeth.

Nobody answered him.

He looked behind him, seeing the men Cosmo called his Demon Security with complete and utter stone looks on their faces. "Are none of you going to tell me I should calm down?"

Roq shook his head. "Not me, man. If she were mine, she wouldn't be able to sit without remembering what it feels like to have my hand firing her ass up for a fucking month."

Axl grunted but looked out the side window on the driver's side. "Double back. I think she was going to take the exit before the one she took like a fucking maniac."

Hollywood's phone rang. "What's up, Keys?"

"You following your girl?"

He brought his hand to his chest, rubbing the spot over the beating organ. "Trying to find the little speed demon."

"Yeah, I saw some footage that was uploaded. Brother, that is one woman who is gonna be hard as fuck to tame. You sure you're up for the challenge?" Keys got quiet, but his ever tapping of a keyboard didn't. "Got her. She's already off the freeway. Why the fuck are you guys so far behind her or rather in front?"

Hollywood looked over at Cosmo who was shaking his head, a little grin on his lips. "You know what, brother? I'm not going to waste my breath explaining the why bullshit. You following her on your fancy computer?"

"You know it. Her dot is going a lot faster than you boys. If you want to catch her, I suggest you tell Cosmo to put some lead in his foot. The area she's in isn't the most well-lit or a safe one I'd want my ole lady in." Keys hesitated for a moment. "She's stopped, and her dot is gone. Either she's gone way underground or the building she entered is lined in lead. Whatever the reason, I've lost her."

"Son-of-a-bitch, Cosmo, step on it. Keys lost her." He rattled off the address the other man gave to him, counting down the seconds it took for them to take the exit.

Roq and Axl sat in the middle row. Had he not known they were back there he'd have thought they'd somehow found a way to disappear. From their very stillness, and the way they both moved, he had no doubt they were trained killers, either by some branch of the military or other. Since they were on his side, he didn't give two shits as long as they were friendly.

"Told you," Axle said a little smugly as they rolled up to a building that from all appearances looked like a garage that wouldn't draw much notice.

The rolls of wire on the roof could be written off as a way to keep kids from trying to break in through that angle, but he was observant and saw the red lights under the overhang. "Infrared alarm system. Kinda high-tech for the area, don't you think?" he asked without expecting an answer.

"She must have a device on her that allows her entry without the need to get out, then once inside, she's sealed up and secure. I wonder what's all inside?" Cosmo drummed his thumb on the steering wheel while they waited for another thirty seconds before he decided to pull down the street a little.

"I'm going to get out and see if I can find a way in other than the front." Hollywood didn't think there was one but sitting in the vehicle waiting wasn't an option.

"What if she comes out while you're out doing a walkabout?" Roq leaned between the seats, his huge hulking form taking up so much space Hollywood wasn't sure how he sat back there comfortably.

"Shit," he growled, looking toward the entrance then the sky. "I fucking hate doing nothing."

"Hey, get in, someone's coming down the road. I recognize that rig from the races." Cosmo had shut the lights off of his own vehicle, but the white Escalade would surely stick out in the neighborhood they were in.

Just as the expensive ride was nearing the entrance where Talena had entered, the door began to open. Her sweet MC20 Maserati eased out, the door gliding down behind her. He could tell when she noticed Louis and his car, a small tap of her brake lights, and then she blew past the fucker. "We won't catch her in that ride either, boys," Hollywood warned Cosmo.

"Why the fuck did you let her have a car, or rather cars—plural—that go that fast? Note to self, my woman will have a scooter, like one of those ones you see little old ladies riding with Life Alert shit." Axl stared straight ahead instead of out the side this time.

"You are in for a rude awakening when you find your woman," Cosmo said, maneuvering his bigger vehicle around corners like he was in a smaller one trying to keep up with the others.

Axl smirked while silence descended.

"My mother and T bought it, without my approval," he bit out, one arm holding onto the oh shit handle to keep from being flung around. "You can bet I'll be taking steps to fix that oversight real damn quick."

"I don't know, she's a damn good driver, man. Look at her," Roq said, a big hand coming between the seats.

Hollywood didn't want anyone else looking at Talena, least of all one of Cosmo's guys, not even when she was driving like a fucking maniac. Just as he was about to tell the other man to shut the fuck up, or keep his eyes to himself, the two faster cars broke away from them.

"Fuck me." He stabbed the number to Keys with his finger, wondering if his phone was going to make it through the night without being broken into a million pieces. "Keys, I need you to keep tabs on Talena's moving dot, brother. She's got a crazy fucker on her ass and they're moving faster than Cosmo's rig can go."

"Got her. I've also got help coming your way. I had a feeling you might need some backup in the way of rides. Don't ask, I won't tell."

Damn ex-SEAL and his secrets. Right then, Hollywood didn't care if Keys knew the damn President and had him on speed dial if it helped Talena. "You gonna give us a hint as to who or what to look for so I don't kill them?"

Keys laughter grated on his very last nerve, which he'd been sure he'd already lost about ten minutes ago.

"You'll know when you see it fly by you. All I ask is you not to kill him or hurt him in any way. He's a friend." Keys grunted, going quiet for long seconds.

A yellow blur flew by them, stilling his words. Hollywood knew what that vehicle was. "Dayumm, a Hennessee Venom GT, Keys?" The car in question could go from zero to sixty in two point four seconds, a hundred miles per hour in four point four seconds, and two hundred miles per hour in just under thirteen seconds. Only a fucking crazy person would drive that car on the freeway after two other fast cars, unless they were adrenalin junkies or nuts. Not to mention, they had to be rich as fuck to afford the ride at close to seven figures.

"He'll make sure he's between your girl and the asshole following her. You need to make sure you catch up and get to wherever she's going. I did some checking on one Louis Valdez. He's one prick that needs taken out, quietly. Note the last word, Hollywood," Keys warned.

"Keys, let me make this really clear so that you understand. That fucker is after my girl. That means he just became Hollywood enemy number one. There is no quietly when it comes to me making sure he's no longer a threat." He wasn't going to lie or play games. He'd killed for his country and he'd killed for his brotherhood. He would kill for Talena, period.

"I figured you'd say that. Cosmo, please try to keep him from going to jail. I'm sure he would get out quickly, but we don't need any incidents right now."

"Is that Hollywood?"

He pinched the bridge of his nose at the angry bark of his club prez. Looking over at Cosmo, he shook his head, then disconnected. "Damn, we lost service. If you feel you need to drop me off, you do that right in front of Talena's car, brother."

Cosmo gave a jerk of his head, the phone on the dash lighting up. "You know, I heard China was a really nice place to visit. I'm sure it sucked you running into that wall and shit while you were over there, fucking up that pretty face of yours. Looks like you healed up nicely, would be a shame if you went to jail. Guess I'll have to make sure that don't happen."

Hollywood didn't look over at Cosmo while he spoke. That wall was a fucking bitch of a family who deserved what they got. He had heard the shit Cosmo's ole lady Tai had gone through long before she'd come to America, had known she'd feared the people who'd sold her to her own government would come looking for her once they realized she wasn't dead. He wasn't willing to allow her or his friend to lose one night of sleep over the fuckers who'd sold her for money, knowing she'd be chopped up for her organs, then either die on the surgery table or be killed after she was used horribly. He'd imagined Talena in her place, and the next thing he'd known, he and a couple others had been knocking on a seemingly upper-class Chinese family's door in a foreign country. He wouldn't lie and say he didn't enjoy beating the fuck out of her older brothers, because he had, immensely. They'd toyed with both of the men, letting them get up, time and again, only to kick the shit out of them all over. Within days, they'd taken out the threat to Tai. Her entire family was gone in a blaze of not so much glory, but a blaze nonetheless. He didn't ask Cosmo to repay him and never would. However, when the other man looked at the phone, then him, before silencing it, Hollywood knew they both were on the same page.

"Well, sheot, that phone done lost signal too. Hmm, guess we are on our own. Let's go fuck some shit up." Roq slapped the sides of both their seats.

Cosmo took a deep breath. "He's like a little kid who doesn't understand he's a big motherfucker."

"I know I'm big. Women tell me that all the time. Oh, Roq, you're too big," he said in a terrible female falsetto.

"How many women tell you you're too big and tell you to stop? I bet I've had more," Axl piped in.

"Don't get started on the dick measuring bullshit," Cosmo warned.

"What the fuck is that?" Hollywood asked. Lights that should be going the opposite direction were coming toward them.

"Ah sheot," Roq muttered.

Hollywood was becoming sick of the other man's twang and use of that word. Anytime he said it, sheot seemed to go sideways.

One of their cage vehicles came across several lanes, Frog, the crazy bastard, laying on the horn as he drove toward traffic as if he was unafraid of colliding with the dozens of vehicles. Fucking King was going to have all their asses. It was the Maserati that blew past them that he was focused on, that and the fact Frog was clearly a distraction as well.

Louis watched the woman he wanted to fuck, after he made her bleed, speed by him in a car he planned to own. His cock got hard beneath his fly.

"That's a sexy ride, Boss."

He glared at Tito through the rearview mirror. "She's mine then I'll let you play, maybe."

"Hey, I thought I was your girl?" Rosalie snarled.

Louis backhanded her, hearing the smack made his dick jump. Oh yeah, when he caught up to the little bitch, he'd make her suck his cock while he let Tito fuck Rosalie. He wondered what the little bitch next to him looked like when she wasn't breathing.

"You're whatever I say you are. Now shut up or I'll make you wish you'd stayed behind." Stupid little cunt had forced her way into his car. Her lips had been wrapped around his cock before the race, giving him a blowjob that had him coming in four damn minutes. He didn't like the smug look she'd given him, like she owned him. Nobody owned him. He did the owning. If he wanted to fuck, or make someone suck his cock, he was the one in charge. The little whore next to him would find out tonight exactly who she'd been toying with, as would the little blonde bitch who thought she was better than him.

He slammed his foot on the gas pedal, enjoying the frightened squeal of Rosalie. A little part of him was tempted to unhook her seatbelt and see if she enjoyed riding with him as much if she wasn't buckled in, but then he'd have to have his car cleaned up. His hand flew out again, making contact with her cheek, eliciting another cry.

"What the fuck are you doing?" she cried.

"Whatever I want, Punta," he told her, staring at her for long seconds, letting her see what most don't because he hid behind the veneer of civility.

"You can't just hit me, Louis. I have friends and family. They'll—" she stopped, pressing herself against the door.

He eased his hand back to the gear shifter once he'd made his point. Little Rosalie wouldn't be telling anyone anything after tonight.

"Play your cards right, and you'll be fine. Keep pushing my buttons and I'll toss your ass out on the highway," he warned.

The feisty little woman held a trembling hand to her cheek but stayed silent. He was glad to find a way to get her to shut the fuck up. The only other times he'd accomplished that task was when he'd shoved his dick in her mouth or stuffed her panties in there when he fucked her. She'd thought it was his kink; when in reality, he just wanted her to shut the fuck up.

"I obviously underestimated that little bitch, Tito. I thought you said she was a loner with nothing and no friends." Louis shifted again, his car nearly bumping the rear of the Maserati.

"I followed her around the races for the last four weeks. She didn't hang out with any particular group, and when she left, she left alone. She never took any calls or nothin', Boss, I swear." Tito's voice was high pitched, almost whiny. Louis hated whiners.

"You missed something. A woman doesn't have shit like that if she's alone. Someone is funding her." He'd take pleasure in finding out who and send them pics of their little bitch with his dick in her. Already he could see it, feel it. His arm shot out, grabbing Rosalie's hand. "Jack me off, Punta."

She tried to keep him from bringing her hand to his lap. Silly bitch, she wasn't as strong as him. He slapped her again, keeping one hand on the wheel, the excitement made his dick nearly ready to blow. "Either do as I say, or I'll slit your fucking throat."

Rosalie's hand fumbled on his zipper, but then she had his dick out, and he pretended it was the blonde. He kept both hands on the wheel while directing her to go faster, squeeze harder until his dick was ready to explode. "In your mouth," he said in a guttural voice.

Like before the race, he didn't last more than four minutes, but he didn't care because he was the one in charge this time.

Chapter Six

How many times can a person say holy shit before the words got stuck in their throat? Talena was pretty sure she was getting to that point as she looked in her review and saw Louis's vehicle gaining on her. How he'd found her she had no clue. How he was able to keep up when she knew he'd used NOS earlier, she didn't know, and didn't care. All she needed to do was get to the next overpass, and then she'd be able to spin her car around and go back the other direction. He was a good driver, but she was too. Not to mention, she was damn good at defensive driving. She hoped he hadn't taken that course. "Please don't be any good," she prayed.

At the last second, she did what she'd planned, downshifting and spinning the wheel until she was going the opposite direction. Her plan was to maneuver into the other lanes going the right direction. Of course, nothing seemed to be going her way tonight. On the fly, she continued turning until she was heading back down the highway the way she'd come. She watched as Louis flew past her, his eyes wide in apparent shock. She didn't hesitate, hitting the accelerator, apologizing to the cars that honked at her when she almost hit them. It was a calculated risk, but dammit, she had to do it. She'd rather collide with another vehicle than be run off the road by the psycho fucker.

"Oh god, if I make it out of this alive, I'm so taking a break from racing," she promised, shifting gears while weaving around cars. Luckily traffic wasn't heavy, making it not so hard for her to steer around the cars traveling east while she drove west. At any moment, she expected to hear sirens or see helicopters overhead, something like when OJ had done a runner.

Like all junkies, her high was dropping. Although her drug of choice was adrenalin, she could feel her body ready to crash. "Just like I'm going to do if I don't stay focused. Fuck what is that?" Bright lights blazed toward her from the left. She wondered if Louis had brought in reinforcements to corral her or some shit. If only she could get to her phone, but then who would she call, Hollywood? Hell no, he'd be so pissed.

She jerked the wheel to the right to avoid another car, hearing the ding dinging she'd been waiting on to happen. Low Fuel blinked up at her like a damn neon light, mocking her. She chanced a look in her rearview, letting out a little breath of relief when she didn't see Louis's car. What she did see was another vehicle, bobbing and weaving causing cars to swerve and collide. "Holy shit, this is bad, sooo bad."

Up ahead in the distance, she saw the overhead signs that meant an onramp was there. She'd have to do some quick maneuvering, but it was the only way for her to get the fuck off. Sending a prayer up, she began moving toward the nearest lane, keeping an eye on the crazy bastard behind her. "Please let me make it out of this alive."

By the skin of her teeth, she was able to spin the small car around and make it off the on ramp without wrecking or running out of gas. Her heart was beating so hard and fast, she didn't think she'd survive if anything else went wrong. Unsure exactly where she was, she looked around for a gas station, groaning when she noticed all the people hanging around the pumps. "Just my luck," she muttered.

Talena rolled her vehicle to the only open gas pump, reaching into the glove box for her gun and credit card. She slid her Sig P365 out, checked it was loaded, before she got out with her jacket on, tucking the gun safely inside her back holster.

She slid her credit card into the reader, pressed the appropriate buttons and waited. All the while, she heard music and voices, paying close attention to her surroundings.

Hollywood and her mom had been very persistent that she learn to defend herself when she'd graduated high school. Not that she minded the training, it had been a way for her to focus and keep fit when she'd needed the outlet. Now she used the training to her advantage as she slid the nozzle into her car, tapping her hand on the handle while she waited. Five gallons. Ten gallons. Hell, that was enough. She pulled the lever down, stopping the fuel flow, feeling the hair on the back of her neck rise.

Without looking up, she replaced the nozzle, screwed on her cap, and was reaching for the slip.

"What's a fine thing like you doing all alone in a place like this?"

Talena closed her eyes and counted to three. When she opened her eyes, she looked at the man who was way too close for her peace of mind and grinned. "I just got off of work and need to return my guy's car to him."

"Told you it wasn't hers. Why don't you let me take it for a little spin? I'm sure your guy wouldn't mind. In fact, he'll never have to know." The blond man with more piercings than sense moved a step closer.

Talena whipped her gun out, pressing it to his forehead. "You see, I'd know, and that's gonna be a problem. Now this is how it's going to go. I'm getting into my car and driving away. You and your friends will continue with your party like nothing happened because nothing did. I was never here."

"Bitch, you pull a gun on me and you think I'll act like nothing happened?"

"You can either do as she says, or I'll put a bullet through your head and that's one hole you won't be putting some jewelry through."

Talena nearly sagged in relief at the familiar sound of Hollywood's voice. The fact she had her gun pressed against a young thug's forehead kept her steady, barely. "Hey," she said.

"Hey, yourself. So, what's it gonna be, boys. You think you can walk through a bullet to the brain? I promise, she's a damn good shot, and even if she wasn't, nobody misses at point blank range." Hollywood stepped closer, a semi-automatic hanging loosely from his arm.

"Who the hell are you?"

"Your worst fucking nightmare if you fuck with me or mine, little boy. Run on back to your friends before you get hurt." Hollywood pushed the guy back with one hand, placing himself in front of Talena, walking backward.

She realized he was herding her back to her car's driver's door. "How did you know I was here?"

"Get in and scoot over to the passenger seat," he bit out.

A white SUV sat idling a few feet away along with the vehicle she'd seen following her on the highway. She was so screwed.

"I can explain," she tried.

"Inside and over or I'm going to bend you over the hood of this car and light that ass up in front of all these motherfuckers, T." Hollywood didn't look at her, his focus on the crowd of young men.

Her hand shook almost too much to where she couldn't get the door to open, but she got it on the second try, crawling over to the passenger seat like he'd told her. Her gun felt heavy in her hand, but she didn't put it away until he was inside with her. He didn't look at her as he started the car. The rumble of the big engine beneath her didn't give her the normal rush. No, this time, she had a feeling the fast vehicle meant she'd be getting whatever punishment he had for her a lot quicker too. When he'd threatened to put her over the hood though, her body hadn't been repulsed, just the opposite in fact.

Calculated thoughts raced through her mind. Like how could she get him to do that very thing? Except she definitely didn't want there to be a bunch of assholes watching who were there to possibly gang rape her and kill him. Yeah, she wasn't there for that. Now, being fucked and spanked by Hollywood? She was so here, there, and everywhere for some of that.

Hollywood needed to calm the fuck down, or he was liable to do some serious damage, or fuck Talena right in front of everyone. Son-of-a-bitch, he was equal parts scared shitless and hard as stone, watching her pull her gun out and threaten the little punk who dared fuck with her. He'd damn near leapt out of the moving SUV when he'd seen the asshole strolling up to where she stood pumping gas in her car, his sly wink enough of a reason for Hollywood to beat the shit out of him. But it was the blade he'd twirled around and then hid in his back pocket that scared him the most. He'd hit the unlock button on Cosmo's rig before they'd come to a rocking stop, leaping out and running across the road like the hounds of Hell were after him.

He held his hand up as he heard her take a deep breath, stopping whatever she planned on saying. "T, my control is held by a very fucking slim thread. I suggest you sit there and be quiet until I get us a few miles down the road, or I'm liable to turn around, kill a parking lot full of idiots, before fucking you senseless in a river of their blood," he bit out, uncaring that he'd just said the filthiest thing to her.

The streets were a blur as he drove through the shitty part of town behind her, anger building as it became obvious her little pit stop was in a dangerous neighborhood. "What the fuck were you thinking?" he barked.

When silence met his question, he took his eyes off the road, looking at her profile. Her usually tan complexion was almost ghostly. Fuck he'd done scared the living shit out of her with his threat. He let out a sigh, reigning in his anger, and tried to still the need to touch her, failing on the last. The memory of her wild driving had him reaching over, touching her cheek. "Dammit, I'm sorry, baby." His voice was softer than moments before.

"I'm sorry, Hollywood. I didn't mean to make you have to face off against those guys. I was almost out of gas, and that was the closest one I saw," she whispered.

His heart banged against his chest. She was apologizing because she thought he was mad because of the fucking gas station bullshit? He wanted to fucking laugh, and at the same time, he wanted to pull her over his lap...not to spank, much. His fingers itched to do that and so much more. "Talena, we have a lot to talk about. Right now, I need to get this ride of yours off the street." He could see Cosmo's big rig keeping up behind them with Frog, the crazy bastard, following. Where he'd parked the trailer with their bikes, he had no clue, but Frog was solid. King was going to make him a brother in the coming weeks, which Hollywood was proud as hell to have the man at his back.

"I know you're mad, but I swear, I had it under control." Talena took a deep breath, turning in her seat so she was facing him.

"Ah, sweetheart, the last fucking thing you had was shit under control. I promise, if you think you did, you were sadly mistaken. Now, if you like sitting down without feeling as though a thousand needles are lighting up that fine ass, I suggest you sit and think about what you are going to say.

Think really hard and remember I don't like liars." He took his eyes off the street for a moment, letting her see the fire burning in his gaze. Some say he had icy blue eyes that changed colors depending on his mood. Those people would say they were positively arctic right now, because he didn't think he'd ever been so angry, scared, and turned on at the same time in all of his adult life. Shit he was sure he'd never felt the way he did in the last couple hours, ever.

"Mom wouldn't like it if you hurt me," she whispered, her lower lip trembling.

He gave a laugh void of humor before he answered, "Mom would hate it even more if she had to plan her daughter's funeral. Mom would loathe it even more if she had to identify the child she's loved, from the moment she laid eyes on her, at the morgue. You want me to repeat the story she told me of when she was given you? She said that even though you were not of her flesh she felt a connection every bit as strong as the one she had when she had me. That's right, little girl, our mother loves you every bit as much as she loves me. So, don't you think for one minute you can wiggle your way out of what I plan to do to you by using her to minimize shit."

A tear rolled down her cheek. "I didn't mean...I'm sorry. I'm such a mess." She swiped her hand over her cheek.

He reached over, taking the fingers she'd used, bringing them to his lips. "Ssh, we'll talk when we get to my place."

If she expected him to apologize or tell her it was okay, she'd be waiting a long damn time. What he would do was kiss her ass, not like a little pussy, but his lips would be caressing every inch of skin on her sexy body. Hell, his cock twitched beneath the fly of his jeans, damn near bursting the metal thing.

He heard her gasp, but this time, he didn't look over to see what the fuck caused the reaction. His control was too flimsy as it was. If he saw her full lips tremble or another tear leak from those beautiful blue eyes, he was sure he'd pull her fucking car over and say to hell with decency and have her on his lap, his dick in her pussy right then and there. He was sure Cosmo and the others had been there, done that.

"You realize you're acting like a...a caveman, right?" Talena's voice was like a lightning strike in the air, setting his blood on fire.

"Ah, baby girl, you've no clue just how close to the truth you are. Big difference between me and cavemen is the fact I got a lot better equipment to make sure my ole lady can't escape."

They drove for another thirty minutes, hopping back onto the freeway toward his place, both staying silent. He didn't mind the quiet. It gave him time to work out his next steps. All his life, he'd been a planner, ensuring he had an idea of where he was going next and a backup plan in case that route was blocked, with a backup to the backup. From what life had dealt him and his family, he'd learned to never just go with the flow. The flow was nothing but shit waiting to blow up in your face.

His beachfront property was the closest, and one that Talena had never been to with the house built into the side of a hill. He had bought it because it was perfect from a defensive standpoint, and it had beautiful views with the beach below and only one way in; a gated driveway a mile down the road that only he had access to. He rolled the driver's side window down, giving Cosmo a wave.

The big white SUV rolled up next to him with Roq now in the passenger seat. Shit he wasn't sure how the man was able to fit into a normal rig the way he barely did Cosmo's Escalade. "Thanks for the backup, brothers. Tell King I'll be at the meeting tomorrow afternoon." Not that he had a choice since it was a mandatory one or that he planned on missing anyhow. Of course, he'd be bringing Talena with him if he had to handcuff her ass to his side.

"No thanks needed. You want us to set up post outside?" Axl asked from the back.

Hollywood tilted his head to the side, a little surprised at the offer, but then again, the men were loyal to Cosmo, which meant they would be loyal to whoever his brother was maybe? Whatever the reasoning, he appreciated the offer. "Nah, I got it handled."

Cosmo leaned forward, one hand resting on the wheel. "You sure?"

He was more than sure. The security at the house was like Fort Knox. Of course, there was always the off chance some fucker could get in. Hollywood would deal with that if and when it happened. "Yep. Go home to Tai and take those crazy bastards with you." He grinned at Roq and Axl. If ever there were men who fit the crazy bill, it was the Demon Security guys Cosmo ran with.

His friend jerked his head up and down once, waiting until his gate opened and closed before executing a turn. Hollywood didn't wait around to watch Cosmo's tail lights disappear before he took him and Talena up the long drive to his place. Although he had a suite he'd claimed at the clubhouse, like most of the Royal Brothers, he would always keep his homes, the places he went to when he needed quiet. While he loved the brotherhood, the feeling of belonging, he'd found the solitude with the military suited him. Not that he was looking for solitude as he drove through the huge garage bay doors. The sound of Talena's swift inhale made him grin. There were very few people who'd been inside his home built into the side of the hill in Malibu, with a staggering price of over forty million. He had land and lush greenery with his own private beach and an infinity pool that didn't get used nearly enough.

"What did you expect, some kind of mancave complete with a dirt floor and bars on the windows? You know me better than that. Besides I have the bars and chains inside." He winked.

She slapped his arm, grinning back toward him. "Don't even try that with me. You know I am fully aware you like your creature comforts as much as the next man. But this..." she pointed toward the garage in front of them.

"What about it?" He parked her Maserati in an open spot, looking around them, wondering what she saw.

"Scott, this space is bigger than most people's homes, and it's your garage. And what is the floor made of, marble?" Talena pushed her door open at the same time he did.

He shook his head, laughing at her assumption. "No, it's not marble. Come on, let's go inside. You can explore the garage another time," he told her, steering her toward the door. He'd purposefully parked near the entrance to the house, aware she clearly had a thing for fast cars. "My contractors used a special concrete that looks like marble, but as you can see, it appears to mimic marble. Don't ask me what because I've no clue. All I know was it cost a shitton, but it was worth every penny as it's easy as shit to keep clean, and it's aesthetically appealing."

She stopped walking, staring up at him with wide eyes. "Are you telling me you...you chose the floor of your garage on the grounds of it being pretty or not?"

Hollywood looked down at her, watching her lips twitch. He'd felt emotions tonight he'd never thought to experience. Fear, worry, anger, and lust all at the same time. She had been part of his life since the day she'd came home from the hospital as a baby. For years, he'd looked at her as a little sister. She'd been the girl he had to protect from the world, and then they'd found out she wasn't his sister, but he still loved her. Blood didn't make you family, he'd told her all those years ago, and he'd meant it.

The woman standing before him wasn't the young girl who needed a big brother anymore, yet he still wanted to wrap her up and keep her safe from any and all hurt. Big difference from when she was a kid though, he had no brotherly feelings toward her now. The things he wanted to do to her, with her...fuck, his dick was so damn hard thinking about them he wasn't sure if he'd last ten minutes once he had his hands on her.

"Why're you looking at me like that?" she asked in a quiet whisper.

"How am I looking at you?" He brushed a few wisps of hair back from her face, watching her the entire time. Hollywood wasn't going to do anything she didn't want him to do. He'd seen the way she looked at him, loved the need she couldn't hide.

"Like that."

He chuckled at her words. Some things never change, no matter what. Talena hated to be confronted and not having the answer when she was. "I'm gonna need a little more than that but let's save it until we're inside. Besides I'm thirsty and want to get the fuck out of these clothes."

A blush stole up her neck and into her cheeks. He was all too aware how far that beautiful hue went, having seen her in all her naked glory. Shit, he needed to quit thinking of her without any clothes on until he got them inside his home.

"Come on," he said, threading his fingers through hers. At the door, he placed his other palm on the electronic plate, waiting for it to read his signature.

The reinforced steel door slid open. He watched Talena take in his security measures, waiting for her to ask him questions, or say something about him being overly precautious. Seconds ticked by while he moved in through the mudroom, kicking his boots off. His feet felt better immediately when they touched the cool tiles. It didn't escape his notice he hadn't released his hold on her, yet she still hadn't said a word or protested him keeping her tethered to his side. Which was good because he had no plans of letting her out of his sight for, well, if he had his way she'd be within his view for a long motherfucking time after the shit he witnessed tonight.

"Scott, your grip is a little tight?"

Her soft voice pulled him from his dark thoughts, making him grimace as he realized what he'd done. "I'm sorry, baby girl. Come on. I need a drink. Are you hungry?"

"Thirsty, but not hungry."

He looked down at her, noticing the faint lines of exhaustion on her beautiful face. Fuck looking at her had him wanting to do all kinds of things, none of them pure, and none wanting to allow her to rest. "When did you sleep last?"

"Hollywood, would you stop mother-henning me? I eat when I'm hungry, and I sleep when I'm tired. I don't need you to nag me. Trust me, I learned my lesson." She put her hand over her mouth.

"What the hell are you talking about, learned your lesson?" He stared down at her, watching her look everywhere but at him, the beautiful blush he loved turning crimson. He felt as if something huge had happened, and he was the only one who was in the dark. "You know I won't let this go until I know what I want."

"Please, Scott, I really don't want to rehash things best left in the past." She licked her lips and wobbled on her feet.

Dammit he was shit for a host. "We'll come back to this."

Chapter Seven

Talena didn't let Hollywood see the relief she felt as he turned away from her. The very last thing she wanted to tell him was how close she'd come to dying because of her own stupidity. She'd rather keep that little secret for as long as she could. Right now, she was enjoying his attention that didn't have anything to do with his need to big brother her, and everything to do with wanting her. The heat that he didn't try to conceal had been everything she'd ever hoped to see, yet she'd also hesitated for a brief second. What if once he sated his desire with her, he moved on like he always did?

"What's made you go quiet and pensive?" He returned with two bottles in his hand. One icy cold beer for him and an orange juice for her.

She accepted the beverage he'd held out, knowing he wouldn't budge and allow her to drink anything else, until he was assured for himself, that she'd drank what he felt was good for her body. The fact she also wanted the refreshing OJ was a moot point. While he sipped his drink, she walked around the huge white kitchen. It was nothing like their family home, which was not to say it wasn't homey, but where their mother's house was all dark wood and filled with things, his space was clean lines with white and stainless steel. The small pops of color kept it from looking too stark, making her wonder who helped him design the space.

"Do you like it?" His question broke into the quietness of the night.

Talena nodded as she ran her hand over the sleek countertop, noticing the little flecks of sparkle in it. "What kind of material is this?"

"It's called Pyrolave Enameled Lava. Eleven thousand years ago the Nugere crater erupted in the Regional Nature Park of the Volcanos of Auvergne, where the Volvic lava used by Pyrolave is extracted. The company will custom make your countertops to your specifications, size, color, everything. Nothing is too extreme for them. If you look at their gallery, they've had some pretty extreme color choices by their clients. I didn't want anything crazy, but I did want something other than a flat white, or as you'll see in the other rooms, the colors I chose for them also have a little sparkle to them."

She finished her orange juice, looking around for the recycling bin. "Where should I toss this?"

"Here I'll take it." Hollywood reached for the small bottle, taking it and his own glass one to a cleverly hidden set of bins inside the cabinet near the mudroom door.

His fingers brushed hers, sending tingles up her arm. She rubbed her hands up and down both sides, feeling the fine hairs standing up and pretending it was from the cold air blowing down on her from the central air vents. Luckily Hollywood appeared to ignore the impact he was having on her, for the moment. Although looking at his face, she saw his eyes twinkle. He wouldn't let her put him at arm's length for long.

Instead of letting him dictate to her like she'd always done, waiting around like a good little girl, she moved to where he was looking at a stack of papers. Not that she wanted to see what he was reading, but she wanted...she wanted him. If she only got him for one night, one hour, one whatever, she was going to take it and store every moment away to pull out whenever she needed a pick me up.

She saw the way his body tensed slightly at her approach. And still, she didn't let that keep her from sliding her hands around his waist. God he was all hard muscles covered in silky soft skin. From the times she'd seen him without a stitch of clothing on, he was nothing short of a girl's wet dream come to life. If he turned her away, Talena didn't think she'd ever be able to face him again.

"What're you doing, baby girl?"

The way he spoke in the deep growly tone let her know she was getting to him. "Hmm, I'm touching you."

"I can feel that. Do you know what happens to little girls who take what they're not told they can?" His fingers trailed over hers, tickling the backs of her hands, keeping his face turned away from her.

She realized he could see her through the mammoth refrigerator with its gleaming exterior reflecting both of them. A little distorted but if she could make them out, he could too.

"I asked you a question, Talena. I expect an answer," he growled.

Talena froze, her mind trying to figure out what he'd said. "I'm sorry, can you repeat the question?"

"Sir," he said.

"Excuse me?"

He turned around, spinning until she was pinned between him and the counter. "There are things I need in a relationship, T. These are non-negotiable. What we start tonight, they're not a one and done thing between us. I'm not going to lie or pretend with you, and I'll expect the same from you. Understand?"

She licked her lips, her heart beating so hard she wondered if he could see it pounding through the thin material of her shirt. "Maybe you should explain it to me."

Hollywood brushed his thumb over Talena's trembling bottom lip, watched as her tongue came out licking at his digit. His cock jerked at the unconscious sexy little action. He was sure she wasn't even aware of the way she had him tied up in knots. Of course, he planned to have her truly tied up before the night was through, if she agreed. Fuck he couldn't even contemplate her not wanting the same things he did.

"You're freaking me out here, Hollywood."

"That's the first thing, baby. When we are here, in our home, I'm Sir, or you can call me Scott, but whatever you call me, I'm in charge, so you will say it with respect. That's what I need. I need my woman to be prepared for whatever I tell her to do." He let his words fall into the quiet of the room, let her register them. With his right hand cradling her face, his fingers spanned her neck, he didn't miss the way her pulse jumped.

"You mean...like in Fifty Shades?" she asked, swallowing audibly.

He laughed at her question, sobering when her eyes closed, seeing his action hurt her. "I'm not laughing at you, baby. I watched that movie, honey, and while I know women seemed to love it, I promise you, that...was nothing like my reality."

"Does that mean you don't have a red room?" she asked, laughter filling her voice.

"I don't nor will I allow you to sleep in another bedroom. I'll want access to you and your body anytime, anywhere I want it. Does that freak you out?" He wondered just how much of the movie she'd quoted she liked and thought he might be willing to recreate some of it for her, maybe.

"I want you. I think I've wanted you for as long as I've known what it was to want a man, maybe longer. Not that I knew what that was at the time, but when I was—" she stopped talking, her hand going over her lips.

"What were you going to say?" He removed her fingers, kissing the tips while holding her gaze.

Talena shook her head, a denial on her lips.

"What did I say about secrets and lies, baby girl?" Hollywood twisted her arm behind her back, pulling her in closer to him. The move wasn't painful, but it showed her he was in control.

"When I was twelve, I was mad at...at Gary for some reason. I can't remember why now, but I ran out to my treehouse to hide and found someone had decided to use it for other purposes." She glared up at him.

He was trying to figure out what she was talking about when it hit him. "Shit."

"I'm pretty sure you didn't use my precious sanctuary as a bathroom. However, after you and your little..."

A look of horror spread over Talena's face as she began to wiggle to get free. "Let me go, Scott."

"Stop it and tell me what's wrong," he ordered, wrapping his arms around her more firmly.

She wouldn't look at him, her breathing turning ragged the more she fought. "Let me go," she snarled. "I need a little space."

"No, baby, you need to tell what the fuck has you so angry."

"Fine I'll tell you. I just realized the person who you were probably fucking on my pretty princess comforter was probably our stepsister Angela." She lifted her face, blue eyes blazing with anger and hurt.

He'd done many things he regretted, screwing Angela was one of them. However, one thing he could correct was Talena's assumption. "T, listen to me. I am not going to lie and tell you I never slept with Angela. We all know I did; that's not ever been a secret. What I didn't do was fuck her in your treehouse or anywhere around the property. I wish like hell I could go back and change the fact I'd taken anyone up to the treehouse, which by the way was mine first," he said, then sighed. "The truth is, I don't even remember the girl's name or what she looked like. That night isn't even a memory I can pull up and recall, but what I do know is it wasn't Angela."

His admission had her shoulders relaxing. Talena lifted her chin, a slight wobble in the stubborn little thing before she controlled it. "I believe you."

"I wouldn't lie to you. I have no reason to. Now what were you saying before you thought it was Angela? And let me reiterate, if you lie to me, I'll know it, and there'll be consequences." She'd learn he said what he meant, and he meant what he said.

"What do you mean?" she asked instead of answering him.

He shook his head, knowing he was going to have to show her he meant business. Before she could say another word, he bent, putting her over his shoulder, swatting her sweetly rounded ass with his palm. Her startled yelp brought a grin to his lips.

"What the hell, Scott?"

"That's the first rule I told you. We'll discuss more once we get to the bedroom. You sure you're not hungry, because I plan to have you tied up for a while?" He left the kitchen area, lights coming on in each space they entered. With the home being built into the hill, most would expect it to be dark, but he'd made sure the entire place appeared light and airy, selecting colors and textures that were smooth and clean, like white and several shades of gray, along with other variations of light colors that fit in well with the clean aesthetic and added lots of recessed lighting.

"Sir, you want me to call you Sir?" She slapped his back, growling angrily.

"You'll need to learn discipline, but that's a start," he agreed, swatting her two fast slaps on each butt cheek, knowing she'd feel the sting. He couldn't wait to see his mark on her flesh.

"That hurt," she cried.

He chuckled, feeling her squirm on his shoulder, not from pain he was sure. "Bullshit, baby girl. You and I both know that you're lying." He dumped her on top of his custom-made bed, watching her bounce slightly as he stood above her. Oh yeah, she was flushed with arousal and a little embarrassed. They'd work on the latter first. "What did I tell you about lying to me?"

Talena shifted backward slightly until the backs of her knees were on the edge of the bed. He gripped her thighs, sliding his fingers between the both of them, eyes locked with hers as he pressed her legs apart. "Answer me, T."

"You said there would be consequences. How do you know I'm lying though?" She licked her lips, first the top, then the bottom.

"First, I can tell because I know you, baby girl. Second, I know because I can see your excitement written all over your body. See this lovely color." He moved until he was between her spread thighs and trailed his fingers up her legs along her ribs on each side until he reached the place on her chest where her shirt gaped. "You blush beautifully," he told her.

"Mom could always tell when I wasn't being truthful because of that unfortunate trait as well," she groused, poking her lower lip out.

Oh, he was onto what she was trying to do. He'd let her too. He wasn't a Dom who didn't like a sub with a little bratty tendency, to a point. However, he'd also show her what he did when she pulled that shit with him. "I really love your lips. Have I told you that, mon pourri?"

"Did you just call me your brat?" Her eyes narrowed on him.

"Mmm," he answered.

Hollywood was done talking. It was time he showed Talena he meant business. Besides his dick was screaming at him to be free and had been for the past hour or so. "I'm going to ask you one last question, and your answer is going to decide how we move forward. I want you, mon pourri. Not for only tonight or in my bed. Although I will have you here, but forever. I'm not playing games, but that is something I enjoy as well. Just not the games that you might be used to. What I'm saying is this"—he took a deep breath, holding her gaze while he continued.—"I've had many women, and I'm not saying that as a way to brag. I'm telling you because I need you to know I know who and what I want, and that is you. I knew when you were seventeen that you would be mine. It took everything in me to let you grow up and spread your wings. I had to leave the country so that I wouldn't fucking act on the needs of a man who was too fucking old to do the things I wanted. Now the only thing that would stop me from claiming you is you. If you don't want me, all of me for more than a sating of lust, then you can go sleep in one of my guest rooms. I'll keep you safe, even from me. Tomorrow we'll figure out where we go from here, and—I'll let you walk away with someone else watching your back." That was a fucking lie. He'd be the one making sure she was safe and kill any fucker who dared harm her.

"You wanted me when I was seventeen?" She shifted on the bed, getting onto her knees so that she was closer to his height.

"Is that all you got from what I just said? Woman, did you listen to me?"

She put her hand over his lips, stopping him mid-sentence. "I wanted you too. I've always wanted you. God, I love you. Everything about you, I love. Even your bossiness,

I love. I might screw up with the calling you Sir thing, but I think I might like the spanking," she whispered.

He nipped one of her fingers over his mouth, making her gasp. "You think, do you? I think we should find out." Not giving her a chance to assimilate his words, he quickly gathered her into his arms, sitting down with her draped over his thighs, that ass he fucking dreamt about wiggling on his lap. He placed one hand over her back, holding her in place as he brought the other down over the jean covered globes. "Settle down, T, or I promise, you won't like your punishment."

"Why am I being punished?" She swiveled slightly, glaring up at him.

"You lied. You were racing in an illegal race that was so damn dangerous you could've been killed. You made an enemy of a very volatile man, who appears to want to harm or kill you at the very least." With each transgression, he landed three swats to each cheek, the crack of his palm loud in the quiet room. "You pulled into a gas station filled with a gang of degenerates, alone. You defied my wishes and lied to my face. You scared me," he whispered the last, rubbing his palm over her ass when he finished the punishment, doing his own mental count of ten.

"I'm so...sorry," she cried.

He pulled her up, settling her on his thighs and used his thumbs to brush the tears from her cheeks. "Not half as sorry as I'd have been if anything had happened to you."

She took a deep shuddering breath, staying silent.

"Are you okay?" He didn't give her a chance to pick a safeword. For them, the rules were going to be different. She was his to protect and he needed her to trust he'd never allow anything or anyone to harm her, not even himself.

"I didn't scream red so that should be a answer in itself." She relaxed against him, wincing slightly.

"That's good because you need to trust that I will never go too far without having a safeword. But if you feel like you need one, then by all means, red it will be." They'd work up to a level of trust where she wouldn't need one.

"So, are you going to do more?" she asked shyly.

His dick jumped at her question. "Oh, baby, I'm going to do so much more."

"You'll have to tell me what to do. Not that I'm a virgin or anything," she stammered.

He narrowed his eyes, hating the image of her and any other man together, which was absolutely absurd since he'd fucked more women than he cared to count. Yet he still wanted to know the names of the men she'd been with so he could hunt them down and kill them. Barbaric? Absofuckinglutely, but he was honest enough to admit it.

"Hollywood Haven, you stop thinking of all the ways you're going to dismember the men I slept with, right this minute." She poked him in the chest. The action was like poking a sleeping bear.

He stood with her in his arms, dumping her in the middle of the bed. "I'll think about it."

What he'd think about, he didn't say. Think about killing the nameless faceless men, or think about not killing them? It was still up for debate. Right then, what he decided to focus on was getting the gorgeous woman lying so innocently on his bed, a bed he'd never had another woman naked. Placing one knee on the bed, he crawled to where she lay until he straddled her body. "I don't want to talk about other men or women anymore. Tonight, is about you and me. Nobody else exists between us. Agreed?"

She nodded.

"Say yes Sir," he instructed her.

Talena licked her lips. "Yes, Sir."

"Ah, mon pourri, very good." He bent, placing his arms beside her head, holding her gaze while he covered her lips with his. When their lips met for the first time, he felt as though his heart turned over. His thumbs skimmed the sides of her neck, feeling her pulse racing. Moving slowly, he continued to kiss her, brushing his lips back and forth, coaxing her lips apart while his right hand glided down her chest, loving the feel of soft skin beneath his calloused palm. Her chest rose and fell with each breath she took, making him acutely aware of the firm mounds of her breasts so fucking close to his palms.

Sucking her bottom lip inside his mouth, he gave a little nip then released it to pull back and look his fill. She had full breasts. He'd bet his left nut were soft yet firm. Holding her stare, he let his fingers trace between the valley over the shirt she wore, holding his weight off her much smaller frame. The caveman in him wanted him to rip the material in half so he could get to the bounty beneath, but the civilized man he was, held himself in check by a thread.

"Damn you have no clue how beautiful you look lying beneath me right now. I need to see more of you." It wasn't a request, but he thought he'd be nice.

Talena shifted beneath him, her hips lifting slightly grazing his dick. He wanted to keep her on the edge but wanted to push her further without forcing her. What the fuck was he doing, becoming a damn pussy? By now, he'd usually have the woman naked and cuffed, begging for him. The thought had him grazing both thumbs over her pebbled nipples, watching her face as he did it. Her tiny gasp of pleasure had him tugging at the little tip, pinching them between thumb and forefinger before releasing them at the same time. "You react so strongly to my touch. Do you like it when I pinch your nipples, baby?" he asked, repeating the same treatment again, doing it a little harder than before to see if she flinched or pulled away. To his delight, she moaned.

In reward for her gift of acceptance, he bent and replaced his fingers with his mouth, first on one hardened tip, sucking on her through her shirt and bra. He then switched to the other one, giving it the same attention before letting her go. "Before this night is through, you'll have my marks all over this gorgeous body," he told her, meaning every word in so many ways.

She shivered, a smile playing about her lips. He loved seeing her happy, would do anything to watch her face light up every second of every day. Right now, though, he wanted to see a different emotion on her beautiful features. He needed to see her looking like he felt. Needy. So fucking needy, he could barely control the urge to rip every stitch of clothing from her, uncaring of the cost or if she particularly loved the items she wore. He was rich as fuck and could buy her a dozen just like them. What kept him from doing what the caveman part of him wanted was the anticipation he knew would build in the both of them by going slow.

"Where should I start?"

"My shirt is really scratchy. I think it should go," she said breathlessly.

She surprised him by her boldness. He'd thought for sure she'd want him to turn the lights off and do missionary. Not that he wouldn't do that for her, but he'd hoped like hell she was adventurous.

With deliberate slowness, he inched her top up. "Lift up for me."

While he had her sitting, he unsnapped the front clasp on her demi bra, freeing her breasts for him to feast his eyes on. "Damn, baby, these are every bit as beautiful as I remember."

He pressed her back down to lay flat on his bed, moving to lay beside her, trailing one hand down the center of her body. His hand had a slight tremor that he hid by exerting pressure on her sternum. Although she was curvy, she was still slim. "When did you get this tattoo?"

Talena glanced down at the words written beneath her right breast. "A few years ago."

Hollywood traced the words that had been inked into her skin, a sick jealousy that someone had been so close to her, had known the reason behind her choice, and he hadn't. "*You can calm her chaos, but you'll never chase away her storm.* Why do you think you're a storm, baby?" He'd known her for all of her twenty-three years. Some might think he was robbing the cradle, or think it was fucked up him wanting a woman who grew up as his younger sister. To them, he gave zero fucks. She didn't share an ounce of blood with him, but he'd bleed anyone who thought to come between them.

"Can we talk about it later?" She shivered under his touch, the diamond hard tips begging for him to pay them some attention.

He was loathed to drop the subject, knowing she was hiding something from him. "For now," he agreed.

She called to him in so many ways, drawing out every possessive male part of him. He ran his palm back up until he reached her neck where he could see her pulse pounding. "Raise your arms over your head, pourri."

Talena pressed her lips together, taking her time before she did as he said.

"Are you prepared to do as I tell you? If you want to be with me, to be my woman, you'll have to understand there's things I need from you. I've never brought a woman here, ever. Clearly, looking around, you can see I've had it fitted out for my needs and what I planned for when I did claim you." He wasn't going to pussyfoot around with her. She'd been his for years; she just hadn't known it.

"You've never had a woman here, Hollywood? Please, pull the other one," she muttered.

Not liking being called a liar, he got up on his knees, staring down at her. "I told you before I wouldn't lie to you, and I expect the same from you. If I don't want to tell you the truth about something, I'll tell you so, but I will not lie."

She blinked several times as if she was fighting tears. Hollywood wasn't going to apologize for being harsh with her, not this time. He waited while she took his words in.

"I'm sorry. It's my own insecurities that are getting the best of me."

He nodded, running his eyes over her, loving the fact she hadn't taken her arms down from above her head. "I want you to trust me to take care of you, not only here in this bed, but in all things. That's my job as your man, your lover, your Dom." He said the last, waiting, watching to see if she understood what he was saying.

"You want to control me."

"It's not just about control. I can control anyone with the right information. I want you to trust that I'll always ensure your needs are taken care of above all else. I'm sure you think because you've watched that movie or read books you know what to expect, but that's not real life, pourri. Real life isn't so cut and dry. There's not a manual that says we have to do A through Z. However, there is one very important thing that I won't bend on, and that's you obeying me when I tell you to do something. Especially if it's about your safety, you will listen, or I'll fire your sexy ass to a red that you'll have a hard time sitting without remembering the feel of my hand."

"And I have to call you Sir?" she whispered.

He noticed she wasn't running from him screaming, but her eyes were dilated with need. "That's up to you. I gave you options. Which is a first for me."

"Stop comparing me to other women, Sir," she spat.

He tweaked the nipple closest to him, making her yelp that quickly turned into a moan. Oh yeah, his little brat liked it a little rough. "There is no comparison, pourri. Any woman before you, are forgotten. Not that I ever disrespected them, but I can't remember a single one with you standing before me."

She snorted, pursing her lips together. "My legs are kind of warm, Sir."

Oh, his little pourri was really pushing her limits, referring to the childish pants on fire was her way of trying to top from the bottom. Hollywood was willing to play games, loved them in fact, but he was also going to have to start how he meant to go on. He decided talking was overrated, and while his cock was dying to be released, he needed to teach her a lesson first.

Scott got off the bed on the opposite side from the door, ignoring her inquiring looks. With decisive moves, he jerked the straps that had been installed on the posts of the headboard, the supple leather cuffs were lined with the softest faux fur to ensure her skin wouldn't be damaged if he kept her chained up for long periods. Which, if she kept testing him, she might find herself tied to his bed more than not. The idea stirred the primal part of him. He didn't pause in his movements, sliding her right arm into the cuff and securing it before moving around to the other side and doing the same with the left.

"You look delectable lying there at my mercy, Talena Haven. How do they feel?" he asked, watching her give an experimental tug on each arm.

"What if I panic and want out?"

He lifted one brow. "You ask your Dom, and if I choose to allow you out, then you will be released. Remember this is about trust."

Chapter Eight

Talena wasn't sure how to express her feelings properly. Exposed for sure but turned on as well. What she really wanted was for him to truly take control and quit asking her every step of the way. How did she tell him that without sounding like a little whore?

"Tell me what you want, T."

"I want you to...to just do it. I want you to take me," she blurted.

His smile was positively wicked and purely masculine. If she'd have been naked, he'd have seen how wet she was already. That smile, good god, that smile had the power to make her pussy weep like a little hussy.

"Good girl." He moved to the end of the bed, climbing up like a predator on the prowl. His hands made short work of undoing her pants, working them down her thighs. This time he didn't ask her to lift up, using his strength to maneuver her how he wanted.

She had always loved watching him when he came over and swam at their house, the way his muscles bunched and flexed before he dove into the pool. "Take your shirt off, please."

"I'm the one in charge here, mon pourri. If I want to feast my eyes on all your nakedness for hours while I keep my own clothes on, that's what I'll do." He trailed his hands down her thighs, his fingers sliding between her legs, pressing them apart.

"Do you wax or shave?" he asked, skimming his thumbs over the cleft at the apex of her.

A moan escaped her, making it almost impossible for her to answer as need consumed her. Goodness gracious. All he'd done was run his hands down her freaking legs and she was a ball of wanton woman.

His hands left her suddenly, then a slap landed on her bare mound, making her cry out.

"I asked you a question." Another tap followed the first, this one a little lower, hitting her exposed clit.

"Neither."

She felt his fingers slide over her skin but kept her eyes locked on his, waiting for his next question.

"Explain," he barked.

Talena hid the smile that threatened to split her lips. "Laser."

"Hmm, you like playing, do you? That's earned you a punishment, mon pourri."

She licked her lips, wondering how much she should push him and just how much of a punishment it would actually be. "Do you not like it?"

His big finger ran between her lower lips. "Ah, baby, I fucking love it. And from the feel of all this wetness, you love this too. You're a kinky little bitch, aren't you?"

"I don't like being called a bitch." She glared up at him, waiting to see what he said or did at her outburst.

"You're mine. My mon pourri. My kinky little bitch. My whatever I call you. Nobody else has the right to you or your body. By me saying that to you it's not a derogatory term, baby." His voice gentled. "What we do with one another, to one another is nobody's business. Now. Tell me why being called a bitch is a trigger for you."

She knew he'd realize there was a reason, dammit. "When I was in high school, some of the kids used to call me a stuck-up bitch because I wouldn't let them come over and hang out when—" She bit her lip to stem the words that were on the tip of her tongue.

"Tell me." He bent, pressing butterfly kisses to her stomach.

Talena closed her eyes, feeling totally exposed, lying naked while he was completely clothed. "Scott, can we discuss this later?"

"No, we're negotiating."

A snort she tried to stop burst from her. "There is no negotiating going on. You're telling me this and that, and I'm to agree. That's how you work."

He shrugged, continuing his kissing that had her melting beneath him.

"They only wanted to come over when they knew you were home. There I said it." If her arms had been free, she'd have crossed them over her chest.

"It wouldn't have mattered if they'd have come over. I wouldn't have noticed anyone but you." He came to rest by her face, nipping her earlobe. "How do your arms feel?"

She rolled her shoulders. "Fine."

"I need you to let me know if you have any discomfort. My first priority is to see to you. If you start to feel your circulation is cut off, or your fingers tingle, you tell me immediately. I want you to feel only pleasure. I get off on knowing you are enjoying what I'm doing to you, not on hurting you, unless that is what I intend.

Relief nearly swamped her until the last of his words hit her. "What do you mean, unless you intend to harm me?"

"If you do something that requires me to discipline you, then you nor I will like it," he said with finality.

"What about you? What if you need punishment?"

Scott leaned down, rubbing his nose with her. "I'd love to see you try to put me over your knee, pourri. Now, if you're done talking, I'd love to start pleasuring you."

He breathed a puff of air over her neck, then kissed her. If she'd wanted to demand more answers, he swept every sane thought away with his masterful mouth. As a child, she'd been drawn to his protectiveness, but now as a woman, she was drawn to everything that was dominant about him. She wasn't going to pretend anymore. Feeling his hands stroke over her, his slight beard brushing over her skin, leaving his marks on her, had her primed for him.

His lips kissed her pulse, tongue sliding across her collarbone. With each kiss and lick, she fell under his spell, knowing no other man would ever, could ever compare to Scott. Not that any ever had.

A ragged moan burst out of her as his lips enclosed her nipple, sucking hard then nipping on it before doing the same to the other. Her breasts had always been sensitive, yet laying under him, they felt as though he'd hooked electricity up to them, shooting little sparks straight to her clit with each pull from his mouth.

"Jesus, I love your mouth," she groaned.

"Mmm, I'm not Jesus, but I do love your tittays." He grinned around the flesh in his mouth while she laughed. Scott flicked the tip with his tongue, his hands moving with expertise precision.

Her laughter was silenced as he trailed a hand down her center, plunging a finger inside her. God, he didn't even give her time to realize what he was going to do before pumping a finger inside her core and adding a second. Her hips lifted, begging him silently.

Scott pulled back, removing his lips and fingers. "Damn, you really are incredible."

She was about to beg him to come back to her but stopped short in disbelief, or maybe it was stunned shock.

Watching him lift his fingers to his mouth, sucking the digits he'd had inside her into his mouth, with his eyes locked on her face. She'd never seen a man take such pleasure in her like him. He said she was incredible, but it was him who was beyond all she'd ever dreamed to find.

Her body was primed, needy.

"Please."

Scott moved away from Talena, easing her thighs farther apart. He wanted to make her come but knew he'd be in her in three seconds if he did that. Instead he pulled away, moving quickly so he could fasten her legs to the ends of the bed. With her body flushed with arousal and need, he figured all he'd have to do was flick her clit a few times, and she'd come, but he didn't want that, not yet.

"What are you doing?"

"I'm taking care of my woman, my dear." He grinned, loving the way her eyes narrowed. His little woman was trying her hardest to be a good sub, but he was pushing her.

"What do you need me to do?" She pulled at the leather straps holding her legs apart, jerking them one at a time.

He let her do it a couple more times, moving to stand beside her. "Are you done yet?"

Her head jerked toward him. "Yes. They don't hurt at all."

With her eyes holding his, he began unbuttoning his shirt, draping it over the chair next to the bed. He found himself almost mesmerized by the heat in her gaze as she followed his movements. He lifted his arms over his head, tugging the T-shirt off from behind, folding it neatly, and placing it on the chair as well. Before moving to his pants, he found her clothing and folded each piece, making sure she watched the care he took with them. Next time, he'd make her do the same thing for the both of them.

"Are you a neat freak or something?" The question seemed to startle her, even though she was the one who blurted it.

"Or something. This is one of those things that will be taken care of by one of us. We don't always need to rush things, mon pourri." His fingers went to the button on his jeans. The erection straining his fly was so fucking hard he almost kept the denim on. In the end, he shucked them, taking care to fold and put them on the chair, hiding his smile from Talena when he heard her little mewl.

Turning back to face her, he opened the drawer, extracting a condom. Her startled gasp made him look up. Fear etched her features. "What is it, baby?"

"That...that's not normal."

Scott looked down his body, then back up at her. "Baby, you'll love the feel of my piercing inside you," he assured her.

She shook her head. "Not that, but we'll get to that. Him, he's...he's bigger than a toddler's arm. Good lord, I thought maybe I was seeing things, or like you had thick underwear or—something. That thing—I just don't think my vajeen is made for something that big. Not that I'm a card-carrying member of the V squad, but..."

Scott moved on top of her, his dick ready to come all over her sassy mouth. "Mon pourri, I suggest you not speak of any other men you've slept with, ever."

He moved until the tip of his cock was close to her lips. "Now kiss him and make him feel better."

Talena licked her lips, her eyes trained on the mushroom shaped tip. "What about the piercing?"

"Play with it. Since your hands are all tied up at the moment, I'll help you." He sifted his left hand through her hair, using his other one, he guided his dick into her mouth. The first lash of her tongue over his tip nearly had his eyes rolling into the back of his head. In short thrusts, he pressed in and out, letting her get used to the size of him. He was a large man, and most women couldn't take all of him into their mouth. He'd work with Talena until she could swallow around him. The thought had him being a little rougher with her. He heard her gag, saw a little tear ease from the corner of her eye.

He pulled back, but she sucked harder, her eyes wide. "I don't want to hurt you, baby. Fuck that feels good."

She lashed the bar below the head of his dick, making him curse as she moved back over the crown, engulfing him within her beautiful mouth.

He'd gotten the frenum piercing for added pleasure for his partners, but he enjoyed it as well, especially when Talena took half his cock in her sweet mouth. It took all of his control to let her suck him without coming like a teen getting his first blowjob, although it was a near thing. After a few more seconds, which was almost three too many, he pulled back from her amazing lips, even though his dick was throbbing with the need to come. He promised himself he would demand names of all the bastards' she'd learned to give head from, later.

"How's your arms feeling?" He reached for the right cuff.

"They're fine, Sir. Please leave them."

It was the Sir that kept his hand from releasing her. He ran his fingers down her slim forearms, testing them, massaging as he went. Slowly he eased his way down, his wet cock leaving a damp trail down the center of her body. Marking her, owning her. "Fuck, you look like a virgin sacrifice laid out on my bed. I wish I had my camera handy. I'd take a picture of you just like this and blow it up to put on my wall."

She bit her bottom lip, a shy little smile on her lips. "Wouldn't the person who blew it up see me naked?"

"I have a friend who would allow me to use their equipment. Now hush, I'm busy." He covered her lips with his, kissing her protest away. Her tongue slid against his, dueling. His teeth nipped as he pulled back, making her yelp.

She moistened her lips, keeping silent as he began kissing a slow path down her neck. He wanted to find everything she liked and didn't like. A small nibble behind her ear made her shiver, then he licked down the column of her neck and bit on her shoulder, not hard enough to bruise, but enough she felt his teeth. Her body jerked, but she lifted toward his mouth, not away. The little tells let him know she liked a bit of pain, which was good because he did too.

From here on out, she would know who the most important person in her life was, him. He had the MC; they were his brothers, but she was his woman. He'd chosen her long before he'd known about the Royal MC, long before he'd ever known what it was to look death in the eye. After tonight, he'd stare the Grim Reaper in the face and dare him to fuck with his ole lady, because if anyone thought they would get to her, they would find out he made the other guys look like choir boys.

He bit the swell of one breast, leaving a visible mark there then kissed it, sucking the tender flesh into his mouth. "So damn soft, baby."

Scott gave the same attention to the other breast, her little cry of arousal sent heat sizzling through his veins. He was going to make sure she was so fucking wet, so turned on when he slid in her she forgot all about her thoughts of him being too big. Fucking toddler arm. He nearly laughed out loud. She didn't mind that he liked it rough or wanted to leave his teeth prints in her. If anything, Talena was encouraging him with her little cries of need, the way her body was lifting toward him even though she was tied down. Damn, she was perfect, exactly what he'd needed for a woman.

The soft sounds she made urged him on as he settled between her thighs, the smooth mound of her pussy a perfect spot for another mark he couldn't resist to nip. His name came out a breathless plea. He loved it, loved her. Using his thumbs, he spread her open, looking at the most perfect pussy ever created. "I have never seen a sweeter piece of heaven." He licked her from her entrance to clit, circling that hard little nub a couple times then back down, lapping up her sweet juices.

Her breathy little moan of Sir was a gift. One he would cherish and reward her for. Blowing a puff of air over her clit, he licked and sucked her folds, running his tongue up one side and down the other. He'd teased her into a state that her little clit was swollen, her hunger for release was close to a boiling point. Each time he flicked that little bit of flesh, she jerked, her pussy fluttering like a vice. The sweet scent of her arousal increased, letting him know it wouldn't take much more for her.

"You ready to come for me, mon pourri?" He lashed his tongue up her right thigh, teasing the both of them then moved back to her clit and flicked it hard, circling it time and time again.

"Scott, please. Oh, Sir, make me come."

He grinned against her, holding one big palm over her abdomen, her core muscles jumping beneath him as her begging became frantic with each lick and suck. Adjusting his grip so his arm lay over her stomach, freeing up his hand to hold her open, he then eased two fingers of his other inside her. Scott sucked her clit inside, watching as he fucked her with his fingers. Her body swayed with his pumping fingers; her breasts heaved with her breathing, and her nipples became hardened peaks showing she loved everything he was doing to her. The entire picture was nothing short of erotic, her and her small, voluptuous frame strapped down on his red silk sheets, her blonde hair fanned out like a golden halo. If he looked close enough, he'd be able to see his marks on her body. Later he'd map them. For now, they both needed her to come.

"Come for me, Talena." He bent back to her, pushing his tongue into her opening, devouring her like she was his last meal, using his thumb to rub her clit. Finally, he replaced his thumb with his mouth, sucking it into his mouth as he pushed two fingers inside, then a third, pumping in and out. Talena's cry came, then her pussy locked down on his digits, her hips thrusting up. He continued to lick at her, letting her come down slowly.

"Please, I need you. I...I need you in me. I feel empty." Her wail had him moving to release first her legs, then her arms, rubbing them to ensure she was okay before he helped move them down.

"Oh," she gasped, her arms coming around his head.

"Are you okay?"

She nodded. "They tingle a little."

He kissed her nose. "I figured they'd been in there long enough this time."

She wiggled beneath him, her heart banging against his. "This time?"

"Baby, I told you, this isn't a one and done, deal." His dick nudged her pussy, sliding between the wetness from her orgasm.

"I'm on the shot. No condom is needed." She looked over to where he'd laid the little foil packet.

He nodded. "I'm clean. My last checkup was two months ago. I haven't been with anyone since then."

After China, he'd had some sixth sense. Getting a clean bill of health had been paramount.

"I haven't been with anyone in over a year. Even before that I've never had unprotected sex." She held his stare, unflinching in his face of anger.

"It's gutting me to keep from asking for names and addresses," he admitted.

Talena lifted first her right leg, then her left, wrapping them around his waist. The feel of her wet pussy gliding along his dick had his eyes crossing. "Let's forget about the past."

"Good idea, Sir." She lifted her hips, riding the ridge of him.

"Are you trying to top from the bottom, mon pourri?" He held himself up off her, glaring down at the beautiful smirking woman who was all his.

"I don't even know what that is, but if it has anything to do with you putting that beautiful cock inside me, then I'm totally here for it."

"My sweet little pussy is going to get fucked good and proper in a few minutes, and we'll see just how much you like trying to top me, baby." He bent, covering her mouth, shifting so he could guide his dick into her.

Chapter Nine

Talena jerked at the pressure between her thighs, crying out at the feel of Hollywood's monster dick entering her. His mouth covering hers kept her from screaming too loudly, but even if she had there wasn't anyone who'd have heard her. She'd known he was too big, but fuck, she'd been sure she could take him.

"Ssh, you can take me," he reassured her, easing backward, then forward.

Oh sure, he could say that because he wasn't the one being split it two by a freaking third arm. And then he shifted, his fingers moving down her body. She could've told him she was only a one clitoris orgasm girl and saved him the work, but he was kissing her again, and lord save her, the man kissed like a fucking god. And then something magical happened, the sensitive bundle of nerves she'd thought she knew began to tingle under his ministrations, little tingles that went from the tips of her toes all the way to her breasts and back. She didn't know how he did it, or...oh god, she was going to come again.

"Right there, please, don't stop," she pleaded,

He tugged on her clit, rubbed his thumb faster, making her need come roaring back.

Just when she was sure he'd send her flying, he knelt up between her thighs, pushing her legs further apart, guiding himself into her with one hand holding his cock.

"Look at me, Talena. Watch me as I take you." He rubbed the mushroom shaped head up and down, getting his cock wet, then pushed inside again.

She took a deep breath, the stretch and burn a pain she craved.

"Keep your fucking eyes open," he demanded.

Talena hadn't realized she'd shut them, her gaze glued to his, then down. Without pause, he slammed inside, pushing through her tightness, robbing her of breath. Her body jerked, accepting him with a spine bending tingle she was sure would rob her of her very soul.

"Motherfuck, you're so damn tight." He rested with his head pressed against hers, his balls against her ass.

"Give me a minute," she breathed, zings of pleasure and pain whipping through her.

Nothing could've prepared her for the feel of him inside her. No wonder the girl was screaming like a banshee in her treehouse. She giggled.

He pulled back, raising a brow.

When she told him, he pulled back, slamming back inside. "A banshee, huh?"

Over and over again, he entered her.

"Yes, Scott, Sir, harder, please." She hoped he didn't take that as topping and stop.

He scooped one arm under her ass, lifting her closer, moving her other leg up higher on his hip. "Fuck, I can't get close enough. Never close enough."

She felt the same way. Lifting her hips, she met his surging thrusts with her own, until he gripped her sides, taking control. He powered in and out, pulling and pushing her, driving them both so hard she wasn't sure how his headboard didn't drive through the wall. And then she wasn't thinking, only feeling, coming around his cock. The feel of the piercing rubbing along her G-spot nobody had ever found before.

"Son of a bitch, your pussy is clamping down on me so fucking tight. God yes, baby, squeeze me," he roared.

The feel of his cock jerking inside her was unbelievable. She'd read about it but had thought it was a myth, or a thing they'd made up. Scott's cock, jerking, spilling with each twitch of his body inside her was felt deep within her. For one crazy moment, she almost wished she hadn't been on any birth control, because she knew that if there was any man, any chance she could have a baby, he was the only one she'd choose. Only she'd fucked her body up so long ago, nearly dying in the process, she didn't think she'd ever be blessed with his beautiful babies.

Her body was still twitching, with Scott hammering in and out of her, but she could tell he was watching her. She focused on the feel of him in her, that sweet feeling of being filled. Her breasts tingled, loving the rasp of his chest over her.

"I swear, that was the most sublime moment. Somewhere between heaven and hell, baby. Now tell me what made you get that clouded look on your face." Scott rested on his elbows, bracketing her head.

Talena shook her head slightly, marveling at the fact he was still hard inside her. "Isn't this when you roll over and offer to get me a washcloth to clean our mess up."

He raised up slightly, looking between them where his cock slid out slightly, showing her the evidence of his come and hers covering him. "Nope, seems pointless when I'm just going to be getting you messy all over again. Besides this way, you're all lubed up. Now you won't need to worry about the baby's arm," he teased.

She slapped his arm, burying her face in his chest.

Unwilling to let her hide from him, he tugged on her hair. "Come on, you and I both know I'm not going to let you get away without telling me."

"Can you let me sit up?"

"Nope, I like my spot. How about this?" He rolled, taking her with him so she was the one on top. "Since you like to try and top, is this better?"

Talena was hiding something from him, and he wasn't going to let her. When she'd come around him, it had almost been painful how tight her pussy had contracted. It had taken all his discipline not to fuck her like a madman, and then he'd seen the way her eyes had clouded. In that moment, he'd recognized the look of someone who wasn't fully in the moment. He'd get to the bottom of what, where, and why. It hadn't taken long for her to come back to what they were doing, but for a man like him, he wouldn't allow his woman to lose herself unless it was to him and their pleasure.

"Tell me," he ordered.

"I was...I'm sorry, Scott. I didn't mean to disappoint you."

He tugged on her hair. "Don't. Don't try that fucking shit with me. Tell me."

"Fine. When we were making love, I was thinking I wished I wasn't on any protection, but then reality slapped me, and I realized it probably didn't matter because I screwed up."

Her words were so angry, then soft, his heart hurt for her. "How did you screw up, baby?"

As he lay beneath her, listening to her explain, he felt a rage unlike any he'd experienced. Impotent and uncontrollable rage. "Why was I never told?" He could've lost her, and he hadn't even known. He rolled her off of him, moving to the side of the bed. His chest ached, the damn thing pounding worse than when he'd been fucking Talena only moments ago.

"I begged mom not to. I promised I'd get better if she didn't. I...I used you as a bargaining chip for me getting better. I didn't want you to see me like that," she whispered.

The shame in her voice made him look over his shoulder, seeing her curled into a ball in the center of his huge bed, her back to him, he saw the bones of her spine. "You weighed eighty-six pounds, T? You're five foot seven, baby," his voice cracked.

She didn't answer him, but with the sliver of light from the moon outside, he could see her body jerk. He moved back to her, curving his bigger body around hers, leaning over so he could see her face. Tears trickled down her cheek. "Baby, don't cry."

"I disappointed you."

"The hell? Talena, I'm angry because I could've lost the best thing in my life. I'm not disappointed in you. You were young, but that shit is never happening again. You hear me? I know that it's an easy slope to fall down, but I want you healthy to carry my baby. If you can't, fuck it, we can adopt. Look at you, you're the best damn thing my mom ever did." He turned her until she was facing him. "I love you, T, everything about you, regardless if you can carry our child. Do you hear me?"

"You still want me?" she asked.

"I'll want you until I'm old and grey and long after that probably. Hell, baby girl, I'll be the one they call for sperm donations in the old folk's home if you're anywhere nearby. As long as you're with me, baby, I don't see my need for you ever stopping. Does this feel like I don't want you?" He pressed his hips against her, letting her feel the truth of his statement.

"I guess it's a good thing I didn't clean up then, because it feels like the toddler's leg has reappeared," she said, snorting.

"And it appears my little brat needs reminding who's the boss." He gave her surprisingly supple ass a firm tap, knowing he would be doing that often. She gave a startled yelp that ended in a moan. "Fuck, and you were wondering if you could handle me, mon pourri? There's nobody in the world more perfect for me."

He flipped her onto her stomach, moving a pillow beneath her hips, keeping a firm grip on her hips. "I like this view." With the light from the moon coming in through the bank of windows he could see her ass perfectly. She looked like a golden goddess.

She whipped her head around, glaring at him over her shoulder. "You just like being in the man position."

Scott wanted to ease her into his lifestyle, but he couldn't allow her to continue to push him, testing his patience. Some things he needed to stay steady. It was a quirk within himself, and he was honest enough to admit it. Using his left hand, he gathered her hair into his fist, pulling on the thick mass, extending her neck toward him at an angle that wasn't natural. It would be a little uncomfortable for her, but he waited until she grimaced before he stopped. "I'm always going to be in the man position, baby. I'll always top you. I think I gave you the wrong impression earlier."

Her eyes dilated; a tiny shiver rolled down her frame. He felt it along his cock nestled between her thighs, and still, he didn't enter her. "I told you before we started what I needed. Do you need a refresher, mon pourri?"

Talena licked her lips. "No, Sir. I understand, and I want it too."

He rolled the fist he held her hair in, wrapping the strands around it. "Good girl." With their eyes locked, her neck still at the angle he wanted her, he slid inside her tight sheath, hissing at the incredible feel of her body welcoming him.

"Oh fuck, you feel bigger than before," she moaned.

Scott grunted, holding his hips flush with her ass. Slowly he unwound his hand from her hair, massaging her neck to relieve some of the stress he'd caused, making her moan. "You feel tighter too, baby. You ready for more?" he asked.

She tensed and would've turned to glare at him if he wasn't holding her neck. Of that, he was sure. Her muffled curse was followed by an inaudible string of words he had to lean forward to hear better. "Repeat that, pourri."

"I said if you had any more dick, then the answer was no, dammit, then rethought saying it because of your penchant for slapping my ass," she muttered.

He laughed, unable to believe she could make him feel every emotion in the span of minutes. "You'd be right." He pulled back, easing his cock out so that just the head was inside her. As he pushed back in, he gave her right cheek a slap, followed by another to the left. "I'm going to need you to count for me, Talena. I said you were owed ten for your punishments you'd racked up. Those two were for the sass you just gave me. Now we begin. If you don't count, then I don't either."

Scott pulled out, and pushed in, giving her ass a slap each time he entered, rubbing the sting each time he exited.

Her voice was loud the first few times she called the numbers, making him proud. He spanked every inch of her ass cheeks, making sure not to hit the same spot, her ass turning a nice red. By the time he was on the seventh count, she was breathless, lifting up into him. He waited for her to say the number before pulling out but was met with silence.

"Still with me, baby?" He rubbed her fiery ass.

"Yes," she moaned.

"What number are we on?" He waited.

"Um, seven?"

"That's your only pass." He thrust back in, his balls drawing up with the need to come. Damn he couldn't remember the last time he'd been ready to blow so quickly. In rapid succession, he landed two swats to her ass, hoping like hell she counted them both.

"Eight, nine," she wailed.

When he pulled out and then slammed back in, he slapped her ass one last time, hearing her yell the number ten unleashed his control.

"Fuck!" He grunted and gripped her hips in a bruising hold.

Talena fell forward, resting on her elbows, her hair obscuring his view of her face. He didn't need to see her to know she was loving what he was doing to her. The feel of her body tightening around his length, her orgasm so close he was sure it would take him with her even if he wasn't already so damn close.

"I could fuck you for hours and never get tired of the feel of your body squeezing my cock. Damn," he moaned as the rippling feel of her pussy nearly strangled his dick.

He stroked in and out of her faster. One, two, three more times, and then he was coming so hard he was sure he had nothing left to give, except when he pulled out, a few drops were still on the tip. Some deep-seated part of him had him rubbing his essence into her reddened flesh, marking his territory. If he'd been an animal, he'd surely have lifted his damn leg and marked her the way they did. The thought had him chuckling.

"Why're you laughing?" she asked drowsily.

Scott sat back on his haunches, looking at her ass in the air with his and her fluids running out of her. "I was thinking how sexy you looked with my marks on you." He wasn't going to tell her what he'd been thinking. He was a smart man and knew women didn't appreciate the way men's minds worked sometimes.

"Come on, let's get you cleaned up. While I love the idea of you with me inside you, I know you'll sleep better after a shower." He scooted off the side, holding out his hand.

Talena groaned, but then she rolled to her back. "You're right."

"Ah, that sounds beautiful." He reached down and swooped her into his arms, carrying her into the ensuite.

She slipped her arms around his shoulders, yawning widely. "I'm not even going to comment since my bum is still sore."

"Smart girl." He pressed the button on the keypad by his shower. Maybe he should've asked her if she liked to take hot or warm showers, but his motto was to start as you mean to go on. Since he liked hot showers, he was doing as he liked. It didn't take anytime for the water to heat up to his preferred temp.

"You can put me down you know?" She didn't wiggle to get let down; her arms stayed locked tightly around him.

"I'm aware." He opened the door, stepped into the huge shower stall with the half a dozen shower heads spraying water all around them. Her little squeal of surprise brought a grin to his lips. Once he had them inside, he lowered her to the ground.

"This is perfect." She held her arms out to the sides, letting the water pelt her.

It was hard for him to not grab her by the waist and fuck her right then and there. His dick was semi-hard again, no shocker. To keep himself from doing what his damn body wanted, he picked up the shampoo from the shelf built into the wall. "Turn around," he ordered her.

Thank fuck she listened since he wasn't sure he would be able to keep from punishing her with his palm or his cock, if she hadn't. His gaze went to her reddened backside. Pride welled up in him at the way she'd taken his discipline without a single complaint. Not that it would've stopped him, but he'd have hated to think she wasn't prepared for what he needed.

After he squirted a large portion of shampoo into his palm, he worked it into her hair, digging his fingers into her scalp.

"Oh lord, that feels amazing. If you weren't, you know rich as Midas, you would make an excellent wash boy." Laughter laced her words.

"The only person I'll ever be washing is my little sub." He ran his finger through her hair, making sure he worked the shampoo through the entire length. "Now rinse."

"So bossy." Her tone was weak like she was getting tired.

"Get used to it." He had a palm full of conditioner waiting for when she had all the shampoo rinsed out. The punch to his solar plexus as she faced him, her blue eyes sparkling like sapphires with happiness, shocked him. He'd known she had feelings for him but the way she was looking at him across the short distance, there was no denying the truth any longer. He'd told her he loved her, and he did. He was sure she felt the same. Now, seeing the walls she'd constructed around herself down, there was no more pretenses any longer. Talena wasn't a little girl with a crush, but his woman who loved him.

"What's wrong?"

"Nothing, baby. Come here." He held his free hand out, letting her come to him, and she did, trusting him to take care of her. The hand with the conditioner came around her, smoothing over the top of her head. His first priority would always be seeing to her comfort, and his little woman was beyond tired. Not wanting to dawdle, he ran his fingers through her hair. While she rinsed, he took care of washing the rest of her, then himself. He made sure they were both clean and then shut the water off, stepping out of the shower first, and grabbed one of the towels from the warming rack. He toweled off quickly before grabbing another for her.

She crossed her arms over her breasts, a shyness he'd never witnessed in her appearing. "You do this for all your...women?"

Before he answered the question, he dried the water from her body then lifted the smaller towel he'd purchased for her hair. It was a little ironic she was standing before him after letting him do what he'd pleased, loving every moment, yet now she appeared almost shy. "Talena, look at me when you ask me questions that clearly have a big impact on you." Seconds ticked by, three to be exact, and then she complied.

"I shouldn't have asked you that. I'm tired." Her yawn attested to the truth of her statement, but obviously she was questioning his motives.

"When I have a woman in my care, then yes, it's my job to take care of her. I said I wasn't going to lie to you, and I'm not. However, I have never had a woman here. Did you notice the shampoo and conditioner I used was your preferred kind?" He let his question settle into her mind. "See this towel?" He held up the microfiber twist towel he had seen his mother buy for Talena. "I have a dozen of them for you because you and I both know I don't need them."

A small smile tipped the corner of her lips. "You have a great head of hair, Hollywood."

All his life he'd been called the golden boy because of his blond hair and blue eyes. In the military, his nickname had become Hollywood not only because he'd come from California but because of his looks. Hearing his woman say something similar had him mock growling, pulling her into his arms; the damn towel he'd bought for her falling to the ground, forgotten. "I'll show you Hollywood, mon pourri." He kissed her, silencing her giggles with a heated kiss, his tongue dueling with hers.

Before he could lose his head, he broke their kiss, panting like he'd run a marathon. "Let's get your hair dry so you can get some sleep."

She didn't put up a fight. He wasn't sure if it was due to her being tired, or if her ass was still sore. He had a sneaking suspicion it had more to do with her tiredness than her learning a lesson. The dominant in him looked forward to the power plays with her in the future. He'd always win, but so would she.

Chapter Ten

Talena stretched, her body aching in places that were pleasantly sore. The room was dark, the bed empty. She would've panicked if she didn't know and trust Scott to have ensured she was safe. The need to go to the bathroom kept her from luxuriating in the huge bed any longer.

She rolled off the side closest to her, happy her eyes had adjusted to the darkness. Her memory kicked in from the night before. While she'd been drying her hair, Scott made quick work of changing the sheets. Although she wouldn't have minded sleeping on their mess, her fastidious guy clearly liked clean. She couldn't wait to mess with his well-ordered existence.

Inside the huge bathroom, she finished up, splashed some cold water on her face, and stared at her reflection. "He must have this place set up like a Smart Home," she said to herself, twisting her neck back and forth to work out the kinks. Although he hadn't hurt her with his rough treatment, she definitely felt the strain in her joints. The slight twinges made her ache for his touch.

She pulled the borrowed T-shirt away to look down at her breasts, remembering the way he'd bitten her. A smile grew on her face as she saw the almost identical marks on each mound. If she could, she'd have Tymber tattoo the marks on each spot, so she'd have a permanent reminder of him.

"What's put that look on your face, mon pourri?" Scott's deep voice had her jumping.

"Good lord, you scared the bejeezus out of me, Hollywood." She pressed her palm flat against her chest, wondering how long he'd been standing in the doorway.

He straightened, moving into the room, wearing a pair of loose sweats that hung low on his hips. "Hmm, I don't think there's a bejeezus in you, but I can be."

She snort-laughed, holding out her hand to stop him. "Oh no you don't. I'm starving, and I need more than your man meat and your succulent jizz to fuel me."

Her words stopped him a foot from her with her palm grazing his chest, his own bark of laughter echoing off the walls. "Jesus fucking Christ, you are seriously hard on my ego. I'll feed you real food, then I'll stuff you with whatever I decide whether you like it or not. Come on, mon pourri, before I change my mind."

Talena stood on her toes, puckering her lips. She'd already brushed her teeth, thankfully. Now she needed a kiss from the sexy-as-sin man in front of her to get her day started.

Hollywood bent, pecked her lips, then bent further, putting his shoulder into her stomach and stood with her draped over his back. A light tap to her rear, followed by a barked order of "Behave," and then he was striding out of the bedroom and back down the hall to the kitchen.

She smelled the bacon first. "Oh, bacon. I love crispy bacon." She tried to see around him since the night before she hadn't a chance.

"I know how you like your food, baby." He stopped and set her down, making sure she was steady on her feet. Gentle fingers drifted down her cheek. "Good morning," he said, bending and giving her a sweet consuming kiss, she'd longed for.

"Can I help?" she asked once he let her up for air.

"There's some cinnamon rolls in the oven over there. When the timer goes off, pull them out. You want some coffee?" he asked, indicating the coffee bar set in a small alcove in the corner.

"Oh, thank the lord. Want me to make you a cup?" She hurried over to the coffee, inspecting his selection. Growing up, they'd always had a coffee bar with the best coffee machines money could buy. She didn't mind admitting she was a bit spoiled when it came to the liquid of the coffee gods, and neither did it seem, was Scott.

They worked together, or rather she helped him get the rest of the breakfast things done, then sat and ate. It was all so normal and domesticated. Her stomach felt as if a million butterflies had settled in it when she finished eating and was getting ready to clean up their mess, only her phone rang, their mom's name on the screen had her freezing.

"It's mom," she whispered.

"I can see that. Let me talk to her." He held his hand out, waiting.

Talena looked at her phone, then his big hand. "What will she think?"

He raised a brow. "Does it matter?"

To him probably not. He was her son, the golden child. She'd been the fuck up, the one everyone always worried about. "What if she doesn't want you seeing me or says she doesn't want me—" She bit her lip.

Scott pulled her off the barstool, settling her onto his lap. "Fuck, I thought you were going to say you didn't want her to know because you were ashamed. Damn, mon pourri, don't scare me like that."

Her face lifted, chin jutting out. "Ashamed of you? Why would I ever be ashamed to say I was with you?"

He ran the pad of his thumb over her bottom lip that was still puffy from his kisses. "Ah, mon pourri, you truly have no clue how precious you are to me and to our mother. You think she would be upset at you for being with me? No, baby, she'd be much more likely to be pissed at me for taking advantage of her sweet little girl. I promise you; she won't be angry at you at all. In fact, I have a feeling our mother will be surprisingly happy we're together."

Talena's phone began to ring again, the ringtone she'd programmed for their mom playing. "You gonna let me answer it this time?"

She took a deep breath, then answered. "Hi mom."

To his pleasure, she pushed the speaker button and placed the device on the counter, staying on his lap. "I'm with Scott."

"Good morning, mother. How're you doing today?" he asked, not even trying to mask the lazy satisfaction rolling off his tongue.

"Obviously not as good as you two. It's seven in the morning so either you two were out late, or you're up early." Tara's words were left to hang in the silence.

"We just finished breakfast, or I'd offer to take you out. What are your plans for lunch?" He was not a child who had to explain himself to a parent, but he would make concessions, since his mother was dealing with the both of them.

"Funny you should ask. I had a call from an investor. I never get calls, you know, not for Haven Corp. It gave me...I don't know how to put it, but the man's voice alone made my skin crawl. Don't get me wrong, he was very polite and said all the right things but call it female intuition if you will. Anyhow, he said he was a friend of Talena's. Which that right there set my mother bear instinct into alarm mode, not that it wasn't already by his smarmy voice. We both know our girl doesn't have men friends like that." Tara harrumphed.

Scott ran his hand between Talena's thighs, feeling the smooth flesh already slightly wet. "Of course, she doesn't," he agreed.

"Anyway, I told him I'd ask if the two of you were free for lunch next week, but he insisted it be today. He said he was only in town for a short window. If I'd been face-to-face with him, I'm sure I'd have seen his pants on fire."

Talena giggled, then moaned as he slid his finger between her thighs, finding her clit without error.

"What was that, Talena dear?"

Talena slapped a hand over her mouth, the other she used to try and push his away from her pussy with. "Talena was laughing at your choice of words, mother. What did you say this man's name was?" He rubbed the little nub, watching Talena's face blossom with a blush.

"Mr. Ferreira. Louis is his first name. He had a slight accent, but I couldn't really place it."

Scott froze, his finger nearly inside Talena's tight body, stopping at the name. "Did you set up an appointment with this Louis?"

"No, I told him I was only a minor shareholder, and that he needed to contact someone on the board. He was most insistent."

There was fear in her voice now, fear he hated to hear. "Where are you now?" If she was at home, she should be safe with the security he'd installed. Nobody but residents could get into the gated community unless they were pre-authorized with a code or the security guard called whoever they were visiting to verify they were legit. However, he wasn't willing to risk his mother's life on should-be scenarios.

"I'm home, son. It's just after seven in the morning for crying out loud," she said with exasperation.

"Call the guard at the gates and tell them you are not expecting visitors and to call you and me if anyone other than a regular visitor shows up for anyone. I'm on my way to you now." He set Talena on the floor, his mind working out who he'd call for backup. His MC brothers were at least a half an hour away. Cosmo would be at the Royal MC compound with his ole lady, but if he'd left a couple of his security guys in the city, they'd be his best bet.

"I need you to listen to me. Make sure the house is locked up and secure. Set the alarm and don't answer any calls except from me. That man might be who he said he was, or he could be a very dangerous adversary. Are there provisions in the Safe Room still?" He'd been extremely glad his father had the foresight to build not just a room, but a suite that would lock down and keep whoever was inside safe during just about any kind of an emergency whether it be fire, tornado, which the West Coast wasn't known for, and even a bomb should someone go that far.

"Scott, you're starting to scare me. I know I said the man gave me the creeps, but I don't think that's necessary. Honestly I'll just get dressed and head to—"

"Mother, do what I said and don't argue with me, please." He hated to cut her off harshly, yet he needed her to understand the situation was serious.

"Please just do as he says. If this is the man I think, he's batshit crazy and will hurt you to get at me."

Talena reached out, putting her hand on his chest, the motion calming him marginally.

"Scott, tell me what is going on?" His mother asked in an even tone.

He pulled Talena into his arms, staring down at the phone, then at the ceiling. "Nothing I can't handle if I know you and T are safe."

"Fine, you two, I'll double check the house is locked up, but I'll expect answers when you get here. You just keep my baby girl safe, or else. Should I send Wilma home?" she asked, gasping like the question just hit her.

Fuck he forgot about the housekeeper. "Has she already arrived?"

"She's just starting, but the house isn't dirty, so she can leave and come back in a week. It's not as if the dust will overwhelm me." His mother sounded a little put out, but he could hear her walking, presumably to find Wilma.

"I don't think I've actually seen any dust," he said, going quiet as he heard Wilma's voice.

His mother and the other woman had a low conversation while he imagined Tara Haven held the cell to her chest, trying to have a little privacy. He could've easily pulled up one of the security cameras and seen for himself what was going on. He didn't though, since he wasn't sure how Talena would react. In all honesty, he didn't feel the need to look, never had since Gary's death, but it was a measure he'd implemented as part of their home security.

"Alright, she's leaving, albeit she was a little startled since she's been coming once a week for the last five years, and I've never cancelled. I guess I'm a creature of habit." She sighed, sounding a little lonely.

"Are you okay?" He pulled Talena into his arms, staring down at her then the cell, wishing he was there with his mom so he could protect them both.

"Ignore me, son. You just take care of Talena and figure out what's going on with our mystery caller. I'm going to make sure Wilma makes it through the gate without incident. Call me when you arrive. I'll be in the safe room," she groused.

He couldn't help but smile. "Always, mom. Now get to getting while I get my shit together."

They both stared at the phone after it went silent.

"I think she misses having a companion." Talena kissed his chest, her small hand rubbing over the area where her lips had been.

"She's a beautiful woman. She should date, find a man who...shit, I can't even imagine her doing—that." He shook his head, then tugged Talena's head back by her hair. "I need to go and make sure she's safe."

"I'm going with you." Her mouth was set in a stubborn line.

Scott could be just as stubborn, even more so. "No way, baby girl. I can't focus on keeping her safe if I'm worried about you. If you're here, I know you're good as long as you stay inside. Nobody knows about this location except Cosmo and his guys."

She opened her mouth to argue with him. Scott couldn't allow her to distract him. He couldn't be swayed, not in the safety of the two women he loved above everyone and everything else. He bent, silencing her protest in a possessive kiss, sweeping his tongue inside, tasting the coffee she'd drank before pulling back. He rested his forehead against hers, inhaling the fresh scent of her shampoo and conditioner. "I'm asking you to please do as I've asked of you." It was as close to begging as he'd ever come.

"You don't play fair." She sniffed.

"You best not be crying, or I swear to all that's holy when I get back, I'll put you over my lap and give you twenty. You haven't seen my playroom, baby. I said I didn't have a red room, and I don't. I have a room that I designed for me and my woman's pleasure. When I get back, I'll show you just what's real that'll make the movie you loved look like child's play." He swooped down for another kiss, this one harder, and then he released her and stepped back.

"I'll hold you to that. Can I explore while you're gone?" she asked, folding her hands in front of her body.

He shook his head, wishing like hell the fucker Louis hadn't decided to sign his own death warrant. Talena stood before him in one of his T-shirts, looking like a virgin ready to be debauched and he had to leave. Fuck he wanted to do all kinds of things like fuck her every which way to Sunday. His dick jumped beneath the loose sweats, precome leaking from the tip, making a wet spot in the front of the damn grey material.

"No, mon pourri, you can't explore that room while I'm gone. It's locked, and only I can open it. You have access to every other space in our home." He made sure to emphasize the word our when he spoke.

"How long will you be gone?" She waved her hands in the air. "Forget it, don't answer that. I'm being needy and stupid. Just go, you need to hurry and stop pandering to me. Mom is the one who needs you right now. I'll be fine here alone. Go on, get dressed, and hurry up." She pushed at his chest, trying to get him to turn toward the bedroom.

"You're every bit as important to me, T." He threaded his fingers through hers, pulling her with him. "Come on, I want you to talk to me while I get dressed. There's things I need to tell you before I leave." Things like where he kept an extra gun she could access and where the safe room was.

Roq looked at his cell, raising a brow at the number on the caller ID. "Howdy, Hollywood, what's up?"

"Are you and your friends close?"

"As in around the block or in close proximity?" Roq flipped Axl off as his friend snorted across the room.

"I need backup now, and it might include dead bodies, however I don't have time to call Cosmo or the others."

"We're about ten minutes from you. We'll meet you outside your gate in thirteen." Roq disconnected the call, getting to his feet already making his next call. Cosmo may not be there, but he wouldn't be taking the team, or part of the team into a situation where they'd be killing and disposing of bodies without letting his brother know about it.

"You calling daddy to let him know we gonna be getting into some trouble?" Cannon asked, his grumpy snarl worse than usual.

"If you don't want to come, you can stay here and play Mario Cart," Axl said, kicking the other man's feet off the table so he could move between it and the bed.

"Fuck you, asshole, I'm playing WOW, and you know it. Besides Mario is the baddest game ever created, and you know it. You're just pissed because Princess Peach would never look at a mushroom hater like you." Cannon stood up, stretching his arms above his head, red welts lined his abdomen where his shirt rode up.

Roq turned away, not wanting to see how his friend and brother dealt with the shit that was their pasts. Each of them owed Cosmo more than just their lives. They owed him their sanity as well. He'd been fourteen, the oldest of their little quartet by a few months, but he hadn't hit his growth spurt until the following year. He often wondered what the prick who called himself his father would've done had he lived until Roq outgrew him. Nah, the fucker probably would've beat him down even if he had, keeping him so weak he wouldn't have been able to do anything except obey like he had all those years.

He shook himself, banishing the dark thoughts that threatened to pull him under. Seeing the welts on Cannon reminded him how close they all were to an edge of a cliff. He, Axl, and Ridley didn't need to be punished like their brother Cannon. He didn't judge the younger man, none of them did. What he'd been through was even worse than all of them. The sick and twisted place they'd found him in still turned his stomach.

"Let's roll," he ordered, shrugging into the lightweight jacket that appeared normal but was made of a thin Kevlar that would stop most bullets from piercing their skin. A head shot? Well in that case they'd be dead if they took one of those.

"Shotgun," Axl called, shoving his way past Ridley.

Ridley and Axl got into a shoving match, reminding him of toddlers he'd seen on TV. "Why do I put up with them?" he asked Cannon, locking the door behind them. They didn't worry about cleaning up the room, since none of them had anything they worried about anyone stealing. It was standard procedure for them to have their shit ready to roll out at the drop of a hat, like now, each man grabbing their gear and rolling, no questions asked.

"Because they'd kill each other or bystanders if you didn't." Cannon's matter-of-fact answer was said without inflection.

Roq was beginning to worry about his brother. They weren't related by blood, none of them were, but the four of them were closer than any birth could've made them. Many times, throughout their first ten years or so, they'd been locked in the same hellholes, made to watch what the others had to endure. Only Cosmo had been saved from that humiliation, since his father was the ringleader. He pushed the memories away, hating that they were trying to make a comeback like an old movie that wanted to remake. "You alright?" he asked Cannon, watching as the wiry man with the mocha-colored skin that made him stand out amongst them get a little ruddy hue to it.

"I'm level, Roqueland, don't you worry non about me." Cannon's Cajun accent became a little more pronounced when he was angry.

"Good to hear. I need all of us to stay on point." The reprimand was said loud enough that Axl and Ridley could hear. Their shoving match immediately stopped at his bark.

Axl, ever the jokester, gave him a salute. "Got it, Captain." He climbed into the front passenger seat while

Ridley walked around to the driver's side, getting into the backseat. Cannon and he both stayed silent, walked toward the vehicle and deposited their bags in the back. The fucking past rearing its head when he needed a little peace screwed shit up.

The SUV rumbled to life, the console lighting up with the coordinates of Hollywood's home on the screen. "We'll follow him at a distance. I think one of us should hang around his place. I have a feeling I don't like in the pit of my stomach."

Axl lifted the panel from the floorboard, taking out a semi-automatic, checking that it was loaded. "I'll stay back," he offered.

"I'll do it. I'm restless so walking around the woods would help me. Nobody will get close to the house, I promise." Cannon spoke without inflection, letting Roq know he was in control of his emotions with that one tell-tale sign.

The sound of the other men checking their weapons filled the interior of the vehicle. He did trust all of the men with him, as did Cosmo. They were a team and had been for what seemed their entire lives. After they'd been freed from their hells, Cosmo had made them finish school, which was easy since they'd all had tutors, then they'd each joined the military. Roq wasn't surprised when one by one they'd all followed him. Becoming a SEAL had saved his sanity, giving him an outlet where he could make a difference and hone his body into a machine. At over six and a half feet tall, he didn't think there was a lot of things he was cut out for, but he'd excelled at being a SEAL, and then Cosmo had created a security firm, pulling him and the others out. If not, he was sure he would've become a criminal or a killer. Not that he'd have killed innocent people, but he'd have found those who deserved it and loved every second of ending their lives.

He always thought that had been Cosmo's fear, worrying they'd go rogue and kill anyone and everything, or some shit, but none of them were that unhinged. They'd have picked and selected their victims carefully, but luckily, they didn't need to do so, since Cosmo gave them a legitimate way.

They rolled up to the gate outside of Hollywood's drive. Seconds later, a platinum G-Wagon came down, the windows so dark he couldn't see who was behind the wheel.

"Nice wheels," Axl said, nodding at the ride easing out of the gate.

Roq rolled his window down as the other vehicle pulled next to them, the driver's window coming down to show

Hollywood wearing a pair of shades. "Cannon is going to hang back and keep an eye on the property." Roq pointed over his right shoulder.

"Did you see anyone on your drive over?" Hollywood looked straight ahead.

He couldn't see the other man's eyes, but he was sure he was looking around to see if he saw anything out of the ordinary.

"No just want to make sure we cover all our bases. Cosmo indicated you and your girl were friends and wanted us to do what we could to ensure we did what we could to keep you both safe." He hid his grin as the other man turned his head toward him, tilted his shades down and pinned him with those eerie blue eyes. Roq had no doubt he was looking at a stone-cold killer. He liked Hollywood, admired the fact he could stare him in the eyes and not hide who he was either.

"Hmm, that's nice. Let's go. Cannon, my girl has instructions not to open the door for anyone so don't even try it. Nothing against you, but she's got explicit instructions to shoot first, ask questions last."

Cannon slid out of the SUV, a humorless smile on his face. "No problem. I don't like talking to most people. See you when I see you."

They watched him jog up the hill, disappearing into the trees.

"Let's roll. You lead and we'll follow. Here," Roq said, tossing a small earpiece into the other vehicle.

Hollywood looked at the little device, then slid it into his right ear.

"That way we can communicate without calling one another. Everyone is mic'd up."

With a wave, Hollywood pulled away, heading toward his mother's home. Roq looked up toward the place he'd seen Cannon enter. Hollywood's property was protected by a fence that appeared to be twelve to fifteen feet high. If he was to guess, the top of the fence wasn't your average run of the mill fencing but razor wire that had been cleverly disguised. Anybody out fucking around the property would get a real nice welcome if they tried to scale it. Luckily for them, Cannon wouldn't be stupid enough to do anything that dumb, he hoped.

Chapter Eleven

Talena paced around Hollywood's home. No, it was their home. He'd made sure to make it a point to call it theirs every time he mentioned the word home. She didn't feel as if it was hers, not with nothing of her own there. However, she could see herself living there. Already she had ideas of where she'd change certain things, if he'd let her. She bit her lip, worry filling her, making her stomach roll.

"How can I be thinking about silly things when things like Louis contacting my mother are going on?" She paced the length of the living and open floor kitchen area. The night before, she hadn't been able to appreciate the craftsmanship of the interior or how amazing the view was. He truly had one of the most stunning ones she'd ever had the pleasure of standing in. If things went according to plan, she would have the right to call it hers as well.

She began to doubt herself and all that she did the more time she had alone. The night before had been amazing. Better than she'd ever dreamed, definitely more than she could ever have envisioned for herself. Now, within the span of twelve hours, shit was spiraling like it always did for her. "It's as if the universe knows I'm not worthy."

She walked to the living room with the floor to ceiling windows overlooking the ocean. The wraparound deck looked as if it spanned out over the rocky cliff with several different seating arrangements all along the space. She could see a fire pit at one end and an outdoor kitchen at the other. Hollywood had told her on the other side of the house there was an infinity pool, but with everything that had happened, he hadn't been able to show her.

The phone rang on the counter, making her jump. "Fuck me," she mumbled, hurrying to see who was calling her. The unknown number had her jerking her hand back, letting it go to voicemail.

Almost immediately, it began to ring again, the unknown caller. Her hand hovered over the phone, but she didn't answer. She picked it up after it quit ringing and called Scott, hating to sound like a scared little bitch.

"Hey, baby, what's wrong?"

His gentle voice made her wish she'd have stayed strong and not called him. Twenty minutes, that's all he'd been gone, and there she was, bugging him.

"T, what's wrong, speak to me?"

"It's going to sound stupid but—" The same number appeared on her screen while she was talking to him. "I've had an unknown caller call me three times. They just called again, and I know they let it ring long enough to get my voicemail, so they know who they're calling."

"Don't answer, baby girl. After I secure mom, I'll be back. Something isn't sitting right with this shit. I'm going to pick her up and bring her back with me."

She sucked in a breath, looking down at her bare legs in nothing but his shirt. "Ok, sounds good. I'll be fine. Be careful."

"I'm always careful, pourri." His voice went deep, sending a shiver of longing through her.

She looked back toward the bank of windows then back toward the bedroom. If he was bringing her mother back with him, she needed to be semi-presentable even if she was wearing what she'd had on yesterday. "I'm going to take a quick shower and make myself not look as though I've been, you know." Her hand went to her cheek even though he couldn't see the blush that was surely heating it.

"Oh, I know alright, and I plan to do it again and a whole lot more. Go get ready and remember not to answer the phone or door. The only person who has access to the house is me, and the only people who should call you should be in your contact list. Love you, baby girl." He ended the call before she could tell him the same thing.

Back in the master bedroom, she looked at the bed first. The sheets were clean since he'd replaced them the night before, so she remade it, making sure it was perfect, exactly how Hollywood would've had it. Next, she went to his closet, looking for something she could borrow that wouldn't look as though she were wearing borrowed clothes. "Good lord, he's got more clothes than I do." She stared at the room he used as a closet. In the center, there was a bench with rows of clothes on each side of it, top and bottom, color coordinated and the shoes, lord he had shoes. A cabinet in the center of the clothing to her left caught her attention. She moved to stand in front of it, smiling down at the rows of watches and other pieces of jewelry he kept locked up. Most days, he wore jeans and leather boots with a black T-shirt and his leather cut with his club patches on it, but damn did the man have clothes that could feed a third world country.

She trailed her hand along the rows of shirts, settling on a blue button down with a thin pinstripe. Her pants from the night before would work well with the stripe and make it appear as though she was trying to be chic. When in all actuality, she was working with what she had, which was a room full of men's clothes. Great clothes, but still, they weren't women's.

After checking the time, she hand-washed her only pair of panties, beggars couldn't be choosers, and quickly showered, making sure she didn't get her hair wet. While she applied makeup and cleaned up the bathroom and kitchen, the tiny scrap of lace dried.

Talena looked at the reflection in the mirror, a little surprised to see she didn't look too terrible with the little bit of makeup she had applied. "Next time, I'm going to make sure I carry a bag of shit with me. Like one of everything from makeup to undies," she told herself, sticking her tongue out.

"I don't think you need anything else," a deep voice cut through the room.

She spun, her hand going to her throat as she stared at the man standing between her and the doorway. "What are you doing here? How did you get in?"

He smiled, moving into the room. The look was wholly evil. "You should know I can get in and out of anywhere I want with the right incentive."

She backed away, trying to figure out a way around him and to the safe room or to the gun she'd left near her purse on the fucking bed. So stupid, Talena. Fuck she was going to be like a damn movie heroine who was too dumb to live.

"I like this situation. I've never taken a woman in her lover-brother's bed before. It's got a sick sort of twist all on its own. Does he have cameras set up to where he can see?" he asked, strolling toward her, moving slowly as if he hadn't a care in the world.

"He's not my real brother, sicko," she snarled.

Like a rattlesnake, he backhanded her as he was within arm's reach of her. She fell to the side, her hip hitting the counter, and bounced off onto her knees. Thinking quickly, she crawled around him, jumping to her feet and ran for the door. A scream ripped from her throat as her hair was grabbed, stopping her.

"Where does Goldilocks think she's going, hmm?" He reined her in by twisting her hair around his fist, each twist tightening the strands to the point she feared he was going to rip out a great hunk of her hair.

"Please let me go," she cried.

"Oh, I will, when I'm done with you. You see, I don't like to lose, especially to a little Punta who shouldn't be playing in a man's world. Now I have to teach you and your little boy toy a lesson. After I finish with you, I think I'll pay a visit to your mamacita. I don't usually like older women, but I will make an exception for her." He licked a slow path up her cheek. "Are you going to cry and scream for me, Punta?" His teeth latched onto her ear, biting down hard.

She refused to cry out for him, knowing that was what he wanted.

His laughter filled her with dread as he pushed her toward the bed she'd just made, the bed she'd made love to Hollywood in only hours before. "I'm going to have so much fun with you. I see he's already got it set up, so I don't need to come up with anything to tie you up. Are you going to be a good girl, or am I going to need to make you lay in the center of that bed for me?"

The question was whispered next to her throbbing ear, wetness dripped down her neck, leaking onto Hollywood's blue shirt. She had no doubt the monster behind her planned to make her suffer no matter if she willingly got on the bed or not. "Fuck you," she snarled.

"That's what I was hoping for, Punta." He shoved her away from him.

Talena barely caught herself before she fell on her face, spinning around to face Louis. He wore black leather pants and a black tank top. His shoes were gone, but his feet looked like he had on webbed socks. She tried to think of a way for her to get out of the room, but with him blocking the only door other than the closet...Shit, Hollywood's closet was huge. If she could get in there, surely, she could find a weapon.

Louis's hands went to his pants, sliding his belt out in a slow motion while he kept that evil grin on his face. She backed toward the bed, making him think she was complying with him. Dumb fucker, she'd never lay down and let him do anything to her without a fight.

The snap of his belt spurred her on, bolting quickly to the cleverly hidden door. His growl made her scream as she slammed the door shut, her eyes darting around the space for something to use. A baseball bat that had been signed by his favorite team was the only thing she saw in the five seconds she had before the door exploded open.

She gripped the bat like she'd been taught all those years ago when she'd wanted to be like her brother. Louis laughed, holding the belt in his hand, the metal end dangling downward.

"Now this is going to be fun." He twirled the belt in a circle by his side.

Talena was pretty sure it wasn't going to be fun. If she got close enough to hit him with the bat, he'd be close enough to nail her with the belt that obviously wasn't an ordinary belt you bought at Neiman Marcus.

"Hollywood, there's movement at your house. Cannon is moving closer, but he said whoever it is was already inside the gates when we pulled off."

Scott heard the other man's words through the device in his ear as they got on the freeway toward his mom's home. "How does he know they were there before we left?"

"He double backed down to the driveway where we'd set up a camera the night before. Call us paranoid if you want. Anyhow, he pulled up the feed and saw a small wiry man climb the fence about five hours ago. He said the man was wearing all black and appeared to know the fence was rigged with razor-wire at the top, because he had equipment to place over the top. When did you set the alarm for the perimeter?" Roq asked.

He scrubbed his hand down his face, thinking about his mom's call. "The house alarm was set before we went to bed. The perimeter after I got the call from my mom, which means anyone I brought in would set the alarm off, so he'd know if there was anyone coming. Fuck. Does Cannon have eyes on him?"

"That's a negative. He said he's working his way over your fence the same as the intruder went. He can trace the other man's steps that way."

"I want to be the one to kill him," he said, uncaring that he'd just told the other men he had no plans to allow the fucker to walk away.

"What about your mother? He could still have a team set to take her."

Hollywood hated hearing Roq speak what he already knew. "Talena is in immediate danger. I'm going to call my mom and have her lock herself in the safe room until I can get to her. I'm going to call Cosmo and have him bring a couple brothers down to help." Fuck, he should've thought of that scenario. Splitting him from the original target was one of the first things a fucker would do.

"Cosmo is already on his way down. Me and my team will continue on to your mom's place. You and Cannon can handle the intruder until Cosmo gets there. Clear the path for us with your mother's security."

Normally he didn't take well to anyone giving him orders. Hell, what was he saying? He wasn't a man who followed orders well, which was why he'd made a good sniper for Delta Force. Yet when Roq made his request, he found himself agreeing and called his mom while exiting the freeway at the next exit.

"Mom, I need you to listen and don't ask me any questions. There are going to be three big motherfuckers who show up at your gate. The one driving is named Roq." He chuckled when she asked if he meant The Rock. "No mom, I'm sorry to say it's not the actor you love, but he's probably as big as him, but he's definitely not Samoan. In fact, I would say he's a southern boy. They'll know our code word. If they don't, shoot them in the dick."

"Scott, you want me to shoot some poor man in his...well, you know where if he doesn't know our code?" She sounded scandalized.

"You got that right, mom. Now get your ass in the safe room and don't come out until they call you on this cell with the code. Got it?" he asked and waited for her affirmation.

Once he was assured that she was safely in the room, he breathed easier.

"You gonna share with the class the code word so we don't get shot in the dick?" Roq asked, the man's voice sounded like he was laughing instead of alarmed.

"I don't know why you're not more afraid than you are, asshole. I like my junk without holes in it, thank you very much," Axl muttered.

"You just need a piercing to make it prettier is all," Ridley announced.

"Would you two shut the fuck up so he can tell us the code, or I'll shoot you both in the damn dick." Roq's words made the other two men groan.

"The code is slim gym," Hollywood informed them.

"Huh, wasn't expecting that," Axl said. "I mean, that's kinda lame unless you have a slim dick or something, but then if your mama knows, I guess then that's like fucked up on another level. Again, we ain't judging that shit because well, I mean, you know, our families were all kinds of fucked up."

"Ignore him. Sometimes he gets diarrhea of the mouth. We got the code, and we'll be sure to use it. None of us want to lose our junk, regardless of *some of us* having issues, Axl." Roq laughed.

Hollywood would've joined in if he wasn't freaking out. "Thanks, I'll owe you."

"Nah you did a solid for Cosmo and his ole lady. We know how much that meant to him, because even though it's something he wanted to do, if he would've done it, Tai might've been upset."

He disconnected after being assured they were entering the gated community with his mom aware they were there. Tara was prepared for the huge men, and he hoped like hell they were prepared for the little spitfire that was his mother.

Scott wasn't so sure Cosmo wouldn't have done it anyhow, but he kept quiet, his mind on Talena. He tried her cell, cursing when it went to voicemail. On the third try, he began getting that sick feeling in his gut he only had when shit was going to go FUBAR. He pulled up the security cameras in his home, seeing nothing but static. "Fuck," he yelled, tossing the cell into the passenger seat. It would take him another ten minutes to get back to his house. Ten motherfucking minutes to his ole lady who was probably in the hands of a sick fuck.

His knuckles were white as he gripped the steering wheel, and the powerful engine roared beneath the hood. If a police officer decided now was a good time to try to pull him over, he'd be in for a chase that would make the OJ Simpson one look like a fool's run.

With the last bit of sanity he had, he pushed the monitor on his dash, remembering he had access to his home security, including the gate that was supposed to keep everyone out. Punching in the backdoor access code only he had, he locked it down. The only thing that would get the fucker open now was him and or a tank. Another series of numbers got the cameras up and running. He didn't have the ability to see all the cameras at once, like on his smartphone, which made his blood boil and his fingers twitch. One by one, he went through the room, looking for any sign of an intruder.

"Your exit is coming up in 1.2 miles." The car's navigation announced at the same moment he saw his worst nightmare in full color. Talena stood in his closet holding a baseball bat like a slugger facing off against a man whirling something that looked like a whip.

"Don't let him get close, baby girl," he whispered, seeing the metal clasp at the end and knowing if he hit her tender flesh with it the damage it could cause.

He couldn't hear what they were saying, but watching Talena, he saw her lips were moving, and fright combined with determination was stamped on her beautiful face. If she could hold off for another five minutes, he'd be there.

The saying time stood still became something he finally understood as Talena's eyes widened. The lips he'd loved opened in what he knew was a scream, and he was utterly helpless to do anything but watch as Louis swung his weapon. "I will kill you," he promised.

The exit loomed ahead with two cars in front of him. Hollywood flew around them, ignoring their blaring horns. His only concern was getting to Talena before the fucker hurt her any worse. He shaved off another minute from the five, making it to the gate where he'd already keyed in the access. The damn thing wasn't opening fast enough, so without missing a beat, he stomped on the gas, busting through the rest of the way.

The sound of his alarm going off blared. He looked back down at the camera where Talena had been, finding his closet empty. "Shit."

His garage door wouldn't rise with his opener at first, then on the second try, it began moving. He hopped out of the SUV, leaving it running, and slid to the side of the bay closest to the opening one, watching to see if anyone was waiting to ambush him. Ducking and rolling, he entered, keeping low and maneuvering around his other vehicles.

Once he was sure the coast was clear, he made his way to the door, searching for clues of the trespasser and his entry point. The palm reader was still activated, scanning his hand. He heard the familiar beep before the huge door slid open. The smell of bacon still lingered as he entered the mudroom. The first thing he noticed was a piece of wax lying on the ground.

"Son-of-a-bitch," he swore. The thin piece of wax-like material held what was clearly a print. "The fucker used me to get into my own home." The how would have to wait until he killed the bastard.

He cleared the kitchen then the living area, seeing little tells that he was aware weren't made by him or Talena. Before he headed toward the master, he pushed on a hidden panel, grabbing one of the guns and the clip that was already loaded. He loaded it, stuffing it into the back of his jeans, then grabbed the other, checking the clip, and slid it inside.

He held the weapon loosely as he walked steadily toward his bedroom. A faint noise coming from the guest suite across the hall had him stopping, flattening himself against the wall, and moving with caution. The closer he got to the entryway, the more he could make out the sound. If Louis hadn't already been dead in his mind, he would've been then.

Chapter Twelve

"You should just give it up, and I'll go easier on you than I did Rosalie. We all took turns with her after she learned her lesson last night. However, I'm sad to say she won't be making any more of the races. Of course, neither will you, Punta. The difference is you can go out easier than she did, or you can go out harder. It's up to you. I prefer the hard way, but that's just me. I don't mind sliding into a woman if she's still warm. I can even use your blood to ease the way." Louis licked his lips.

She saw his muscles bunch, even though he was trying to distract her with his disgusting words of what he planned to do to her. She may have hated Rosalie, but if what he said was true then...shit, he was a murderer and a sadistic asshole. Just as he struck with his wicked looking belt, she ducked, hearing the whistle it made as it barely missed her. Using all her strength, she rolled with the bat in her arms, coming up right in front of him, nailing his knees with a satisfying crack.

"You fucking whore," he yelled.

Talena didn't wait around. Jumping to her feet and hitting the door with the palm of her hand, she slammed the door behind her and ran. She knew she should've taken the time to inspect the entire house earlier, but couldn't change the past, so she went to the first door across the hall. The lights came on automatically when she entered, making her wish she knew how to shut the fuckers off. Her only hope was that he wouldn't be able to see beneath the door. The lock was a simple turn style, but she feared if she locked it, he'd know she was inside. Indecision warred within her, and in the end, she ran behind the desk, opened one of the cabinets then another, looking for one that would hide her.

"Oh, Lucy, come out, come out, wherever you are," Louis cheered.

She twisted to stare at the door, then the desk, and finally the door on the other side of the room. No way was she going out that way since she had no clue where it led. Hiding under the desk was so freaking cliché and it had no out if he came around it. "Think," she whispered, panic making her heart race with images of him bursting into the room while she raced around the large space that was getting smaller with each second. She noticed the space behind the door would be the only place that she'd have any way of hiding and possibly a chance to get away. Her hands were sweating, making the grip on the bat slippery. A minute ticked by then two. The doorknob turned slowly, and she knew this was it. He'd found her, or he was eliminating the rooms one-by-one. The bat was heavy after holding it up in the same position for so long, and she wondered if she'd even be able to swing it with enough force to hurt him, let alone get her out of the room.

The door didn't ease open. She was prepared for any situation, keeping her body pressed into the corner so the door would hit the wall. Louis was a psycho, but he was smart. He'd proven that by getting into Scott's home. She wasn't going to underestimate him. All she needed to do was stay alive long enough for Scott or someone to realize there was an intruder. She had to believe that was going to happen.

"Fuck, where are you?" he roared. The sound of the belt cracking against something and glass shattering kept her silent. She held her breath, not daring to breathe lest he hear even a whisper of sound.

"When I find you, I'm going to tie you to that bastard's bed, then I'm going to whip the skin off you before I fuck you. I think I'll wait until you're about to take your last breath so you can fill your lungs with me and my scent. Does that turn you on?"

"What turns me on is picturing you with my fist breaking every fucking bone in your face, following that up with pain," Scott growled.

She whimpered, relief and panic at the thought of what was going to happen between Louis and the man she loved.

"Ah, the little Punta was right there the entire time." Louis's voice sounded excited.

"Too bad you and I are going to be the ones playing though. You talk a big game for a little man, Louie. Come on, you like to scare little girls, but you don't appear to like to take on men—well I was going to say your own size, but I am way outta your league in more ways than one. How about we even the playing field some?" Hollywood unloaded the clip in the gun he held, making sure the little weasel could see the gun was empty. "See how's that for evening the field? You still got your little weapon. You feel big enough to play, boy?"

Louis let the belt hang down, the metal hitting on shattered glass beneath him. "Ah, pretty boy, you're going to wish you'd kept your gun. I'm going to kill you then I'm going to kill your whore. After I finish with the both of you,

I'm going to go to your mother's house and fuck her with your blood on my hands." He lashed out with the leather, the metal end hitting Scott on the arm.

Scott grimaced but moved further into the room, pushing the empty gun and clip against the door so it would stay open and keep Talena hidden. "Is that all you got, little man?"

When Louis swung again, Scott ducked, lunging forward. The smaller man stumbled backward, swinging his weapon in a wild arc. One of Scott's favorite vases became a casualty, a shard nicking him in the neck. The next swing he waited and timed, reaching for the belt. He met the other man's dark gaze as he held the metal clasp and began to pull. Scott smiled a feral flash of his teeth. "You really shouldn't have come to my home, Louis. In fact, you really shouldn't have fucked with me and mine."

By the time the other man was an arm's length away, he tried to release the belt, but Scott was prepared and wasn't going to let him get far. He moved forward, striking Louis with the fist wrapped in the belt, blood spraying like a geyser from his shattered nose.

Scott let out a sigh, shaking his head. "Look what you did, boy. You done fucked up my office, and now you're bleeding all over my expensive carpet. Guess if we're gonna fuck it up, might as well do it all the way, hmm?"

When he'd gone to China and beat the fuck out of Tai's brothers, he'd had fun with them before they'd ultimately killed them. Staring at the man who said he was going to tie his woman up and fuck her in his own bed, rage unlike any he's ever felt sizzled through his veins. He hit Louis again and again, holding him by the back of the hair when he tried to fall. And then he did fall, but Scott followed him down, unwilling to allow him to get away with the shit he'd said he was going to do.

His fist ached, blood made his knuckles slide off the...hell, he wasn't sure what the fuck was below him.

"Please, Scott, it's okay. I'm okay."

"Yo, King, I think you might need to come and get your boy off the hamburger meat in here."

"What the fuck, Hollywood. Come on, brother, your ole lady needs you to chill. Come on, we got cleaners here." King's voice boomed through the quiet room.

The sound of his prez's voice and Talena's scared one filtered in through the red haze, bringing him out of the place he'd gone. He looked down at the bastard, or what was left of

Louis. In a second, he would get up and face T and know she wouldn't want him after seeing what he could do. Hell, his own club would probably kick him out. He got to his feet, wiping his bloody hands on the front of his jeans. Not that it did any good, what with the amount of the stuff on him. Fuck.

"I like him. He's my people," Cannon said, coming up next to him with a towel. "Here, it's a lucky thing you have black ones, you know, on account of all the blood and shit."

Hollywood looked at the towel then at the crazy bastard who handed it to him. "You realize I just killed a man with my bare hands, right?"

Cannon shrugged. "Yeah, sorry about that. I didn't realize anyone had slipped past me. I killed his two friends, stupid fuckers. Not as, er, creatively as you, but dead is dead I always say."

"Gotdammit, Cannon, are you comparing killing again? I told you, we don't discuss that shit like we're talking about the weather. Whoa, alrighty then, maybe we can discuss it around here. Dude, that's some shit. Who's on cleanup?" Roq asked, his southern twang heavier than normal as he spoke as he came to stand over the bloody mess.

Scott inhaled, looking King in the eyes but addressed the room. "I have no clue who Gotdammit is, but he had nothing to do with this shit. I'm thinking the answer is yes, you realize I killed, and you clearly have no problem. As to him slipping past you. I think he was already inside the gates when you got here, Cannon." He took the towel from Cannon.

"Makes sense. Not many get past me and my Spidey senses." Cannon wiggled his fingers like he was shooting nets out of his hands, then walked back toward Roq.

King stared at the two men, then at Hollywood. "Are they for real?"

"Afraid so," Hollywood said with a negligent shrug.

"I had a feeling you were going to say that. Go get cleaned up and take your girl with you. We'll handle this shit, and I'll find out from crazy one over there about the other dead fuckers. I would like to have one week or two, where shit don't blow the fuck up, for once." King ran his hand down his beard, a small smile tipped his lips.

"Maybe you can ask Santa for that since Christmas is next month," Roq said, his deep baritone sounded bored.

King and Scott both looked up at Roq. "Are you going to dress up like Santa and slide down the chimney in a red suit?" King asked without cracking a grin.

Roq put his hands on his hips, looked down at his boots, then up at King. "Well, you see, I was going to, but then I tried to put in an order for the Santa outfit, and found out they don't come in my size, partner. I'm sure the ladies are all gonna be most upset, but I did find a nice pair of red boxer briefs that's got gold bells right over my package. I'll be glad to come and deliver some presents in it, if you fellas need me to...slide in anywhere." Roq began swinging his hips back and forth while Axl made dinging noises.

"I don't know how Cosmo hasn't killed you yet," King growled.

Scott dropped the black towel after wiping as much blood as he could off his hands before he faced Talena. He had put off looking at her until that moment, and what he saw nearly sent him to his knees. Silent tears streaked her cheeks, making her blue eyes look luminous.

"I'm sorry, baby." He dropped his eyes, wishing he had the right to hold her, to tell her he loved her.

A solid body hit him, her sweet scent filling his lungs. "I knew you'd save me. I knew if I could just hide and stay safe long enough, you'd save me."

His head came up, his arms wrapping around the only thing that mattered in that moment. "You aren't scared of me?"

"What?" Talena asked, wrapping her legs around his hips.

Scott wasn't sure what the hell was going on. One moment he was thinking he'd lost whatever chance he'd had with Talena, to wrapping his arms around her ass, pulling her flush against him like he wouldn't ever let her go. "Sweetheart, did you see what I'm capable of?"

What the hell was he doing for Christ sake? If he could he'd cut his own tongue out, but in truth he had to make sure she was aware of the danger that was being with him. Not that he was a walking timebomb, but he had the ability to do what she'd witnessed. He kept a tight leash on that savage part of himself, never allowing anyone to see the things he was capable of. However, he would destroy the entire fucking world if his loved ones were in danger.

"I'll admit it was a little scary watching you thrash Louis, but he totally deserved it. I'm glad he's not going to be able to do what he said he was to me or anyone else. I...I think he killed Rosalie and probably a lot of others too," she whispered.

They were in his bathroom now, and the clear indication that his home had been invaded was everywhere. Already he was making plans to put the home on the market, not wanting the taint of Louis to mar a life with Talena and him. "I know, baby girl. He was pure evil. We can't go looking for Rosalie, or it would lead the authorities back to us. We have to make him disappear along with his men." And for that, he hated that the victims wouldn't get any kind of resolution.

"That's okay, just knowing that he can't ever harm another person makes it okay. Can we take a shower and then talk? I feel dirty," she said, kissing his cheek.

His little miracle kissed him as if he hadn't just made mincemeat out of a man in the middle of his office and then left the mess to be cleaned up by his friends. He didn't know what he'd done to deserve her, but he'd be damned if he'd ever give her up. Years ago, when he'd been a little boy, he'd looked up at the sky and asked for one thing, someone to love him as he was. He'd known his mother loved him and always would, but he'd wanted a soulmate. It had taken him a long time to realize his wish had come true.

"Thank you for loving me, for giving me a chance." He stripped himself and her outside the shower, then pulled them both inside, letting the hot water wash away the blood and doubts.

Epilogue

Talena twisted her hands on the steering wheel, wondering if Scott was going to freak out when he saw his surprise?

"Honey, why are you so nervous?" Tara Haven asked, reaching over and patting Talena's knee.

"Because it's Christmas Eve, and you know how Scott is about the holidays." She bit her lip to stifle the rest of her words. Since the incident at the beach house, or rather mansion, he'd been working overtime to sell the property. What he didn't know was she was working just as hard to foil his efforts. She almost felt bad for doing it, but she loved the home and just because some bastard had tried to do bad things there didn't make it a bad place. Which she'd told him a dozen or so times.

"If you don't quit grinding your teeth, you're going to need veneers, dear," her mother warned.

Talena rolled her eyes, but did stop, or tried to stop working her jaw so ferociously. "Now you know that this is an MC, mother, right?"

One of the things she'd been working on was preparing their mom for what they were walking into. Scott, aka Hollywood, was a member of the club, and as a member he had a brotherhood and loyalty that transcended mere friendship. She'd witnessed the depths of their loyalty six weeks ago as the men had come and helped take care of things at their home, ensuring there was no evidence left of what went down that day. Although she still wasn't sure about the three men who had come with Cosmo, since she hadn't seen or heard anything about them since that day, but she would forever be grateful for those men.

"Yes, dear. I do know what an MC is and does. I did some research, and while I was a little worried, I realized that he's been a part of this club for some time. If they were unsavory, then he'd have ended up in trouble a long time ago. I think they're just the opposite to what you read about. In fact, I'd say they helped save him." Tara nodded, crossing her arms over her chest with a harumph.

Talena didn't bother to deny it since the men had, in fact, done just that a few weeks prior. Nope, sometimes ignorance is bliss. The entrance to the compound was next, so she hit the blinker, and then they entered, knowing her mother was going to be shocked at the size of the estates.

"Holy lord," Tara breathed.

She kept her lips sealed, driving down to the clubhouse past King's huge home, and the two other new ones that had been built. All three were easily the size of her mother's.

"Here we are, mom. Mouth closed now. We don't want to attract flies," she teased.

Her mom slapped her arm after Talena shifted into park and turned the car off. "You said this was a bar and that...that they lived in houses on the property. Talena, these aren't normal homes, and that's not a normal bar."

With a laugh, she got out, bending down to look her mother in the eye. "Welcome to the Royal MC Clubhouse, Mama. Come on, let's go see if Santa's arrived."

Her mother growled, getting out of the low-slung sports car. "Help me get the presents out of the trunk, you little brat."

"That's what I call her too."

She was sure she'd never stop getting butterflies when she heard his voice or when she saw Scott. Like now, watching him walk down the steps wearing his black jeans, black T-shirt, and leather cut, she thought he was the most gorgeous man in the world. "Hi," she said breathlessly.

"Hi yourself, mon pourri." He tugged her to him, giving her a kiss that left no doubt they were a couple.

He pulled away, licking his lips. "Mmm, you taste like strawberries. Hi, mom. You need some help?"

Scott kept one arm around Talena while he met his mother at the back of his G-Wagon.

"Hello, sweetheart. What a lovely place." Tara turned her cheek for a kiss.

"The Royal brothers have done a fine job of building it up," he agreed.

"Don't let him bullshit you, ma'am. Your son has been a huge investor and so have all the brothers. My name is King. I'm glad you could join us for Christmas Eve. My ole lady is really excited for the holidays this year." King came down the stairs with a smile on his face, not looking nearly as scary as Talena remembered.

"Hello, young man. Thank you for having us. Here come help us bring in the gifts." Tara waved at King.

Talena buried her face against Scott's chest so King wouldn't see the laughter she was trying to suppress.

Another car pulled up next to them, a silver Mercedes with blacked out windows. Talena had never seen the silver haired gentleman who got out of the vehicle, but when he looked at her mother, there was no denying the interest in his gaze. Scott's muscles hardened beneath her hand on his chest. "Don't," she whispered, knowing without looking up he was going to say something.

"Dammit, he's Doc," he muttered.

"Um, is he a doctor then?" she asked, blinking up at him.

Scott stared across at Doc and then his mother before looking down at Talena. "Yes, he's a doctor, and he goes by the name Doc. His daughter is Duke's ole lady." He didn't like the way the older man was looking at his mother though, like he could see her without her clothes on, and he liked it. Nope, Scott was not okay with that at all.

"Well let's have a nice night and don't be...mean." She patted his chest again.

"Baby girl, you are racking up the punishments. You know that, right?" He brought her hand up to his lips, nipping her palm.

The little shiver that went down her slight frame made him wish they could skip the festivities and head straight to his room in the back of the clubhouse. Of course, since his mother was there, he couldn't very well do that without her knowing he was fucking her baby girl six ways to Sunday, dammit. "Let's go before I toss you over my shoulder and take you to King's house for a little privacy."

"What the hell? I don't remember giving you permission?" King asked, then shook his head. He had his arms full of a box overflowing with packages. "I suppose I'd allow it, but only the basement, not my upstairs master suite."

"Don't even think of disappearing on me, you two. Come on, there's more in here." Tara waved toward the G-Wagon.

"Here, let me help," Doc offered.

Twenty minutes later, Scott sat around the clubhouse, which had been turned into a Christmas extravaganza, sipping a beer while he held Talena in his lap. "You happy, baby?"

Frog was playing bartender with lights all around the bar and more strands dangling above, and on every surface, even the dance floor. The only thing that wasn't wrapped in lights or garland was the stripper poles, but he had a feeling that was only because they feared an injury would occur if one of the women were to slide down the smooth surface.

She leaned against him, her arm around his shoulder. "Very. How about you?"

He bit her earlobe, blowing a puff of air over the little sting. "Hmm, I am. I would be a whole lot happier if we were alone."

"Hey, I need to borrow your girl," Ayesha announced from beside him. Lennox was standing back a little, but she too had a little gleam in her eye that had him tensing.

Scott sighed, giving Talena a kiss before helping her stand. "Fine, but no crazy shit."

Ayesha put her hand over her heart, feigning hurt. "Why, Hollywood. How dare you suggest I do anything of the kind. Why I'm the epitome of good girl, and Lennox, why she's just plain good."

"Yeah, you're both the epitome of good girls gone bad. Listen to Hollywood and behave." King slapped Ayesha on the ass, making her squeal.

"I swear, women are the best thing that God created." Duke held his bottle up, waiting for them to agree, and clank their drinks to his. He winked at his woman who sashayed away.

Hollywood tapped his with Duke's then King's, nodding. "That they are, brother."

"What's the matter, Hollywood? You still look like a man who's running." King took a sip of his whiskey looking toward the door the girls had gone through.

"I think T is hiding something. Hell, brother, she's probably rethinking being with me." He shrugged, swallowing the last of his beer.

King took another long sip, then sat his cup down. "Hollywood, you can't defeat your demons if they're still your friends. You know what I mean?"

He stared at his prez, wondering if he'd drank too much or maybe smoked some bad shit, then it hit him. "Me. I'm my own worst enemy."

King lifted his glass, raising it in the air. "There you go. You see, you're the only one who's hung up on shit that happened. I saw the way she looked at you that day, brother, and I can promise you she wasn't looking at you like you were some kind of freak or murderer. More like you were her hero. Our ole ladies, they're not like other women. It takes a certain kind of female to be with men like us. Your girl, Talena, she's like my Ayesha, and Cosmo's Tai, and like the other women who find their way into our lives. They got grit and pride, and they know how to handle our bullshit, but still know how things are done. I saw her, and you, brother, need to see her too." King slapped his shoulder.

"Damn I hate when he's all poetic and shit, but he's right. Talena is a ride or die bitch, brother. I know my ole lady said that if a chick was all up in her face, like if their eyelashes be braiding, that Talena would cut her. She said in the name of Jesus, she swore T would be her girl because Talena said she would cut her and bury her in her grandma's back forty." Duke tossed the last of his drink back.

"King, what the fuck is he drinking or taking? Did he eat a weed brownie and decide to cook another pizza at fifteen degrees for four hundred minutes so now he's mangry?" Scott asked, taking the empty beer bottle and sniffing it.

Duke looked between King and Scott, grabbing for the bottle. "What the fuck is mangry?"

"It's like when a female is hangry and gets all irrational, but in your case, it's mangry, which you're obviously not only irrational but a dumbfuck too," King muttered.

"Hey, guys, you might want to gather round. I think the women are about to come out with presents." Doc's voice boomed, pulling them from the argument that was about to ensue.

The overhead lights dimmed, leaving the multi-colored Christmas lights that had been strung about the room, along with the huge Christmas tree that was lit up, the only illumination in the huge space. All of a sudden, Mariah Carey's song *All I Want For Christmas* began playing over the speakers and out came the girls onto the stage. Tara, Hollywood's mother, leading the way, wearing a red silk dress that showed off her curves that he was sure no son should have to witness other men ogling. And then, Talena came out last, and his thoughts scattered.

"Jesus fucking Christ," he whispered, hearing the other men mutter things that mirrored his own thoughts. Out of the corner of his eye, he thought he saw Doc move closer, but then Talena and Ayesha stepped in front of his mom with Lennox right behind them.

"If my ole lady strips, I am going to beat her ass so damn good she ain't going to sit for a week," King said, rubbing his hands together.

"Take it off," cheered Duke.

King elbowed his brother Duke, who smiled back at him.

Hollywood ignored them both, his stare riveted to the stage.

The women danced to the song, articles of clothing did indeed start coming off. He heard King growling and muttering as his prez moved closer and closer. Before Ayesha could get down to what was probably a sexy teddy, he had her over his shoulder, his preferred mode of exit, and strode toward the door. "See you tomorrow, assholes. I'm gonna get my Christmas present early." King swatted Ayesha's ass, the slap echoing around the room.

Doc held his hand up for Tara to step off the stage, which Hollywood was glad to see his mother hadn't removed a stitch of clothing. He'd have had to gouge out every fucker's eyes there.

"Mon pourri, you want to continue, or are you ready to come down from there?" he asked, watching her eye the pole.

She grinned down at him. "I practiced this amazing routine though."

"Oh yeah she did," Lennox cheered.

"You coming down, or am I coming to get you?" Duke asked, arms crossed over his chest with his beer bottle dangling from his fingers, standing a foot from the stage like he was fully prepared to leap up and snatch his ole lady.

"Now, Duke, you know I was only doing my duty as...well as the only professional dancer amongst us," Lennox said, moving toward Duke.

Hollywood kept his lips sealed since her professional dancing wasn't pole or lap dancing, yet she and the others, minus his mother, had done a damn fine job of shaking their assets while taking their clothes off. Nope, he most definitely wasn't going to rattle that cage.

He folded his arms over his chest, waiting. Over his shoulder, he looked to see how the others in the room were taking in the show, and to his surprise, they'd all turned their backs. Goddamn, he loved his brothers. "Well, let's see it then."

Talena grabbed the bar, her movements fluid and sure to the music. He was utterly transfixed by the play of muscles in her arms and stomach with each twirl and flip she executed while holding onto the pole, keeping up with the tempo. When the song was coming to an end, Talena flipped her entire body up and around, legs spreading wide until she slid to the floor, the only thing holding her was her arms. He had an image of her riding his cock with her legs spread the exact same way and couldn't wait to get her alone. If he turned around, every person there would have no doubt how much he wanted her with the huge bulge in his jeans. His dick was going to have the indent of his zipper if he didn't get himself under control.

Taking a few deep breaths, he held his hand up and waited for her to take it. If he'd had a couple hundred in dollar bills, he'd have stuffed them in her outfit. He couldn't believe the skill she executed, but then again, his girl was amazing at anything she put her mind to. "That was perfect, mon pourri. How long have you been practicing?"

"It was Ayesha's idea," she said quickly, then bit her lip. "I added the pole part at the end though. I asked Lennox and her to teach me how to work the thing properly. Are you mad?"

He gripped her by the ass, holding her tight to his body, letting her feel his dick throbbing for her. "Hell no, baby. Horny as fuck and unable to do anything about it until we get home."

The thought of the beach house had his dick going semi-soft.

"Hey, you two. Um, Doc is going to give me a ride home." Tara held her hand up. "Don't give me any shit, Scott

Haven. I'm your mother, and I'm a big girl who can get a ride from a nice man."

Scott looked at Doc then at his mom. "You take her home, and you treat her like you'd want your daughter treated on a first meeting. You feel me?" He'd bury Doc's cold lifeless body if he fucked with his mother.

Doc grinned. "I feel you, Hollywood. Don't worry, I'll treat her like a proper lady. You have my word."

His mother kissed his cheek then Talena's. "That was some really amazing dancing, honey. Please tell me that you're not um, you know, planning to do that as a career though. Not that there's anything wrong with that of course. It's just that I don't think Scott's heart could handle watching you do that in front of other men."

He growled an agreement and then watched Doc help his mom into his Mercedes while he stood with his arm around Talena.

"Excuse me, brother, but I gotta go. My ole lady has informed me we are starting a month of love tonight." Duke held up his fist and bumped his knuckles against Scott's, walking out with his arm around Lennox.

"What the hell is that?" Keys asked, carrying his sleeping boy from the kitchen.

"King's woman was talking about it the other day. Whatever it was had his eyes going all slumberous and shit, and Duke said he was going to find out. Guess he did." Hollywood looked down at Talena's laughing face.

"How about you, Hollywood, you here for the month of love too?" she asked.

"What is it exactly?" He pulled her in front of him, holding her by the hips.

Talena stood up on her toes, kissing his chin. "It's where you make love every day for a month."

He snorted. "We already make love every day, sometimes twice a day."

"Yeah, but we can do it and say we're doing the month of love. It makes it more romantic." She bit his chin.

"Woman, I'll give you romance." He decided if she wanted to take a page out of King's book, he would do too. Tossing her over his shoulder and swatting her ass, he realized his friend had the right idea.

"I love it when you go caveman on me, Hollywood." She wiggled her ass on his shoulder, almost making him drop her.

He'd thought he was happy with life, chugging along, and watching others find love, then he realized happiness doesn't depend on what you have or who you are. It solely relies on what you think. He decided he could turn his life around one thought at a time, one choice at a time. Choosing to love the right woman made everything in his life not only happy but fulfilled.

"Tonight, when I make love to you, Talena, I promise to make sure all your wishes come true."

"You're all I wish for, Hollywood Haven."

He shifted her from his shoulder, sliding her down so he could see her face. She wrapped her legs around his waist, filling his palms with her firm ass.

"Ah, mon pourri, I hope you wish for a lot better than me." He ran the back of his scarred knuckles down her soft cheek knowing she deserved a lot more than him, but he'd be damned if he'd ever give her up.

"Look up." She tilted her head toward the ceiling and the twinkling lights.

He was sure King would've had a fit seeing the clubhouse decorated with trees and more lights than the Macy's freaking parade, but to his surprise, the man had been smiling from ear to ear all night. Doing as Talena had instructed, he couldn't help but grin himself, seeing the bundle of greenery just over the entryway. "Is that mistletoe?"

"Why I do believe it is, and you know what that means?"

Scott was sure he knew the answer, only wanting to hear what his clever girl came up with kept him silent. However, he did let his hand find her nicely rounded ass again, swatting each cheek one more time while he waited.

"Hollywood Haven, that is not nice," she complained.

"Ah, see, that's where you made your mistake, baby girl. I never said I was nice. Just because the outside veneer looks good and clean most days, doesn't mean the inside is. Now tell me what I want to hear." He rubbed the sting, loving the way she moaned under his palm.

"It means if you kiss someone under it on Christmas Eve then your wish will come true." She gasped as he slipped his fingers between her thighs, running them along the seam shielding her pussy.

"Baby girl, don't you know your dreams will always come true if you ask me for them?" He unhooked her legs from his waist, settling her in front of him, making sure she was steady in the mile-high heels she had one. Fuck he was so going to fuck her with them on. Already he could imagine what the points digging into his back would feel like and couldn't wait to see if they were as sharp as they appeared.

"What're you doing?" She pushed her long hair off of her face, blinking up at him with the rainbow-colored lights from the Christmas decorations creating a halo behind her.

"Why I'm gonna kiss my girl under the fucking mistletoe of course." Scott held her face between his palms, tipping her head up to his. Her smile widened moments before he covered her lips with his, tasting her sweetness and the flavor of the sweet drink she'd had combined. If the world ended tomorrow, he knew he would die happy, knowing he had her with him.

"Get a room, asshole."

Hollywood pressed his forehead against Talena's, murmuring low so only she could hear words he didn't think he would have to ever say. "Don't kill him, Cosmo would be pissed."

"Nah he'd only be slightly miffed. There's four of us, so he's got three others." Ridley slapped his back on his way out.

"How the fuck did he hear me?"

"I got super hearing like Spidey senses," Ridley hollered back without breaking stride, heading toward the SUV they'd come in. "Shotgun," he yelled.

"The fuck you do. Get out of that front seat if you value your life and balls, boy." Roq slapped Hollywood on the shoulder as he too passed him, shaking his head.

Scott barely kept from falling over when the other man hit him. "Roq, you really need to learn to be a little more...gentle, brother."

Roq stopped walking, turned on his cowboy boots that looked to be a size eighteen, and stared back at Hollywood and Talena. "Shit, man, next you'll tell me I need to be all friendly to the locals and all that bull that my counselors suggested. Ain't having any of that kumbayashit, man. Nope, I ain't doing it. I'll try to be a little less manly around you fellers," Roq said with a wink.

Hollywood lifted his right hand, flipping the big bastard the bird. "I'll show you less manly, asshole."

Cannon and Axl walked out, carrying a bottle of liquor each. Makers if he wasn't mistaken.

"Don't worry, we paid for these. That bartender is a tough negotiator," Axl muttered, glaring over his shoulder at Frog who stood behind the long bar wiping the top with a rag and grinned.

He didn't give a shit what they paid or didn't pay; he only wanted to finish kissing his ole lady, and then get her back to his room and fuck her in nothing but the heels she wore. Was that too much to ask, dammit?

A horn blared, making Axl shove Cannon off the steps, the other man barely catching himself before he faceplanted. Then the four men were loaded up and backing out, probably off to kill someone, but he didn't give a shit. All Hollywood cared about was the woman in his arms. "Guess what time it is?" he asked Talena, swaying back and forth, still standing beneath the damn greenery.

"Time to whisk me off to your room of debauchery and take advantage of me?" she asked, running her hands up his chest, then in a totally Talena move, she hopped up, wrapping her legs back around his waist.

"First of all, fuck me, baby, you're going to hurt my dick if you don't settle down. Second, who the hell says whisk in this day and age. And last, but certainly not least, you read my mind because I'm most definitely going to debauch the fuck out of you. But you didn't guess what time it was." He gripped her ass tighter, happier than he could ever remember being in all his life.

"Are you going to tell me since I don't have a watch on, and my phone had nowhere to go in this outfit?" She shifted rubbing purposefully up and down on the ridge of his dick.

Scott groaned and dug his fingers into her ass. "It's Christmas."

"Then my wish is coming true already," she whispered, licking her lips.

He didn't stand around to hear what she had wished for knowing it was more than likely going to injure his dick even more if he didn't get them to his room. He carried her back through the bar, paying no attention to those still inside drinking. All the brothers with ole ladies had taken off, presumably to do the same thing as him. Or close to what he planned. The long hall with doors lining it was quiet as he made his way to the end. The suite he took her to once belonged to Cosmo, but since the brother had built a fucking small mansion on the compound, he was gracious enough to let Scott take it over. Before he didn't give a shit what his room at the club looked like, although it was always clean and serviceable. That was before he had Talena.

Like his home, he'd had it customized with security that opened with his palm print or retinal scanner. Of course, he'd upped his security measure with the screen wiping after he entered and making it have a heat signature match as well. No bastard was going to be able to match him like before.

"Scott, you're squeezing me. While I like it when you get frisky, I don't like it when you do it and look feral."

He kicked the door shut, making sure it latched. "Sorry, my mind went back where it shouldn't." Hell, he wasn't one who claimed to have PTSD after his years in the military, yet one fucked up situation where Talena's life was almost lost, and he was a twitchy bastard.

"I bet I can help you get your mind on better things," she whispered, her arms circled his head tighter, bringing him closer to her breasts.

"You think so?" He continued walking through the suite, ignoring the living area, and going straight for the bedroom he'd had redone to his specifications. Poor Cosmo would probably have a conniption if he knew the changes he'd had done, but then again, Cosmo would also enjoy the hell out of the new toys too.

"Oh my," Talena said, her voice a little high pitched.

"I hope you like one of your Christmas presents, mon pourri." He let her slide down his body, his fingers keeping hold of the tiny scrap of silk, pulling it further up her back until she moaned.

"Did you leave any lights at the store for other people?"

He let her turn around so her back was facing him, wrapping his arms around her so he could cup her breasts. She'd kept the two pieces of triangles that covered her chest on while she'd danced, but the red silk topped with white fur was even more enticing with what it hid, than what it showed. He scooped the tips of his fingers in the top, teasing the hardened tips. "I'm sure there were a few for anyone who came after me. Alright, tell me which do you want to try first? This is your one and only chance to decide, baby girl."

"Let's see? I can be tied to the cross or that bench thing? Sounds like you have some kinky things planned?"

He released her, walking over to the dresser where he had laid out some of his favorite toys. "What I have planned is what I love to do with you, and that's maximizing ecstasy and minimizing all risk." He lifted a length of rope, running it through his hand. "You see this rope? I wouldn't use it on you until I've held it, touched it, smoothed it between my hands enough to know there isn't a part of it that would cause you injury...unless that is what I chose." He put the rope back, lifting another item he hoped she'd love as much as he did.

She looked at what he held. "Is that a flogger?"

"This is a light flogger, and this is a leather whip." He showed her the different ones in the chest next to the St. Andrews Cross. Her eyes widened when she spied the whips with multiple tails. He purposefully ran his fingers over them so she could see he was comfortable with touching them and would be using them on her. "I have several I'll use on you but not tonight."

"That looks more comfortable yet more confining," Talena whispered, walking closer to the bench.

He nodded, walking to where she stood. "This is a custom piece. You would lay here, rest your legs here, and place your arms here. See these cuffs? I made sure the leather is the softest and are lined so they won't mar your delicate flesh. Only I'm allowed to do that. Now, if you select the cross, I had it custom created as well, but as you might know, all crosses are basically the same. What makes mine unique is the material the frame is made of, which I won't bore you with. Suffice it to say, you won't be injured unless it's what I desire. Now choose, mon pourri." He put a bit of steel to his tone, letting her know the time for leniency was over.

"The cross," she said.

"Good girl." He held his hand out to her, waiting for her to take it. This was the way he needed her to show she was with him. "Do you need a safeword?"

"Do I?"

He helped her into position, admiring the way the red on the leather framed her from behind. "I said you didn't need one before, but for tonight, choose one. I can see you're scared and if it would make you feel better then choose one."

She took a deep breath, then let it out. "No, I trust you."

He ran his hand down her cheek, smiling at her trust. "Ah, you don't know how much that means to me, baby girl."

The last cuff slid over her ankle. He kissed right above it, then stood up, admiring how beautiful she looked. "I need to take a picture of you just like that."

"What? Oh my god, what if someone sees it?" she asked.

Scott lifted the camera from the cabinet, coming to stand in front of her and gripped her chin. "Nobody will see you like this unless I allow it, mon pourri, do you understand me?"

Talena licked her lips then nodded. "Yes. I just...I know things on the internet get leaked sometimes."

He pinched her chin, then kissed her hard. "Nothing will get leaked, baby girl." He took a step back and snapped a couple pics before shaking his head. "No that's not good."

Settling the camera on the ground, he stood up and with a wicked smile, he ripped the tiny scraps of material from her body. Her shocked gasp was swallowed by his mouth as he let his hands roam her body, tweaking her nipples into hardened points then smoothing down her stomach until he reached the juncture between her thighs. "Are you wet, baby?"

She nodded.

"I need to hear you. What do you say?" he asked, tracing her folds without touching where she was most needy.

"Yes, yes I'm wet, Sir."

The sound of her calling him Sir had him ready to say fuck the scene he was creating. "I think someone is being a very good girl. You know what good girls get?"

"They get fucked?" she asked with a hopeful expression.

"Eventually," he agreed.

His fingers pressed between her legs and then spread her lower lips apart, making her cry out from that small touch. "Are you close to coming before I ever even touch you?"

She shifted her hips, trying to get him where she wanted him. Scott gave her mound a tap, stilling her movements. "Behave or I'll stop touching you with my hands and grab one of my floggers."

His threat had her freezing. "Please, Scott."

For the next forty-two minutes and thirty-six seconds, he did just that...pleased himself without letting her come. He took her up, building the pleasure to where she was shaking with the need to come, only to back off. "Ssh, it's okay, baby girl. I got you. Are you ready to come?"

"Yes, damn you," she wailed, sweat glistening on her skin.

He took off his jeans, folding them neatly, and placed them on a chair before returning to where she hung, glassy-eyed and panting. "Damn me, you say?"

Talena licked her lips, locking her eyes on his hand as he pumped it up and down his cock.

"I'm sorry, please, I need you to fuck me, Sir."

Scott bent, releasing her ankles first, massaging each one, then moved to her left arm, making sure he helped her move it down so that she wasn't in pain and then did the right. He lifted her into his arms and carried her over to the bed, sliding between her thighs as he walked. They both moaned as the head of his cock entered her. Although she was soaking wet and ready, he still took his time. "Damn, you're so tight."

"No, you're just huge. Oh, yes," she cried.

He pushed all the way in, holding still while her body twitched around him, her orgasm catching him off guard. "Damn, I'd punish you for coming without permission, but that felt fucking amazing. I think I'll need to feel you do that a couple more times."

She panted, chest rising and falling, but she didn't open her eyes. "I don't think I can. You've killed me."

Scott laughed, pulling his hips back until just the tip of his dick was inside. "Hmm, well, I guess I'll just have to fuck you back to life."

Talena's eyes opened, love shining back at him. "I'll love you until the day I die and beyond, Scott Haven."

He pressed all the way in, holding himself above the only woman who held his heart. "Ah, baby girl, I love you even more than that. My parents had that magical kind of love. I knew what I felt for you was like that because when I was with you, I felt complete. My life was me existing, but not living, until I had you right where you are. With me, under me, beside me. That magical love is the kind I have for you."

She sniffed, tears falling from both eyes. "My love, I don't know what I did to deserve you, but you're the light that brightened the darkness and the rain that comes after a storm, you know the cleansing kind, that's you. You're my light and my own personal rain that's helped me grow into the woman I am. I am so in love with you now and will love you forever with my whole heart and soul."

Scott brushed the wetness from her cheeks with his thumbs, smiling at her words. "That's good to hear because you're stuck with me, baby girl."

He began moving, loving her with his body as much as his heart. No woman on Earth could be loved as much as his Talena. In, out he pushed, slowly building up the pleasure for her again, swiveling his hips on each downward thrust. He watched her face as he moved, paying attention to every nuance and adjusted his movements when he noticed what had her gasping and what had her clenching on him.

When he felt her inner muscles begin to flutter and saw her chest rising faster, he moved his hands under her ass, tilting her up for a better angle.

"Oh yes, right there, please."

He wasn't going to get onto her for not calling him Sir, not when her pussy was fluttering, tightening around him and her nails were raking his back as her pleasure pulled him over the edge.

"Fuck yes, baby, come for me. Let me feel you come on my cock," he ordered.

"Yes, I need. I need you harder."

He reared back, slamming into her harder, his balls slapping her ass. One, two, five times and then he was coming right after she had. He continued to pump even after he was sure he had no more to give, his dick not caring. "Shit, baby, I think you're going to kill me," he gasped, falling to the side half on, half off Talena.

"What a way to go," she gasped.

Scott chuckled, running his hand down her chest in a lazy motion. "Let me rest a moment then I'll get us cleaned up."

"Okay, daddy," she whispered.

He froze. "What?"

The soft sound of her even breathing made him wonder if he'd heard her wrong. Yet his hand went to her flat stomach. He would love to have a little girl who looked like Talena and acted like her too. Surely, she was just tired and called him that instead of Sir since she was new to the world.

Talena woke first, sliding out of bed before Scott. She couldn't believe she fell asleep before she could get cleaned up. He lay next to her with one big tattooed arm over his face. Her bladder was making itself known in the most annoying way, so she eased off the bed, trying not to wake him. She looked down at her body, shocked to see she was— clean. He must've done so after she passed out. Her hand went to her stomach as she hurried into the bathroom and shut the door. Oh lord, she wondered if he had any clue. She had been on the shot, but then the incident happened, and she'd spaced going to get the one she'd been scheduled for.

She'd been sure she couldn't get pregnant, not after...well, clearly, she'd been wrong and so had the doctor at the clinic.

After she finished, she washed her hands and looked at herself in the mirror. The shower beckoned, so she hopped in washing off the sweat from the night before. The door opened behind her; the familiar form of Scott eased in.

"I missed you this morning." He kissed her neck.

She couldn't help but laugh. "I've been gone all of ten minutes."

"The longest ten minutes of my life," he agreed.

Her quick shower turned into a much longer, much dirtier one before she was stepping out with Scott right behind her. If anyone would have seen her, there would be no denying the glow she had was from amazing sex, yet she also had a secret.

"Once you get dressed come on out to the living area so you can open your presents." Scott kissed her after he gave her the order.

She sighed, watching him walk out of the bathroom naked as the day he was born. "Dear lord, that man is seriously the sexiest thing since sliced bread."

Since she hadn't washed her hair, it didn't take her long to get dressed and apply a little tinted moisturizer to her face and a little mascara. If she was going to tell him about his pending fatherhood, she didn't want to put it off too much longer.

When she walked out of the bathroom, she came to a hard stop at the sight that met her eyes. There in the middle of the room was a huge Christmas tree and Scott in front of it down on one knee. "What are you doing?"

He waved her forward. "C'mere," he said.

She moved slowly, holding his gaze.

"Last night, I was going to do this, but then you fell asleep. Today I'm on my knee, asking you to be my wife. To love me for the rest of our lives and make me the happiest man on Earth? Will you marry me?" He opened his palm, a velvet box sat inside.

Talena nodded. "Yes. Oh, yes, I'll marry you."

"You haven't even seen the ring." He lifted the lid, showing her the diamond ring inside. With deft fingers, he lifted the jewelry out, standing up with it between his fingers.

"That box could've been empty, and I'd have said yes. I...I have to tell you something."

Scott grabbed her hand, sliding the ring on her finger. "Perfect fit. What do you have to tell me?"

"I'm pregnant," she blurted, tears threatened to fall, but she forced them back. If he wanted to call the almost engagement off, she'd let him.

"You called me daddy last night. I thought, I hoped it was true. A baby?" He pressed his hand over her stomach, then dropped to his knees, pressing his lips to her stomach. "You're having our baby," he said with awe in his tone.

She ran her hands through his hair, tears falling down her cheeks unchecked. "You're not mad?"

He wrapped his arms around her stomach and looked up at her. "You are having a little you. Why would I be mad? This is the best day of my life. We need to call mom." He raised her shirt and kissed her stomach before getting to his feet.

"Whoa, shouldn't we wait and like, break one thing to her at a time?" She held the ring up to his face.

Scott waved her words away. "She already knew about that."

Talena groaned. "She's gonna kill me."

He scooped her up into his arms, striding over to the large chair facing the fireplace. "She's going to be so excited. This is the best Christmas ever, baby girl."

Talena sat on Scott's lap, feeling like she was on top of the world. She'd made a lot of fucked up decisions in her life but choosing Hollywood and having him chose her as the one he wanted to be with was truly a Christmas miracle. Now they just had to hope their mom didn't freak out when they told her their happy news.

"Good morning, grandma," Scott said.

"Are you serious?" Tara cheered.

"Are you okay, Tara?"

"Who the fuck is that?" Scott asked his mother.

"Doc, I'm going to be a Mimi."

"I'm gonna kill him." Hollywood tried to get up, but Talena kept her arms around him, hitting the disconnect button.

"Scott, she's a grown woman who has been alone for a very long time," she reminded him.

His jaw bunched. "I don't like it."

She pressed her lips against his. "She's excited to be a Mimi."

"I'm going to be a daddy."

"Oh yeah you are," she agreed.

He stood up, keeping hold of her. "We should get a lot of fucking in before the baby gets here. I think I heard that kids cut into sexy times."

Talena laughed but didn't utter a protest.

Tara stared at the phone in her hand then over at the man she'd met the evening before. She hadn't felt a connection to another man in over thirty years, not since she'd met and fell in love with Scott Haven. No other man had ever held a candle to her first husband, the only man she'd ever loved. "This is a miracle," she whispered, wiping a tear from her cheek.

"You don't mind your children becoming a couple?"

Her head snapped up, glaring at Doc. "God no. They're not related by blood and if ever two people belong together and deserve happiness it's my babies."

Doc held up his hands, a grin tipping his lips. "I didn't mean no harm. I agree with you. Your son is a fine young man. While I don't know much about Talena, I know she must be a remarkable woman if she's anything like you."

She held her ground as he moved closer. They'd left the clubhouse last night and went for breakfast at a truck stop along the interstate, spending the night talking, getting to know more about one another. She'd told him more than she'd ever divulged to another human being. Many nights she'd cried herself to sleep, her little dog she'd gotten after Scott's death for her son became her faithful companion. The only problem with that was he didn't talk back, but he did let her cuddle him. Of course, like all the men other than her son, Roscoe passed away after fourteen short years and she couldn't bring herself to get another. Gary of course was against animals, so it hadn't been an issue.

"Hey where did you go?" Doc brushed his knuckles over her cheek.

She blinked, trying to dispel old anger. "Sorry, I was thinking about old pets." Which was the truth.

"You should get a guard dog since you live alone in this big house," Doc said.

He was standing so close she could smell the scent of his cologne and the coffee he'd had. "I'm not sure I could train a dog."

He smiled, showing off perfect white teeth. "I can help you find one that's already trained. I know a guy."

Tara laughed, unable to contain herself at his choice of words. "I swear, anytime I hear a man say those words it spells nothing but trouble, but for some reason I trust you."

Doc took a deep breath. "That's good, sweetheart. I want you to trust me. I'm not good at relationships. I'll be honest with you. I haven't had what you'd call a relationship since Lennox's mom passed away. I'm not saying I've been celibate, but—" He raked his hand through his hair, holding her gaze.

"I get what you're saying. I need to tell you I haven't...I mean, I have been celibate since Scott's dad was killed." There, she said it. Her son knew and now this man did. If he walked out because he thought she was a freak, then so be it.

"But you were married again?"

She nodded, letting her silence fill the air.

"She was a cold bitch who didn't want me touching her, but she's clearly decided to come out of the deep freeze with the likes of you."

Tara spun at the sound of Gary's voice, shock holding her in place. "You're dead."

"Did you miss me, darling?" Gary moved out of the darkness, entering the living room with a gun in his hand. "It's really quite easy to fake your death if you have the right connections and money you know. Thanks to Haven Corp I had both. I had planned to sneak in and get what I'd left behind, but then I overheard your conversation and saw you with that. You really sunk low, my dear. Your beloved Scott wouldn't approve," Gary sneered.

"You're a real tough guy when you're holding a gun," Doc growled.

"You think I'll sink to your level and resort to a fist fight? Not gonna happen, old man. Let's make this easy on all of us and the two of you move on into the bedroom, which I'm sure was where this little meeting was moving anyhow," Gary said, waving the gun toward the master suite.

"You won't get away with this," Tara warned.

"I already did, sweetheart," Gary mocked, looking down at his tailored slacks and polo shirt.

Doc moved, placing Tara on the outside so that he was closer to Gary. She recognized what he was doing and wished she could scream at the injustice of what was happening. Just when her life was becoming beautiful again, the worst mistake of her life returned to ruin it. Her one saving grace was that Talena was safe with Scott, and she knew he'd protect her and their unborn baby with his life.

"Let's go, move it. I'll even let him see you naked before I kill you and then him. It'll be a lasting memory he can take to his grave. See I'm not a total bastard."

"You're worse than a bastard, Gary. You're a rapist, a pedophile, and a monster," she yelled.

Gary lunged toward her, making her scream when she'd thought she'd pushed him too far.

Doc seemed unfazed; his reflexes faster than she'd have thought, grabbed the arm holding the gun with one hand and punched Gary in the face with the other. The crunch was audible as Doc's fist connected with her ex-husband's nose; blood poured down her ex's face onto his pristine pale blue polo shirt.

She fell back against the wall, feeling as though she was in a movie, unable to do anything but watch the two men grapple with the weapon. Her mind kept seeing the gun go off like in the movies. She looked around the room something to help Doc when a crash pulled her attention back to the fighting pair.

"Oh god," she whispered, horrified to see Gary on the ground, his throat slit from ear-to-ear.

"I'm sorry, baby," Doc growled standing up and wiping the bloody scalpel on Gary's shirt before sliding the weapon back into his boot.

She held up her hand, stopping him. "Is he really dead this time?" They'd all thought he'd died all those years ago when the company jet had crashed into the ocean. She should've known he'd faked his death, killing the pilot and the flight attendant clearly hadn't been an issue for him.

Doc looked down at the body then back at her. "Yeah, you don't get any more dead than that."

Tara took a shaky breath, licking her lips. "How do I explain to the cops about...this?"

Doc pulled out his phone. "I'll handle it. He's already dead, right? You've had a funeral and collected insurance, correct?"

"Yes, years ago. God, this is a mess." She looked away from the body covering her face with one hand.

"I'm so fucking sorry, Tara." Doc pulled her hand away from her eyes.

"What? No, this isn't your fault. You saved me. He'd have killed me if you hadn't been here. Oh my god, he's been alive all this time and could've killed all of us anytime he wanted."

Tara couldn't stop the hysterical laughing-cry from falling from her lips. When Doc pulled her into his arms, she let him hold her, needing his support, wanting his support. "Thank you," she whispered against his muscular chest.

"You don't have to thank me, Tara." His hand palmed the back of her head, massaging the ache away.

"Well, sheot, I missed the party. PS. Miss. Tara, your security wasn't set. So, we'll just do some cleanup and be on our way. Doc, you might not want to boink Hollywood's mom until you clear it with him though. He's kinda mean."

Tara pulled back from Doc, stunned to see one of the men from earlier standing in the shadows. "Axl?"

"Yeah, it's me, your favorite. Ouch, mothereffer, she totally said I was her favorite earlier." Axl stepped out of the shadow followed by Ridley and Cannon.

"Where's Roq?" Doc asked.

"He's in the truck. He said we could handle shit. We're handling shit, but clearly not well. He's gonna be pissed as fuck. However, we'll just take the body and go. Ridley and Cannon grab him and, Tara, don't you worry, we were never here." Axl put his finger to his lips.

She watched as the two men grabbed the rug and rolled her ex up in it. In a matter of minutes, Gary and any sign of what had happened was gone, except for the space where the rug had been. "I need a new rug."

"I'll buy you one," Doc offered.

"Do they carry chemicals with them all the time you think?" She was still a little in shock from when she'd witnessed Roq walk in with a bucket and tools. If they'd began hacking up Gary she'd have been done.

"I'd say it's best to not ask things you really don't want the answers for." Doc ran his hand up and down her back as he spoke, the action soothing her.

"Scott is going to have a fit," she groaned.

He turned her into his body, wrapping his arms around her. "Of course, but now at least we know you won't have any more problems from Gary."

She slapped his chest with a little laugh. "I wasn't supposed to have problems with him before, but I see your point. God I'm tired."

"Come on, let's put you to bed and I'll see myself out." Doc tried to move back.

Tara tightened her hold. "Stay with me?"

"Your son might try to kill me." He didn't sound scared.

"We'll tell him you saved me first."

Doc shook his head, but he held her hand as she led him to her bedroom, the one she hadn't shared with another man since her first marriage. Her daughter had told her to make a wish for Christmas, which she'd laughed about at the time. However, she'd wished for happiness for all of them. Last night, both her babies had given her more happiness than she'd thought she deserved, gifting her with the news of their love and this morning the news of a grandchild to come. When Gary almost took her life, she was ready to accept her fate because she'd tasted joy, but now with her hand engulfed in a man who was making butterflies dance in her stomach, Tara was certain she was being given a second chance. With her eyes closed, she sent a prayer up to her first love, knowing he had to be looking down on her. She'd loved with her whole heart once before, and now it was time to love again.

The End

Thank you for reading Scott aka Hollywood and Talena's story. I hope you enjoyed it as much as I loved writing it. I don't know if you noticed a few characters from Cosmo's book—Roq, Axl, Ridley, and Cannon, but they're getting their own spinoff next with Roq and Netty who you met in my Navy SEALs series. I hope you're ready for one heck of a Royally Secured story with Roq up first as he and the other Demon Security guy's head off on a mission that lands them in a bar where Netty happens to be singing, albeit poorly, and then he has to save her from an ex who won't take no for an answer. Of course, things aren't as easy as that when it comes to my heroes and their ladies.

Read on for a look at Royally Secured the first book in the Demon Security Series, Roq and Netty's story:

Royally Secured

Netty sat at Naughty Girls and pounded on the bar. "Give me another one." She held the empty shot glass up.

Traci filled the glass with another shot of tequila. "Girl, I'm not holding your hair."

She rolled her eyes, and tossed the drink back, no longer feeling the burn. "Men suck. I mean like big hairy donkey balls. I think I'm going to switch to the other team." She covered her mouth when she burped 'cause she was still a lady, dammit.

Her best friend's eyes widened. "Don't look at me, girl. I ain't going downtown to lady-town on nobody. Nope. I mean you're gorgeous, but I like men. Big strong men with big dicks." Traci held her hands apart, indicating the size she liked.

Several men seated around groaned.

"Come on Traci, that ain't even natural," an older cowboy said.

Traci shrugged. "Well, I'm just sayin'. I can teach a cowboy with a big bull how to ride, but if he's got a small you know what…well, I just can't. The answer is no. I like big dicks, and I cannot lie. You know the song, ladies."

Netty sat up as the song in question began playing, a smile forming on her face. She and Traci both went to opposite ends of the long wooden bar, climbing up the stairs that had been cleverly designed by Traci and built by one of her old boyfriends. They each grabbed a microphone one of the ladies behind the bar gave them, even though she stumbled a bit while Traci was all smooth and sober. Netty was pretty sure she was too drunk to maneuver so far off the ground, not to mention she was in a skirt that was too short, and any man seated on a barstool would get an eyeful of her cute panties. However, she'd had just enough to drink, and her give a damn had done gone and went.

She'd just started on the chorus when a familiar figure walked in. Shep Calhoun, the dirty, rotten, cheating bastard. Netty ignored him and shuffled across the polished surface, dancing and singing, pretending like he didn't matter. He really didn't and never had. It was more the fact he'd cheated and tried to make it her fault that pissed her off.

Traci began bumping hips with her, mixing the words up with liking big cocks instead of butts, which really had her laughing more than singing. She heard her name being hollered in that all too familiar country drawl that was too classy to be good ole boy. Fucking Shep the prick.

Pretending she didn't hear him, Netty turned her back to the room. The mirrored wall gave her a perfect view, defeating the purpose. Just when the song was about to end, the door opened, and a man walked in with three other men. Her mouth dried as she made eye contact with the first who entered. Good god, she didn't think she'd ever seen a man as handsome as the ones she'd met at her cousin Jaqui's wedding, even though she thought Shep was close, this man was right up there with them. Actually, that man who was staring right back at her was not only heads and shoulders above all the men in the room, he was heads and shoulders...wait, that doesn't sound right, but whatever, he was way better looking than any man she'd ever laid eyes on. And holy lord, did she want to lay something on him, like her hands and her tongue.

She watched his eyes narrow, then felt herself being pulled down. Fear had a scream ripping from her throat. Traci's yell was drowned out by the sound of her own heart beating double time, and then she was falling over Shep's shoulder.

"Put me down, you limp-dick fucker." She hit his back, looking around for someone to help her. Everyone there was scared of crossing the Calhoun's, the rich fuckers who thought they owned everyone in the entire damn state. They didn't own her, and Shep needed to learn that really quick. Besides he was a terrible lay with a limp-dick for real.

"Shut the hell up. I'm getting you out of here before you make any more of an ass out of yourself," Shep growled.

She wiggled, hitting him harder. "You are taking me nowhere. I'll call the cops. Put me down now. Traci, help me."

Traci came around the bar with a shotgun in her hand. "Put her down now, Shep, or I swear to my mama, I'll pepper your ass."

The sound of her best friend cocking her gun had her trying to get down, but the jackhole holding her only tightened his grip. "You better think really hard, darlin'. You don't want to make an enemy of me and my daddy."

"I don't think the little thing wants to go with you. How 'bout you put her down, and I'll buy you a drink."

Netty's body froze at the deep southern drawl. She twisted and tried to see who spoke, but then Shep hit her so hard on her ass, it brought tears to her eyes, making her cry out.

"Damn, I guess we do this the hard way."

"Fucking-A, Roq. We're here not even a minute and already you starting something."

"I'll buy you a beer after we teach these boys how to treat a woman, Axl." Roq cracked his knuckles.

"Hell Yeah!" Axl cheered.

"Do I get a say in any of this? I mean, I didn't even bring my good shitkickers for kicking shitheads' asses."

"What are good shitkickers compared to what you got on, Cannon?"

"They'd have those shiny things like he's got. Oh well, I guess we'll have to work with what we got. Lead on, Roq."

Roq knew without a doubt his friends had his back, and the little lady over the guy called Shep shoulder, was not there willingly. He looked at the smaller man, knowing he wasn't going to let go without a fight. He sighed and handed his Stetson to Axl. No way in hell was he going to get his favorite hat dirty or beat up in a bar fight. Damn, he sure did love it when they could go an entire day without busting heads.

"Axl, if you allow my hat to get dirty, I'm gonna be pissed as hell," he warned.

"Why do I gotta babysit the hat?"

"Because I'm gonna need someone who can keep a level head and not kill. Sadly, brother, that's you."

Axl swore. "That's the worst thing you've ever said to me. Just because I'm not a blood thirsty fucker like you three. Fine, I'll hold your hat, but I'm killing the first bastard I can next time."

"I think I like you boys. Will he really get Netty away from Shep?"

Roq looked at the sexy little redhead standing next to Axl and Ridley and nodded. "Ridley, gonna need you to make sure she doesn't get hurt while I whoop his ass."

"Fuck you. You ain't whooping nothing," Shep yelled.

"We'll see about that, won't we?" Roq smirked but didn't say another word, moving faster than the other man probably thought he could. Many men thought because he was so big that he couldn't be swift. Huge mistake on their part, which he took advantage of. Like he did now, plucking the feisty little woman off Shep the dipshit's shoulder and setting her behind him, where Axl waited, secure in the knowledge she'd be safe, same as his favorite hat. Cannon and Ridley split up, taking care of the men who stood with the idiot, and then it was just Roq and Shep.

He stared down at the little bastard who tried to puff his chest out. Little Shep had probably perfected that move in grade school. What the little shit didn't know, was that Roq hadn't attended grade school. None of the men with him had. They'd all been in hell of one sort or another, being used and abused, beaten and worse. Until Cosmo had come along and rescued them. Now they were the ones who rescued others. If they happened to do a little slicing and dicing as they went, well that was collateral damage. Thank you USA Delta Force and...other factions.

"You're going to pay for messing with me, boy," Shep warned.

Roq tossed his head back, laughing at the other man's words. He had heard the same thing too many times. So many in fact, he'd lost count. Bending so he was close to Shep's ear. Roq whispered while wrapping his fist in the pressed button-down shirt. "Boy, I ain't been a boy since you were knee high to a grasshopper, probably longer. Matter of fact, pretty sure I was never a boy. And guess what, *boy*? I've lost my patience," he growled.

"Ah, sheot," Ridley said.

"What's that mean?" Netty asked.

"Sweetheart, that means we need to clear the bar," Axl said, an ear-splitting whistle followed.

Roq smiled as he stood to his full height, twisting his head to the left and then the right. "I'll give you to the count of three to run along, little man. That's more than you were gonna give her. One, two," he said, starting the countdown, skipping three because really, who ever got to three was an idiot.

"Sheot, run, fucker," Cannon yelled.

Roq didn't say three, didn't figure it would do any good. Ole Shep was thinking he was on the winning side, what with him having a bar full of cowboys while Roq only had himself and three of his brothers. Stupid fool. He pulled his right fist back, hitting him with his left while Shep prepared for the other one to hit. Roq moved, lifting Shep with his hand around his throat, taking the gun from the back of his pants as he did and pointing at the little bastard who had been sneaking up on his right. "One more step and you'll be pushing up daisies."

He flipped the gun around, whipping the little shit upside the head with it. The entire time, he kept pressure on Shep's throat, aware he could crush his windpipe at any second.

"Have you decided to run along yet, *boy*, or do I need to pistol whip your dumbass too?"

Hatred glared back at him, but the dark eyes closed, then opened. "Let me go so I can leave."

"What's that?" Roq asked, wanting to hear him repeat his words.

Shep tried to swallow, which Roq made almost impossible, so he released the pressure a little. "Go ahead, *boy*," he sneered, putting his face in front of Shep's. "The next time you want to threaten someone, I suggest you make sure they're someone your size. Oh shit, you did threaten me. I'm bigger than you too. I guess next time, you better make sure you got more than your mouth to back you, *boy*. I don't play games, and you and your daddy don't scare me."

Roq gave him a shake that would be making his brain rattle for a good while before releasing him, uncaring the move made Shep fall on his ass.

Shep got to his feet, wiping off his jean clad ass. "This isn't over," he promised.

"You don't want to start something you can't finish, little man. Best remember that, boy," Roq held his hand out for the hat Axl held without taking his eyes off of Shep.

"I think he shit his pants, brother." Ridley clapped him on the shoulder, his words loud enough everyone in the quiet bar heard.

"Mister, I think you just made a really bad enemy, but I want to say thank you very much. If he'd have left with me I...I don't know what he'd have done."

Roq looked down at the tiny woman, his heart beating a little harder than normal against his chest. Damn she was sexy and cute all wrapped together in a dynamite package. "Was he your boyfriend or—" He trailed off waiting to see if she'd fill in the gap.

"He was my ex-boyfriend. Should've been my never boyfriend." She rubbed at her ass, wincing.

"Can I buy you a drink?" Roq asked.

"Drink's on the house."

Roq looked up to see the woman with the shotgun who threatened to shoot the asshole standing there. She too was a tiny thing, more curvaceous than her friend, but still gorgeous. What the hell? Women in California were all gorgeous, that was a given. Yet here in this small little southern town, he was a little shocked to find three women who outshone all the women who paraded up and down Hollywood. As he looked over at his brothers by choice, he saw Axl staring at the women with a look he'd never seen on his face, the same looks on Ridley and Cannon as well. Shit, for all their sakes, he hoped like hell his brothers weren't interested in the woman before him. "What's your name, sweetheart?"

"Netty," she said.

"My name's Roq," he told her, tipping his hat and waving for her to proceed him to the bar. They'd come to find a missing girl and landed in the middle of a bar where he wasn't sure if he'd found a heap of trouble and probably even more. One thing was for certain though, he wasn't going to let a little thing like Shep Calhoun, or his brothers, keep him from finding out why a tiny slip of a woman made him want things he thought he'd never have.

Thank You

Thank you for reading Royally Chosen Christmas and the glimpse of what's to come with the other books! I hope you loved it and my heroes and heroines as much as I do!

Did you enjoy meeting Hollywood aka Scott and Talena in their story and getting to see some of the others from previous books? I tried to write this so you could enjoy it without having to read the others and hope like heck I did a good job. Up next is going to be Roq and Netty which actually started a long time ago, but Roq has totally become someone else, and I can't wait to write all the guys from the Demon Security spinoff series. Roq, Axl, and Ridley for sure, and maybe Cannon (at first, I was going to off him, but then I didn't soo who knows) wink.

You can also join my Facebook group, Elle Boon's Bombshells, to discuss all things Elle Boon books and see what's going on or coming up in my book world.

Want to stay up to date on upcoming releases in all my series? Be sure to join my VIP newsletter. I promise your inbox will be filled with the hottest dominating Alphas and exclusive content.

XOXO,

ELLE BOON

About Elle Boon

Elle Boon is a reader first and foremost...and of course if you know her, she's the crazy lady with purple hair. She's also a USA Today Bestselling Author who lives in Middle-Merica as she likes to say…with her husband and Kally Kay, her black lab who also thinks she's her writing partner. (She happens to sit next to her begging for treats and so takes a lot of credit). She has two amazing kids, Jazz and Goob, and is a MiMi to one adorable little nugget named Romy or RomyGirl (greatest job EVER) who has totally won over everyone who sees hers (If anyone says a hair bow is too big, they're crazy). She's known for saying "Bless Your Heart" and dropping lots of F-bombs (I mean lots of F-BOMBS, but who is keeping track?).

She loves where this new journey has taken her and has no plans on stopping. She writes what she loves to read, and that's romance, whether it's about Navy SEALs, HOT as F**K MC heroes, or paranormal alphas. #dontlookdown is a thing you will need to google. "Wink" With all her stories, you're guaranteed a happily ever after, no matter what twisted thing her mind has come up with. Her biggest hope is that after readers have read one of her stories, they fall in love with her characters as much as she has. She loves creating new worlds and has more just waiting to be written. Elle believes in happily ever after and can guarantee you will always get one within the pages of her books.

Connect with Elle online. She loves to hear from you:
www.elleboon.com
https://www.facebook.com/elle.boon
https://www.facebook.com/Elle-Boon-Author-1429718517289545/

https://twitter.com/ElleBoon1

https://www.facebook.com/groups/RacyReads/

https://www.facebook.com/groups/1405756769719931/

https://www.goodreads.com/author/show/8120085.Elle_Boon

https://www.bookbub.com/authors/elle-boon

https://www.instagram.com/elleboon/

http://www.elleboon.com/newsletter

Other Books by Elle Boon

Ravens of War

Selena's Men

Two For Tamara

Jaklyn's Saviors

Kira's Warriors

Akra's Demons

Mystic Wolves

Accidentally Wolf

His Perfect Wolf

Jett's Wild Wolf

Bronx's Wounded Wolf

A Fey's Wolf

Their Wicked Wolf

Atlas's Forbidden Wolf

SmokeJumpers

FireStarter

Berserker's Rage

A SmokeJumpers Christmas

Choosing His Mate, A Prequel to FireStarter is Available in The Glittering World Anthology

Iron Wolves MC

Lyric's Accidental Mate

Xan's Feisty Mate

Kellen's Tempting Mate

Slater's Enchanted Mate

Dark Lovers
Bodhi's Synful Mate
Turo's Fated Mate
Arynn's Chosen Mate
Coti's Unclaimed Mate

Miami Nights
Miami Inferno
Rescuing Miami

Standalone
Wild and Dirty, Wild Irish Series

SEAL Team Phantom Series
Delta Salvation
Delta Recon
Delta Rogue
Delta Redemption
Mission Saving Shayna
Protecting Teagan

The Dark Legacy Series
Dark Embrace

The Royal Sons MC Series
Royally Twisted
Royally Taken
Royally Tempted
Royally Treasured
Royally Broken

Royally F**ked
Royally Chosen Christmas
Royally Baited Coming November 2021

Demon Security – Royal MC Spinoff
Royally Secured ROQ - Coming Soon
Royally Complete RIDLEY - Coming Soon
Royally Shielded AXL– Coming Soon
Royally Caged CANNON – Coming Soon

Magic and Mayhem
The Lion's Witchy Mate
The Leopards Witchy Mate

Standalone
Shaw's Wild Mate, Coming Soon

A Cursed Hallows Eve Anthology
Their Dragon Mate

Made in the USA
Monee, IL
20 May 2021

69114102R00193